DANGER ON DECK!

Marty reached the deck and took in a deep breath of fresh sea air, which smelled like perfume compared to the greasy galley. The dark sky was moonless, lit by millions of stars. The *Coelacanth* was anchored. He walked over to the rail and looked down at the water. Somewhere beneath the dark water a giant squid awaited.

Tomorrow, if things are going well in the galley, I'll spend the day on deck getting some sun, he thought.

Something slammed into his back and he was falling over the wrong side of the rail. One of his flailing hands managed to snag the edge of the scupper and he came to a shoulder-wrenching stop. He managed to get his other hand onto the scupper, but his position was still precarious. He tried to pull himself up, but he didn't have enough strength. He began to yell his head off. The sharp edge of the scupper was cutting off the circulation to his fingers. If someone didn't hear him in a minute or so, he was going to drop into the dark sea and never be heard from again.

CLES

ROLAND SMITH

SCHOLASTIC INC.
New York Toronto London Auckland
Sydney Mexico City New Delhi Hong Kong

No part of this publication may be reproduced, stored in a retrieval system, or transmitted in any form or by any means, electronic, mechanical, photocopying, recording, or otherwise, without written permission of the publisher. For information regarding permission, write to Scholastic Inc., Attention: Permissions Department, 557 Broadway, New York, NY 10012.

This book was originally published in hardcover by Scholastic Press in 2009.

ISBN 978-0-545-17816-7

12 11 10 9 8 7 6 5 4 3 2 1   11 12 13 14 15 16/0

Printed in the U.S.A.   40
This edition first printing, February 2011

The text type was set in Futura Std.
The display type was set in Bank Gothic & Agency.
Book design by Phil Falco

cryp·to·zo·ol·o·gy (krip-ta-zō-ă-la-jē) *noun* The study of animals, such as the Sasquatch, the Yeti, the Loch Ness Monster, the Chupacabra, kraken, and others, whose existence has not yet been proven scientifically. There are thought to be more than two hundred **cryptids** in existence today. – **cryp·to·zo·o·log·i·cal** (-zō-a-´lä-ji-kal) *adj,* – **cryp·to·zo·ol·o·gist** (-´ä-la-jist) *noun*

Marty O'Hara Wolfe's nephew. Grace's cousin (formerly thought to be her twin). Thirteen years old. Brown hair, gray eyes, a foot taller than Grace. Talented artist. Master chef. Scuba diver. Mountain climber. His parents, Timothy and Sylvia (the most famous photographer/journalist team in the world), are missing after a terrible helicopter crash in the Amazon rain forest.

Grace Wolfe Wolfe's only daughter (although for most of her life she thought she was Timothy and Sylvia O'Hara's daughter and Marty's twin sister). Black hair, blue eyes the color of robin's eggs. Born at Lake Télé in the Congo. Twelve years old. Small for her age, but a foot *smarter* than Marty. Fluent in several languages. Habitual journal-writer. Lock-picker. Genius.

Luther Percival Smyth, IV Marty's best friend and former roommate at Omega Opportunity Preparatory School (OOPS) in Switzerland, where they got into a lot of trouble and coauthored graphic novels. Sleeps like a vampire. Gangly, with wild orange hair. Expert computer hacker and video gamer.

Dr. Travis Wolfe Called "Wolfe" by his friends — and foes. Grace's father. Marty's uncle. Cryptozoologist. Veterinarian. Oceanographer. A giant of a man – just under seven feet tall. Unruly black hair, bushy black beard, brown eyes, wears size-fifteen shoes. Cofounder and owner of eWolfe with Ted Bronson. His right leg was bitten off by a Mokélé-mbembé as he tried to save his wife, Rose Blackwood. He now wears a high-tech prosthesis invented by Ted Bronson.

Dr. Noah Blackwood Father of Wolfe's deceased wife, Rose. Grace's grandfather. Environmental superstar — but he is not who he appears to be. Wealthy. Powerful. Owner of several animal theme parks around the world, all called Noah's Ark. He hunts and breeds endangered animals and cryptids, and displays them at his parks. In their prime he kills the animals, has them stuffed, and stages them in his private diorama.

Butch McCall Noah Blackwood's henchman. Dangerous. Tattooed. Tough. Expert field biologist. More comfortable in the woods than under a roof. Sworn enemy of Travis Wolfe, who "stole" Rose away from him.

Bertha Bishop Ex–Army Ranger general; can kill a person 106 different ways with her bare hands. She is extra-large, but solid as a rock. Wolfe's head cook. Phil's wife.

Phil Bishop Ex–Air Force colonel. Former combat pilot. Wolfe's chief pilot. Bertha's husband.

Dr. Laurel Lee Wolfe's cultural anthropologist. Birdlike. Athletic. Former circus aerialist. Taught Grace to walk on a high wire to help her focus and overcome her fears. Laurel and Wolfe are sweet on each other.

Dr. Ted Bronson Wolfe's closest friend and partner at eWolfe. Eccentric genius. Inventor. Recluse. Rumored to have not left the Quonset hut on Cryptos Island (where he develops his marvelous gadgets) in more than three years.

Theo Sonborn A cohort of Wolfe's since the beginning. Surly. Pugnacious. Obnoxious. Jack-of-all-trades, master of none.

Bo Female bonobo chimpanzee; orphaned and adopted by Wolfe years ago in central Africa. Pals around with PD and Congo. Fond of Luther's orange hair. Sworn enemy of Winkin, Blinkin, and Nod.

PD Short for "Pocket Dog"; black-haired teacup poodle. Best friends with Bo. Does not get along with Congo. Jumps into a pocket upon hearing the word *snake*.

Winkin, Blinkin, and Nod Wolfe's three bottle-nosed dolphins, who all love teasing Bo.

Congo African gray parrot who belonged to Rose, Grace's mother, when she was in central Africa. Grace brought him back to Cryptos Island after their adventure with Mokélé-mbembé.

Monkey A plush toy resembling a primate. Covered with patches and stitches. Its mouth and left eye are missing. Grace has had it since she was a baby. Because of its tattered appearance, Marty refers to it as the Frankenstein Monkey. Between the cousins, a promise is sealed by giving Monkey's arm a squeeze.

GIANT SQUID (Genus: *Architeuthis*)

Pushing water in rhythmic pulses through its spherical-shaped body, or **mantle** (a), and steering by use of its **caudal fin** (b), the giant squid is jet-propelled. On average, the mantle is six feet long.

More than one foot in diameter, the **eyes** (c) of the giant squid are among the largest of any living creature. The larger the eye, the better to detect light, which is scarce in deep, dark water.

Giant squid have eight **arms** (d) and two **tentacles** (e). The insides of both are lined with hundreds of **suction cups** (f) ringed with sharp, finely serrated circles of *chitin*. The combined gripping action of the suckers and their pointy teeth attaches the squid to its prey.

The bases of both of the tentacles and all of the arms join to encircle a single, parrotlike **beak** (g), which shreds food with the aid of the *radula* – a tongue with tiny, file-edged teeth.

PART ONE—BON VOYAGE

LUTHER

Marty O'Hara did not realize how much he had missed his best friend, Luther Smyth, until Luther jumped out of the seaplane onto the dock at Cryptos Island. In fact, he was so excited to see Luther he didn't even notice the other, rather odd-looking passenger who had flown in with his gangly, fluorescent-carrot-headed classmate.

The lanky Luther ran up to Marty, sporting his trademark goofy grin and a small backpack slung over his bony shoulder.

"You weren't lying, nose-picker!" Luther said. "Cryptos Island is real and very weird!"

Marty returned Luther's grin. "Duh *du jour*," he said (meaning, "Duh of the day," one of his and Luther's favorite sayings).

Just then, almost as if to accent Marty's point, a chimpanzee ambled down the wooden dock, came to an abrupt stop directly in front of Luther, and hooted.

"This is Bo," Marty said. "And you're the nose-picker."

Luther ignored the insult and squatted down in front of Bo before Marty could warn him.

Bo grabbed a handful of Luther's bizarre hair and yanked it out.

"Ouch!" Luther fell over backward and would have fallen into the water if Marty hadn't grabbed his arm.

"Thanks," Luther said.

"No problem," Marty said.

Bo hooted again, ran back up the dock with her treasure, scaled the chain-link security gate, and disappeared into the trees.

"Hair-picker!" Luther yelled after her.

Marty shook his head. "I wondered what she was going to think of your hair."

Luther rubbed his sore scalp. "I guess she doesn't like it."

"Wrong," Marty corrected. "She wants it."

"How much did she take?"

Marty looked at his friend's head. "A pretty good chunk, but no one will notice."

Luther's hair had always stuck up all over the place in one giant cowlick that not even Elmer's glue could keep down. (Luther had actually tried Elmer's glue once, but it had just made things worse.) The missing hair already forgotten, Luther looked over at the giant ship moored to the dock.

"So that's the *Coelacanth*," he said, pronouncing the name *koh-eel-uh-kanth*.

"It's pronounced *see-la-kanth*, you dunce," Marty said. "Named after a fish thought to have gone extinct sixty-five million years ago, until it was rediscovered in South Africa by a woman named Marjorie Courtenay-Latimer in 1938. Wolfe has a breeding pair in an aquarium up in the library."

"Well, that *ship* looks like it's sixty-five million years old," Luther said. "You sure that rusty bucket of bolts can make it to New Zealand?"

"It'll make it," Marty said, not mentioning the scuttlebutt on the island that the *Coelacanth* was haunted. Badly haunted. The ship had drifted into U.S. coastal waters ten years earlier — minus its cargo and its crew of nearly fifty men and women, except for the captain's freshly severed head lying on the pillow in his berth.

Grace had gotten the information off the Internet, but there was no point in scaring Luther by recounting the ship's grisly history. Marty's uncle, Travis Wolfe, had bought the ship at an auction for a fraction of what it was worth because he was the only bidder. No one else wanted to touch the bad-luck ship. "Their ridiculous superstition was my *good* luck," Wolfe had explained. "I had enough money left over to retrofit the interior." Clearly, Wolfe was not concerned with what it looked like on the outside.

The *Coelacanth* was buzzing with activity: people hauling gear, cranes lowering crates into the cargo holds, deckhands battening down a helicopter to a landing pad behind the bridge. Marty was certain that none of them had heard the story of what had happened on the ship, and he wished that he'd never heard it, either.

"We're shipping out in a couple of weeks?" Luther asked.

"Maybe sooner," Marty said. "People have been coming in by airplane, chopper, and boat every day for the past week. They go right onto the ship. Wolfe hasn't let any of them onto the island for security reasons."

"Yeah," Luther said, pointing. "Like that guy walking up the gangplank. He came in on the seaplane with me. His name is Dr. Seth A. Lepod. Barely said a word during the whole flight. I pegged him as a squid scientist. He has longer legs and arms than I do, and he smells like a dead fish. Even Phil was put off by the stench. He kept looking back at the guy, wondering what the problem was."

Phil was Phil Bishop, a retired Air Force colonel and one of Travis Wolfe's pilots. He was married to Bertha Bishop, a retired Army Ranger general with the ability to kill someone 106 ways with her bare hands. She was now Wolfe's chief cook and mother to Phyllis Bishop, a.k.a. Phil Jr., another retired Air Force veteran and Wolfe's chief pilot.

"Have the Mokélé-mbembé eggs hatched?" Luther asked.

"Not yet," Marty answered. "But Wolfe expects them to start cracking any day now."

"I can't believe you guys saw an actual, living dinosaur in the Congo. Are you sure the eggs are real?" Luther said.

"As real as Bo yanking your hair from your scalp," Marty answered. "Let's head up to the Fort."

"Fort?" Luther asked.

"You'll see."

"I'd better get the rest of my gear."

Luther started toward the seaplane, but Marty stopped him. "Don't bother. Phil will have someone haul it up and put it in your room after they search it."

"Search it?" Luther said.

Marty nodded. "After what happened in the Congo, Wolfe hardened island security. About a week ago a guy named Albert

Ikes took over island security. He used to work for the Central Intelligence Agency and he's a complete paranoid nutcase. I don't think he even trusts Wolfe, and Wolfe is his boss . . . at least I think he is."

"Is this Albert Ikes guy going to New Zealand with us?" Luther asked.

"Unfortunately," Marty said. "And don't call him Albert. Call him Al or he might shoot you. Come on. Oh—" He stopped and handed Luther a silver chain with a square piece of carrot-colored plastic hanging from it.

"This is the tracking tag you wrote me about," Luther said.

"Yeah, but these tags are new and improved," Marty explained, pointing to the gray plastic square hanging from the chain around his own neck. "Put it on and don't ever take it off—even when you're in the shower. Don't ask me how, but they know when you're wearing it and when you're not. The second day I had mine, I took it off in my sleep because it got tangled around my neck and I thought I was choking to death. Within minutes, two of Al's stormtroopers burst into my bedroom with guns drawn. I almost had a heart attack."

Luther slipped the chain over his head and tucked the square under his sweatshirt. "You're not joking about any of this."

"No joke," Marty said.

"Why all the security?"

Marty counted the reasons out on his fingers. "Noah Blackwood, Mokélé-mbembé eggs, Ted Bronson's top secret work for the government, and Grace."

"Grace? What does your sister—I mean, your cousin—have to do with all this?"

Marty started walking down the dock. "I'll tell you all about it after we get through the metal detector."

"Metal detector?" Luther asked.

Marty pointed to the end of the dock, where two armed security men were guarding the chain-link gate. They wore camouflage fatigues and deadly serious expressions. "The guys with the shaved heads are a couple of Al's stormtroopers, who are actually ex–Navy SEALs. They pretty much stick to the perimeter of the island, watching for intruders—except at the Fort, where Al has two guys on station 24/7. Once we get past them, everything on the island is a lot more relaxed. I would have emailed you about the changes, but Al cut off our email because he didn't want anyone on the outside to know about the new security measures."

Marty and Luther walked up to the two bullet-headed men.

"Empty your pockets and turn them inside out. You know the drill," Bullet Head #1 said, slapping a plastic tray onto the stainless steel table.

"I already did," Marty said. "I left all my stuff here with you so I didn't have to be searched again. Remember?"

"Turn your pockets inside out anyway," Bullet Head #2 said.

Marty turned his empty pockets inside out again.

Bullet Head #1 frisked him (making sure he hadn't slipped a nuclear device into his undershorts while they weren't looking), then had Marty pass through the metal detector.

"You're next," Bullet Head #2 said, glaring at Luther.

"You asked for it," Luther said, relieving his first pocket of a half-dozen colored pencils, a pencil sharpener, candy wrappers, a small sketch pad, a pair of sunglasses, a comb (useless in Luther's case), a handheld video game player, two flash drives, a digital camera, stereo earbuds, a stick of gum, an iPhone, and dental floss. "I started with the easy pocket first," he said, then began emptying the second pocket.

The Bullet Heads rolled their eyes as they watched the mound of stuff grow.

"Did you cram everything you own into your pockets?" Marty asked.

"Nah," Luther answered. "The big stuff is down at the dock. Three humongous suitcases. I didn't know what to expect, so I brought everything I had at Omega Prep except my bed. I could have gotten everything into two suitcases, but I needed a third for those diaries Grace asked me to bring back for her."

"Moleskines," Marty said. "Three hundred and fifteen of them." Grace had kept a diary ever since she had learned how to write at the age of five.

"Yeah," Luther said. "That suitcase weighs about a thousand pounds. The valuable gear is here in the backpack. Didn't want to risk losing it if they lost my luggage at the airport. Phil could hardly squeeze the suitcases in with all the junk Dr. Fish Stink brought along." He nodded at the Bullet Heads. "These guys are lucky they aren't checking *his* stuff. It smelled worse than he did. Bouquet of roadkill. One whiff of that and these two security guards would be retching."

"We are not security guards," Bullet Head #1 muttered.

"Didn't mean to offend you," Luther said cheerfully.

Marty had forgotten how pleasantly annoying Luther could be when someone was annoying *him*. Cryptos was going to be much more fun with Luther around.

"We are Security Specialists," Bullet Head #2 said.

"Sorry," Luther said. "You act like security guards and I just thought . . ." He turned his last pocket inside out. "That does it for the pockets." He held his arms out from his sides. "I'm ready for the pat down, but I have to warn you, I'm a little ticklish. Oh, and I have this rash that's highly contagious. The doctors don't know what it is or how to get rid of it."

Bullet Head #2 snapped on a pair of disposable rubber gloves and frisked Luther more roughly than he had Marty. Luther giggled through the entire process.

"What's on the flash drives?" Bullet Head #1 asked.

"Stuff," Luther said.

"We'll examine the *stuff* and give the drives back to you . . . maybe. We'll keep the camera and the video game player, too."

"And the cell phone," Bullet Head #2 added.

"I need the iPhone," Luther said. "My parents are going to be calling. I don't think they'd be happy with you if you took it away."

Luther's parents were billionaires and barely knew they had a son. Marty had never even met them, and he'd known Luther since they'd attended first grade together at the Omega Opportunity Preparatory School in Switzerland. He doubted Luther's parents would be calling.

"It's the *rules*," Bullet Head #1 said. "You got a problem with the *rules*, you can take it up with Mr. Ikes or Dr. Wolfe."

"Don't worry about it," Marty said. "You can use my Gizmo to call your parents or to have them call you."

"You mean I don't get my own Gizmo?" Luther asked, disappointed.

"Afraid not," Marty said. "Only a few people have them. Grace doesn't have one, either. Al decided to limit the units for security reasons. To make a call out or get one in we'll have to get his or Wolfe's permission."

"Why did they give you a Gizmo?" Luther asked.

Marty looked at the guards. "I'll tell you later. You won't believe the improvements Ted Bronson has made to them."

Ted Bronson was Wolfe's partner in eWolfe, a software development and technology company. Marty had never laid eyes on Ted, but not for lack of trying. It was rumored that the eccentric genius hadn't stepped outside the Quonset hut where he invented things in more than three years.

Luther reached for his pack.

"That stays here," Bullet Head #1 said. "We'll give it back to you after we've had a chance to examine the contents."

"When?" Luther asked.

"That's hard to say," Bullet Head #2 said. "We're kind of backed up."

Luther looked at the abandoned dock. Phil had already taken off in the seaplane to pick up more people from the mainland. "I can see that," Luther said. "Let me just take one thing with me. It never leaves my side. If I can't take it, then I'll just have to wait here with you until you're done."

"Let's see what it is," Bullet Head #1 said, clearly not happy about the prospect of spending another minute with Luther Smyth.

"Close your eyes," Luther told Marty.

"Why?"

"Because it's a present for you and Grace, you dunce."

Marty closed his eyes and heard pages being turned.

"This is just a bunch of—"

"Shh!" Luther said. "Do you want to wreck the surprise?"

"Just take it with you and get out of here," Bullet Head #1 said.

Marty opened his eyes and saw that whatever Luther had taken out of his pack was now stuffed under his sweatshirt. They walked through the gate and over to a beat-up four-wheeler. Marty strapped on a helmet and swung onto the front. Luther did the same and climbed on behind him. While Marty tried to get the four-wheeler started, Luther turned around and shouted at the Bullet Heads, "I wasn't kidding about the rash. The last doctor who looked at it was infected within an hour and he still has it. He was wearing gloves, too. I'm really sorry."

The four-wheeler belched to life and Marty peeled out.

"Jeez!" Luther said. "It *is* a fort."

They were standing outside a three-story building made of black granite blocks.

"It's actually Wolfe's house," Marty said. "And it's a little less forbidding on the inside, but not by much. Hey, you don't really have an incurable rash, do you?"

"Duh *du jour*," Luther said. "But when I took your present out of my pack, I managed to open the itching powder Brenda Scrivens invented in chemistry class. Those guys are going to think they have an incurable rash as soon as they go through my stuff."

Marty laughed. He and Luther were going to have a blast — if the Bullet Heads didn't shoot his friend before they even shipped out.

Wolfe's massive stone house sat atop a high promontory overlooking the Pacific Ocean. Luther walked over to the edge of the cliff and looked down. Marty joined him.

"How far is Cryptos from the Washington coast?" Luther asked.

"About a hundred and fifty miles," Marty answered.

"So is it part of Washington State? Is it part of the United States?"

"Of course," Marty said, but he didn't really know. He'd heard that the island had been a secret base during World War Two, and that Wolfe had gotten it in exchange for some work he and Ted Bronson had done for the government. Grace had tried to find the island on a nautical map, but it was as if the island didn't exist. The name *Cryptos* came from the word *cryptic*, which meant "secret"—and there were certainly a lot of secrets on the island.

"So how's the birthday girl?" Luther asked.

Marty thought about the question for a second, then said, "Grace is not the same Grace you knew at Omega Prep."

"I figured that," Luther said. "I mean, when you and she left school, she was your twin sister. Now it turns out she's your cousin."

"There's more to it than that," Marty said. "A lot more."

Grace was in the library. She was as excited as Marty about Luther's arrival, but for different reasons. Marty hadn't mentioned it much, but she knew he was worried about their parents—*his* parents, she corrected herself mentally. Some days, she still had to remind herself that she was now Grace Wolfe, not Grace O'Hara. Luther's presence on the island and aboard the *Coelacanth* would be a welcome diversion for Marty—something to keep his mind off the ongoing tragedy.

And, Grace thought selfishly, with Luther there she might be able to get something accomplished. She loved Marty, but he had a tendency to dominate every waking moment of her life. She'd barely had time to think since they had returned from the Congo. The dinosaur eggs were nothing compared to what she had discovered about herself and her past.

Just then, Marty and Luther burst into the library.

Grace watched Luther dart around the large room like a hungry mosquito, taking in everything at once with open-mouthed enthusiasm. He had more energy than any other human being she had ever met. It was as if he were on fire beneath his pale, freckled skin. Back at Omega Prep they used to make bets on how long he could remain seated in his chair. Eight minutes and thirty-six seconds was his record, and the only reason he lasted that long was because the headmaster, Dr. Bartholomew Beasel, was standing above him, ready to push him back down if he popped up. Oddly enough, Luther was just the opposite when he slept. Waking him was like trying to rouse a corpse.

Luther's first stop was one of the two large saltwater aquariums bracketing the giant fireplace at the far end of the library.

"Coelacanths, huh?" he said, tapping the thick glass. "With those armored scales, they look medieval, like they're ready to joust."

"They just sit there most of the time," Marty said. "They're kind of boring."

"But not these!" Luther said, rushing over to the second tank. "Squid!"

"A common variety," Marty explained. "Wolfe caught them off the end of the dock one night. He used a flashlight to attract them, and when they rose to the surface, he just scooped them up with a net."

"But we're going after the *giant* squid in New Zealand," Luther said. "In Nordic mythology they're called kraken. Supposedly they lived off the coasts of Scandinavian countries and attacked ships. I've been doing some reading about them. Tennyson even wrote a poem about one, back in the nineteenth century. I can't remember how it goes, but their scientific name is—"

"The kraken and the giant squid may not be the same animal," Grace said. "The kraken might be a cryptid. The giant squid is not. We know the giant squid exists, and the scientific name is *Architeuthis*."

Luther looked around in confusion. He couldn't see her.

Marty pointed his index finger at the ceiling.

Luther looked up, and for once he was speechless.

Grace was balanced on the middle of a high wire stretched tautly between the rails surrounding the circular second-floor library, eighteen feet above their heads. From aloft, she recited the opening lines of Tennyson's poem:

> "Below the thunders of the upper deep;
> Far far beneath in the abysmal sea,
> His ancient, dreamless, uninvaded sleep
> The Kraken sleepeth—"

"What the heck are you doing up there?" Luther asked.

"Focusing," Grace answered.

"There's no net. If you fall, you'll break your neck."

"I won't fall," Grace said. She spread her arms and started walking backward on the wire toward the rail. "How was your flight?"

"Uh . . . rough," Luther answered. "They made me stay in my seat."

"That must have been hard all the way from Switzerland."

"Yeah. I brought all your diaries."

"My Moleskines," Grace said. "Thank you."

"I told you she had changed," Marty said.

"Yeah," Luther said. "But you didn't tell me that she had joined the circus."

Grace reached the rail, climbed over, and made her way to the spiral staircase leading to the ground floor. She joined the boys in front of the squid tank.

"Happy birthday," Luther said.

"Thank you."

"How'd you learn to . . ." Luther pointed up at the wire. ". . . you know . . ."

"Laurel Lee taught me," Grace said. "I started out low and worked my way up. It's helped me learn to focus and overcome some of my fears."

Marty's right, Luther thought, *Grace* has *changed.* He looked at Marty. "You told me Dr. Lee was a cultural anthropologist. You didn't mention that she was an acrobat, too."

"I guess it slipped my mind," Marty said.

Luther looked back at Grace. "Is Dr. Lee here?"

"I wish she were," Grace said sadly. "She's still in Africa."

"So, what do you have planned for your birthday?"

"I don't know," Grace said. "That's not up to me."

Luther grinned and pulled a sketchbook out from under his sweatshirt. "I made something for you. Well, it's actually for both you and Marty, but mostly you because it's your birthday." He took the pad over to a laboratory bench and cleared a space. Marty and Grace joined him.

"It's a graphic novel of what happened to you in the Congo," Luther explained. "Of course, I wasn't there, so all I had to go on was what Marty told me. It's a little crude and I'm not as good of an artist as Marty, but . . ."

"Oh, stop it, Luther," Grace said. "Just show us."

Luther opened the pad.

The first drawing was of a helicopter crashing in a jungle.

Marty and Grace stared at the image in silence.

"Maybe this wasn't such a good idea," Luther said. "I mean . . ."

"No, it's fine," Marty said. He pointed at the drawing. "That's my parents crashing in South America."

"Yeah, well, that's what started all of this, you guys leaving school, going to live with your uncle — Marty's uncle — so I figured . . ." Luther hesitated, then asked, "Has there been any news?"

Marty shook his head. "But Wolfe still has people looking. He won't give up."

"And I think they're still alive," Grace added. "If they weren't, I'd know it." She looked at Marty with her robin's-egg-blue eyes. "I would feel it."

Luther looked away. Marty's parents had been missing for more than six months in the Brazilian rain forest, one of the most hostile areas on the planet. The chances of their still being alive were just about zero.

"If Grace says they're alive, then I think they're alive," Marty said. "So don't sweat it. Let's see the rest of your drawings."

Luther began flipping pages.

Marty was not impressed with Luther's drawings, but the story they told was pretty accurate, considering that Luther had pieced it together from the few emails Marty had sent him during and after their ordeal.

The next drawing showed Marty and Grace landing on Cryptos Island to meet Travis Wolfe, the uncle they didn't know they had, followed by the arrival of Dr. Laurel Lee from the Congo with an egg the size of a soccer ball, belonging to the legendary Mokélé-mbembé — the last living dinosaur.

As Luther continued to turn the pages, Marty looked over at Grace. The last few months had been a shock for him, but they had completely turned Grace's life upside down. To learn that she had actually been born in the Congo; that Wolfe was in fact her father and had given her to his sister and her husband, Marty's parents, to raise as their own child; that he had done this to protect her from her own grandfather, world-famous conservationist Noah Blackwood — the whole story was pretty incredible. Grace was handling it well, all things considered.

Marty turned back to Luther's graphic novel.

"See, this is supposed to be Butch McCall, that guy who works for your grandfather," Luther was telling Grace.

"The guy who kidnapped me," Grace clarified.

Marty, Grace, and Luther spent the next half hour reading the rest of Luther's masterpiece, which concluded with Wolfe, Laurel Lee, and Bertha Bishop commandeering Noah Blackwood's helicopter, stranding Noah and Butch McCall in the Congo, and returning triumphantly to Cryptos Island with the Mokélé-mbembé eggs.

"It's great," Marty said. "Really."

"It's excellent," Grace said. "You put a lot of work into this."

"It's just a draft," Luther said, flushing a little. He looked at Marty. "I thought that we could spruce it up on our way to New Zealand."

"Sure," Marty said. "We could add a few things here and there, and I might be able to touch up some of the illustrations a little." *Meaning I'll completely redraw them,* he thought. *But it is a great piece of work, considering Luther drew it from Switzerland, thousands of miles north of the Congo.*

"We have something for you, too," Marty said, opening one of the cabinets beneath the laboratory bench.

"But it's not *my* birthday," Luther protested.

Marty ignored him. One of the problems with getting Luther anything was that Luther had everything—at least everything he wanted. His absentee parents made sure of that. Another problem was that Luther didn't want much and was not interested in *normal* things.

Marty set a glass jar filled with salt on top of the bench.

"How thoughtful," Luther said. "A saltshaker. That's the one thing I didn't bring with me from Omega Prep."

"Just open it," Marty said.

Luther carefully unscrewed the lid, then dipped his little finger into the white crystals and touched it to his tongue. "Mmm," he said. "Sodium chloride. Delicious!"

"Right," Marty said. "Salt. Dump it out."

Luther dumped the contents into the lab sink. Buried in the salt was a desiccated object with fangs. He held it up and blew the salt off, tears welling in his eyes. "This is the greatest gift anyone has ever given to me," Luther said. "It's the head of the green mamba you killed in the Congo, right?"

Marty nodded. "We thought you'd like it," he said, delighted at Luther's reaction but not surprised. "It's from both Grace and me. The venom sacs are still intact, so I would keep it in the jar if I were you."

Luther put the snake head back in the jar and scooped most of the salt back on top of it. "I don't know what to say."

Marty was about to tell him that it was no big deal when the library door burst open. Travis Wolfe strode in, accompanied by Al Ikes. Wolfe was smiling. Al was frowning. They made an odd couple. Wolfe was a giant, well over six feet tall, with unruly black hair and a bushy black beard. He wore a gray sweatshirt, baggy cargo pants, and size fifteen sneakers. Al was clean-shaven and dressed in a three-piece suit and polished wing tips. The top of his carefully groomed brown hair barely reached Wolfe's broad shoulder.

"This is my friend Luther Smyth," Marty said to Wolfe, totally ignoring the perpetually irked Al Ikes.

Wolfe's smile broadened as he stepped forward and shook Luther's hand. "Welcome aboard," he said. "I'm glad you're here."

"Thanks for inviting me," Luther said. He stole a quick glance at Wolfe's right leg, which had been bitten off by a Mokélé-mbembé in the Congo when Grace was two years old. In its place Wolfe wore a high-tech prosthesis invented by the mysterious Ted Bronson.

"We've had a little change of plans," Wolfe said. "We'll be sailing tonight."

"Tonight?" Grace and Marty said. They often spoke in unison like twins do, even though they were no longer twins.

Wolfe nodded. "You're going to need to get your gear down to the ship as soon as possible."

"What about Grace's birthday?" Marty asked. "I was going to bake a cake."

"You'll have to bake it aboard ship," Wolfe said. "We'll have the birthday party after we're underway."

"And there's another problem," Al said, glaring at Marty. "Did you leave the keys in your four-wheeler?"

Marty checked his pockets. The keys weren't there. One of Al's security measures was that the keys to all vehicles on Cryptos were to be taken out of the ignitions. Marty had no idea why this was important. Where could a car thief go on the tiny island?

"Sorry," Marty said. "I'll run out and get them."

Al shook his head. "It's too late. The four-wheeler has been stolen."

"By who?" Marty asked.

"Not by who," Al answered. "By *it*."

Marty glanced at Wolfe, who was doing his best to stop himself from laughing.

It was what Al called Bo. He hated the chimpanzee, and the feeling was mutual. Bo delighted in tweaking Al and his men whenever and wherever she could.

"And she has that little dog with her," Al added.

The little dog was PD—short for Pocket Dog—a three-pound teacup poodle who jumped into pockets when she heard the word *snake* because she was terrified of the reptiles. Bo and PD were best friends, and Bo was always carrying the tiny poodle around on her adventures.

"I didn't know Bo knew how to drive a four-wheeler," Marty said.

"From the reports we've gotten, she doesn't drive it very well," Wolfe said. "You and Luther better go out and try to catch her before she kills herself or someone else. Luther's gear is already on the ship. While you're out chasing the renegade chimp, Grace can pack your stuff. When you catch up with Bo, take her and PD down to the *Coelacanth*. But I'm warning you ahead of time . . . Bo is terrified of ships, especially the *Coelacanth*."

Marty didn't blame her. He and Bo were the only ones on the island who had any sense about the haunted ship.

"Is her tracking tag active?" he asked.

"I'm afraid not," Wolfe answered. "I haven't had time to put in another subcutaneous tag compatible with the new Gizmos."

"Subcutaneous?" Luther asked.

"Under the skin," Marty answered. "If she had to wear one around her neck like we do, she'd just tear it off." Marty looked back at his uncle. "So, how am I supposed to find and catch her?"

Wolfe grinned. "She's the only chimp on the island riding a four-wheeler. I'm sure you'll figure something out."

Al looked at his watch. "If we're going to ship out tonight, I have things to attend to."

"Nice to meet you, Albert," Luther said.

Al glared at him and hurried out of the library.

"I wonder if he's going to wear three-piece suits on board the *Coelacanth*," Marty said.

"What do you want me to pack?" Grace asked.

"I haven't even *un*packed since we got back from the Congo. Just put the loose stuff into my bags." He looked at Luther. "We'd better go."

"There's another four-wheeler parked outside," Wolfe said. "And don't forget to wear your helmets."

Marty doubted Bo and PD had helmets, but he and Luther slipped theirs on and ran out of the library.

Wolfe watched them go, shaking his head, then turned his attention to the high wire stretched across the balcony.

"That makes me very nervous," he said.

"Don't worry," Grace said. "I'm very careful when I'm up there."

"Maybe when we get back we can set up something in the hangar with a net below it . . . just in case."

"Good idea," Grace said, then changed the subject. "How's Congo?"

Congo was the African gray parrot they had brought back with them from the continent. He had belonged to Grace's mother, Rose. Noah Blackwood's henchman, Butch McCall, had broken Congo's wing when the parrot tried to stop him from kidnapping Grace. Her father, Travis Wolfe, was not only a biologist, oceanographer, and cryptozoologist . . . he was also a veterinarian.

"His bones mended well," Wolfe replied. "I took the bandages off and sent him down to the *Coelacanth* along with the Mokélé-mbembé eggs. Secretly, of course. We still don't want anyone to know about the eggs. It will be a while before Congo can use his wing, but he'll be flying around soon."

"I thought you wanted to wait for the eggs to hatch before we left for New Zealand," Grace said.

"I did. It would be a lot better to have them hatch on the island than on the open sea, but a little problem has come up." An uncharacteristic look of worry flashed across Wolfe's rugged but handsome face. "Your grandfather, Noah Blackwood, got back to Seattle last night," he said.

BLACKWOOD & BUTCH

Dr. Noah Blackwood was holding a press conference in front of the giant panda exhibit at his Seattle Ark. Three black-and-white cubs rollicked behind him on a field of green grass, but the irresistibly cute cubs were all but ignored by the reporters in attendance. Very few people on earth—perhaps no one else on earth—could command that kind of attention against such a tantalizing background.

Dr. Blackwood's mesmerizing blue eyes were offset by a bronze tan and a lion's mane of snow-white hair. He was smiling at the reporters with his perfectly white teeth, hiding the raging anger burning inside his famously cheerful exterior. Standing next to Noah was a gaunt Butch McCall. With his bushy mustache, bald head, and tattoos, Butch looked as if he had just stepped out of solitary confinement at a state penitentiary.

"As you know," Noah was saying in his deep baritone voice, "my only child, Rose, disappeared in the Congo eleven years ago. Not a day . . ." He wiped a tear from his eye and cleared his throat. ". . . not an hour goes by that I don't feel the heartbreaking loss I wrote about in my autobiography, *My Wondrous Wild Life*. The mystery of Rose's disappearance has never been solved." He looked at Butch and put a manicured hand on Butch's shoulder. "My friend and chief field biologist, Butch McCall, loved Rose almost as much as I. He felt compelled to revisit the Lake Télé region of the Congo, where Rose was last seen, hoping to uncover new evidence of what happened to her. Sadly, he failed in this endeavor, and in the process was injured and became hopelessly lost. . . ."

It took all of Butch McCall's considerable willpower to stop himself from scowling. This was the only part of Noah Blackwood's outrageous lie that he had a problem with. The idea that Butch McCall could get lost in the wilderness, or anywhere else, was utterly ridiculous. He prided himself on his ability to know exactly where he was at all times, and with good reason. But today he had to swallow his pride. The only thing in the world that Butch feared was the white-haired old man standing next to him.

Noah continued. "Fortunately, I was able to locate him and carry him out of that terribly hostile environment."

Butch gritted his teeth. It had taken them over a week to reach the nearest settlement. And it had been Butch who had carried *Noah* out of the jungle.

Instead of heading back to the Seattle Ark, Noah had his private jet drop him at an exclusive private spa in the south of France to recuperate from his ordeal, leaving Butch in the Congo in much less lavish circumstances to lick his own wounds.

"As luck would have it, while I was searching for Butch in the Congo I made two very important scientific discoveries," Noah went on.

It was Butch who had made the discoveries, and only one was scientific—the other was personal. And this was the second reason Butch was putting up with this charade. He had managed to let both discoveries slip through his callused hands, and Noah Blackwood was furious with him. Butch wanted the discoveries back. The only way to get them was with Noah's considerable wealth and power.

Predictably, the reporters asked Noah what these discoveries were. And just as predictably, Noah, with his familiar sly smile and a mischievous blue-eyed glint, said, "I am afraid I cannot tell you."

The reporters let out a collective disappointed groan.

"At least not yet," Noah added. "You know my policy and the name of my other bestselling book, *Wildlife First*. It's not just a title, it is the lifeblood of my soul. Wildlife first, without exception."

"Did you discover a new animal species?" one of the reporters asked.

"No comment at this time," Noah said. "But you have my word that I will let you know what I discovered as soon as I possibly can." He stared at the group for a moment, then began again. "The reason I called this press conference was to thank everyone for the outpouring of concern and prayers for my safety during the past two weeks." He smiled again. "I'm afraid that the rumors of my death have been greatly exaggerated."

The reporters laughed at the famous quote by the writer Mark Twain. What they didn't know was that the *rumors* of Noah Blackwood's death had actually been circulated by Noah himself while he was undergoing his spa treatments. When

Noah had sufficiently recovered, he snuck back into the Congo and stumbled out of the forest cradling Butch in his arms—no easy task because of Butch's size, but luckily it was only a distance of thirty feet.

Coincidentally, there was a camera crew in the very village Noah staggered into.

NOAH BLACKWOOD ALIVE!
DR. BLACKWOOD SAVES COLLEAGUE
FROM DEADLY JUNGLE!

. . . were the lead stories on television and in magazines and newspapers all around the world.

Noah's disappearance and miraculous reappearance had added millions of dollars to his considerable bank account. Aside from his highly rated wildlife television show, he owned several popular animal theme parks around the world called Noah's Ark. During his two-week disappearance, visitors had flooded through the gates of his parks, and his television show rerun ratings had never been higher. He had made more money missing or presumed dead than he had when he was alive, making him wonder why he hadn't tried the disappearing act before.

Noah lived in a mansion on a hill perched above his Seattle Ark. When the press conference was over, he was planning to tour the park and talk to visitors, which always made great footage on the five o'clock news. The Noah Blackwood everyone knew was a man of the people, an accessible man, a kind man, but a merciless warrior when it came to protecting the world's wildlife.

"The only thing I can tell you now is that what I have discovered will rock the scientific community to its very foundation," Noah said.

"What do you think of Northwest Zoo and Aquarium's plans to capture and exhibit a giant squid?" a woman reporter asked.

Noah blinked. This was the first time he'd heard about it. NZA was his main competitor in Washington State. He believed that every dollar spent at NZA was a dollar stolen from him. Why hadn't his spy at NZA told him about this?

"I wish them luck," he said with a strained smile, as if it were old news. "But it will be no easy task. A living specimen of *Architeuthis* has never been captured."

"They're pretty confident they can bring one back alive," the reporter persisted. "We haven't been able to verify it, but the rumor is that they've contracted eWolfe to capture the squid in Kaikoura Canyon off the coast of New Zealand."

At the mention of eWolfe, Noah's smile failed him.

"Didn't Travis Wolfe work for you?" the reporter asked.

"Yes," Noah said tightly. "A long time ago."

"He and his partner, Ted Bronson, captured that great white shark for you, didn't they?"

"Actually, I captured and brought the great white in," Noah lied. "Travis and Ted were deckhands at the time." Noah gave the woman a smile and chuckled. "And not very good ones at that."

Some of the other reporters laughed along with him.

"After the great white died at your park," the reporter continued without smiling, "I always wondered why you didn't replace it. It was a very popular exhibit."

"Yes, it was," Noah said. "But the great white is hardly endangered. We used the empty tank for an endangered species of porpoise. My Arks are conservation facilities, not amusement parks."

The truth was that Blackwood's parks were gold mines and breeding grounds where he grew animals for the unusual collection he kept on the top floor of his mansion.

Noah leaned over to Butch and whispered, "Act like you're ill. This press conference is over. And before we leave, get that reporter's name. Her career is over."

Butch didn't know how to *act ill,* having rarely been sick a day in his life, but he gave it his best shot. He started to wobble as if he were going to pass out.

"Are you all right, Butch?" Noah grabbed Butch's arm to stop him from falling. "I told Butch he didn't have to attend the press conference," Noah told the reporters with deep concern. "In addition to his other injuries, he's suffering from a bout of malaria. I'm afraid we'll have to cut this short." Noah started leading Butch through the crowd of reporters to the electric cart that would drive them back up to the mansion.

As they passed the reporter who had brought up the shark question, Butch asked her what her name was. She told him. Butch smiled, knowing that by the end of the week the reporter would be looking for a new occupation. Noah would see to that.

Butch was relieved to be back inside the mansion and away from the cameras, where he could drop the rescued victim charade.

Unfortunately, Noah had also dropped the kind and caring Noah Blackwood charade. He was fuming as Butch followed him upstairs to his inner sanctum on the top floor. It was a large room few people had ever seen, and with good reason—it was the lair of the real Noah Blackwood.

The world was used to seeing Noah Blackwood holding and petting baby animals on late-night television shows, giving impassioned lectures on wildlife conservation, and pursuing evil animal poachers and bringing them to justice. But in this room, filled with the most exotic and endangered animals on earth, only two animals were breathing: Noah Blackwood and Butch McCall.

Butch walked around the hermetically sealed, climate-controlled glass dioramas filled with exquisite taxidermy. The animals looked better in death than they had in life. And Butch knew these stuffed animals well, having killed or captured more than half of them. He stopped before the window of a new occupant. It was a young female Caspian tiger in her prime, attacking an ibex. Her name was Natasha. Butch had not killed Natasha, but he had captured her parents in Afghanistan several years earlier and smuggled them into the Seattle Ark. The Caspian tiger was thought to have gone extinct in the early 1900s. It hadn't, but it was extinct now.

Butch turned to Noah, who was sitting behind a huge spotless desk, glaring angrily at the only thing on it—a large flat-screen computer monitor.

"Natasha never looked better," Butch said, trying to lighten the tension in the room.

"Henrico botched the job," Noah retorted sourly. "If you look at the right upper canine, you can see there's a hairline crack."

Henrico was Noah's personal taxidermist. Butch had never seen him. His workshop was in the basement of the mansion and could only be reached by a private elevator to which Noah alone had the key. As far as Butch knew, Henrico had not left the basement in more than twenty years—and in all that time he had seen and talked to no one but Noah Blackwood.

"Henrico is getting old," Noah said. "He's losing his artistic touch. We are going to have to get an apprentice for him soon so he can pass on what he knows before he dies."

"That's not going to be easy," Butch said. "Where are you going to find someone willing to spend twenty years underground with a bunch of dead animals?"

"Who said Henrico was willing?" Noah said. "Who said he had a choice when I found him on the streets of Rio picking tourists' pockets? He had a very light touch, which all good pickpockets have. That's why I chose him. He was trained by my father's taxidermist. You'd be surprised how good you become at something when you are locked in a basement with absolutely nothing else to do. He was resistant at first, but now he's a true artist." Noah swept his elegant hand across the beautiful dioramas. "In Rio he would have been imprisoned, or murdered, or would have died of disease. Instead, he has created a legacy of work that will make him immortal."

Noah turned his attention back to the computer monitor and punched a button on a keyboard. There was a short ring over a speaker, then a nervous-sounding woman came on the line.

"Dr. Blackwood, I'm so relieved you're safe. I was afraid you—"

"Stop wasting my time," Noah said. "Why wasn't I told about the expedition for the giant squid?"

The woman paused. Butch could sense the fear in her hesitation.

"I didn't know about it," the woman answered shakily. "They kept it a secret."

"I pay you to know about everything going on at NZA," Noah said. "It's difficult to believe that an expedition of this magnitude could be kept secret. I was just told about it by an obnoxious reporter. You are supposed to give me news *before* it becomes news. When did you learn about this so-called secret?"

"Two days ago."

"Why didn't you call me two days ago?"

"I thought you were dead."

Butch turned toward the diorama of the Caspian tiger to hide his relief. He didn't know the woman, but he was sure that right about now she wished the rumors of Noah Blackwood's death had been true. Butch hoped Noah's anger toward her might lessen the anger Noah was feeling toward him. He was surprised that Noah hadn't fired him (or worse) after he lost the Mokélé-mbembé eggs and Noah's granddaughter, Grace, at Lake Télé. He was certain Noah would make him pay for these failures, but the old man had yet to inform him how, or what the price would be. If Butch could somehow get Grace back, retrieve the dinosaur eggs, and possibly stop Wolfe and NZA from snagging a giant squid, his boss might just retire the debt and maybe even add a little money to his bank account.

"Why all the secrecy?" Noah shouted at the receiver.

"I don't know," the woman answered.

Butch knew. So did Noah Blackwood. A few months earlier NZA had launched an expedition to catch a pair of whale sharks. They might have succeeded if their research ship hadn't had a mysterious fire that all but destroyed the vessel. When they were towed back into harbor, they found out that their insurance payments weren't up-to-date, and they lost the ship. Butch had started the fire, and Noah had disrupted the insurance policy. The director of NZA publicly accused Noah Blackwood of sabotage, but few people believed him. Noah's reputation was restored a week later when NZA had a major failure of their filtration system. NZA tried to call in Travis Wolfe to fix the problem, but he was in South America searching for his sister, Sylvia, and his brother-in-law, Timothy O'Hara—that brat Marty's parents—after their tragic helicopter crash in the Brazilian Amazon. Noah graciously stepped in to save NZA's dying fish by loaning his technicians. After this, no one doubted Dr. Blackwood's intentions. Why would a man sabotage NZA's expedition, then a week later save the aquarium from total ruin?

It had been a wonderful year, Butch thought, *until the Congo.*

"Get me the details of the giant squid expedition by the end of the day," Noah said. "Then I suggest you move out of your downtown waterfront condo, which I own, I might add, and get out of town as fast as you can. And leave the keys to the Mini

Cooper in the condo. I own that as well. I'll be waiting." He ended the call and looked at Butch.

"NZA is broke," he said. "They could not possibly have raised the funds to launch an expedition this big without my knowing about it. Which means that Travis Wolfe is fronting them the money and expertise, and getting a percentage of the take if they succeed in bringing in a giant squid alive. He'd make millions of dollars. Dollars that belong to me. With all that money he'd be able to search the world for cryptids for the rest of his miserable life and keep me away from Grace in the process. We have to stop him!"

"Fire?" Butch asked, smiling. (Butch loved a good fire.)

"No," Noah said. "A suspicious fire aboard a second ship would cast the blame back on me. And there's a chance that Grace might be on board the *Coelacanth* along with the Mokélé-mbembé eggs. We can't risk losing Grace—or those eggs."

"If the eggs are even fertile," Butch pointed out. "And if they are, they might have already hatched. Maybe Wolfe won't take Grace or Marty with him on the expedition. When he leaves, I'll sneak onto Cryptos Island and grab the hatchlings and your granddaughter." *And even the score with the boy,* Butch thought.

"Travis is not about to leave his only child and the greatest discovery of the last millennium behind on the island," Noah said angrily. "Your fatal flaw, Butch, is that you have always underestimated Travis Wolfe. That's how you lost Grace and the eggs in the Congo. Our only chance—*your* only chance—is to get on that island before they leave and take back what is rightfully mine."

"I'll go tomorrow," Butch said, already starting to calculate what he would need and how he would do it.

Noah shook his head. "We need more time. We're talking about kidnapping. We have to find a place to take Grace where no one will find her. And the eggs or the hatchlings? Where are we going to hide them until we come up with a plausible story as to how they were acquired? I laid the foundation with those reporters, but it will take at least a week to get the rest of the story in place. You are underestimating Travis again. He knows we're back. He knows that we are going to come after Grace and the eggs. He's taken precautions."

"Like what?" Butch asked.

"I'm not sure yet. I have people working for me on Cryptos, but I haven't been able to get in touch with any of them since Travis got back to the island. And don't think that Travis hasn't documented his discovery. He has records of those eggs. Videos, scientific data, photos . . . We would have to take everything he has so he couldn't come back at us and prove that we stole his discovery. The only mistake Travis made in the Congo was letting us live. He should have put a bullet in our heads— and that's Travis Wolfe's fatal flaw. He's a coward at heart. He is incapable of pulling a trigger unless he's holding a tranquilizer gun."

"I don't have that flaw," Butch said. "I'll pull a real trigger on Wolfe the second I get him in my sights."

Noah laughed sarcastically. "You don't think Travis knows that? Just because you don't like him doesn't mean he's stupid. Travis started planning what he was going to do the moment he commandeered our chopper and ditched us in the jungle. The problem is that I don't know what his plan is, and until I do, we cannot move on him. We need to—"

A buzzer sounded on the desk. Irritated, Noah punched a button on his keyboard. "What is it?"

"There's someone here to see you," a woman's voice replied. "He says it's urgent. He said to tell you that he's from the island."

Noah Blackwood smiled. "Send him right up."

A minute later there was a knock on Noah's door. He opened it, and a little man stepped inside.

"What's going on?" Noah asked without saying hello.

"Wolfe told everyone on Cryptos that you and Butch had died in the Congo," the man said.

Noah looked at Butch. "See? Travis knew we had people on the island. If he convinced them that we were dead they wouldn't try to get in touch with us. What would be the point?" He turned back to the man and narrowed his blue eyes. "But that doesn't explain why you didn't answer my calls. I've tried to reach you and the others a hundred times since I got out of the Congo."

"Total blackout," the man said. "No calls to or off the island without authorization. Ted Bronson set up some kind of jamming device that fried the satellite phones you gave us. And Wolfe hired some security specialist named Albert Ikes. Ex-military—"

"I think he's ex–Central Intelligence Agency," Noah corrected. "I've heard of him. He's one of the best in the business, and his services are very expensive."

"Whoever he is, he brought in a paramilitary outfit," the man continued. "Cryptos Island is like an armed fortress. Only a handful of people have been let off the island since Wolfe returned, and even those are under twenty-four-hour surveillance."

"How'd you get off the island?" Butch asked.

The man smiled up at him. "My size," he said. "I've been working aboard the *Coelacanth* for the past week. Phil Bishop has been shuttling supplies and people onto the island several times a day. During his last haul I squeezed into the cargo area of his seaplane. I don't know how much time I have, or whether I can smuggle myself back onto the seaplane. When we heard you were alive last night on TV, we decided one of us had to get off Cryptos and tell you what's going on — even if it meant not getting back onto the island."

"Good work," Noah said. "Excellent! How long before they miss you?"

The man looked at his watch. "I have someone covering for me on the ship. I'll have to be back on board in a few hours or they'll know I left." He reached under his shirt collar and pulled out a black-and-white tracking tag. "And then there's this thing. They do random tracking checks. If they do one while I'm here, the game is up. They'll never let me back on the ship or the island."

"How often do they check?"

The man shrugged. "No one knows."

"We'll get you back," Noah said confidently. "Now tell me what you know about the expedition."

"They're shipping out tonight," the man said.

"Tonight!" Noah shouted.

"That's why I jumped ship," the man hurriedly explained. "We didn't know we were leaving tonight until this afternoon. We thought we had two weeks."

"What about the eggs?" Noah asked.

"What eggs?"

Noah's face flushed in anger. "What did they have on board the jet when they returned from the Congo?"

"I don't know," the man answered. "As soon as the jet landed, they towed it into the hangar and closed the doors. No one was allowed in. The next day several employees were given a pay bonus and laid off. Most of us left on Cryptos were sent down to the *Coelacanth* and we haven't been allowed back on the island since."

"And Grace?"

"Wolfe's niece?" the man asked. "I haven't seen her. She hasn't been down to the ship, that I know of. But I did see Wolfe's nephew, Marty, today. Phil Bishop flew in a friend of his."

"So, Grace is probably still on the island," Noah said. "Is Wolfe taking the kids with him?"

"Definitely," the man said. "They're in adjoining cabins. One for Grace, and one for Marty and his pal. I hauled his stuff aboard and stowed it in Marty's cabin just before I slipped off the ship."

"What's the friend's name?" Noah asked.

The man smiled. "Yeah, I got a chance to go through the kid's junk. His name is Luther Smyth. He was Marty's roomie at that private school they went to in Switzerland. I copied some information down." He pulled a crumpled piece of paper out of his pocket and gave it to Noah. "Parents' names, addresses, etc. I don't know if it will do you any good."

Noah scanned the piece of paper. "Anything else?"

"One of his suitcases was crammed with diaries. Hundreds of them, but they weren't his. They belong to Grace. He must have hauled them all the way from Switzerland."

"Did you take any?"

"Couldn't," the man answered. "They're numbered. I figured she'd know if I lifted one."

"Did you go through Grace's cabin?"

The man shook his head. "I was going to toss it, but there was this gray attack parrot in the cabin sitting on a perch. It came at me screaming its black beak off. You could hear it all over the ship. I had to get out of there quick so I didn't get caught."

Butch rubbed his hand where the parrot had bitten him back in the Congo. *I should have thrown him against the tree harder,* he thought.

"How many people are on the ship?" Noah asked.

"I'm not sure. Counting the crew, maybe fifty or so. They've flown in scientists and technicians from all over the world. I don't know a third of them."

"Who's covering for you on the ship?"

The man told him.

Noah smiled. "Excellent. You did well. Why don't you wait downstairs. Butch will be down in a minute, and he'll get you back onto the island."

After the man left, Noah stared at Butch for a long time.

"What?" Butch asked, beginning to sweat in the air-conditioned room.

"I want you to shave your mustache," Noah said.

He might as well have asked Butch to cut off his right arm — Butch had had the mustache for almost as long.

"We'll have to make some other changes as well, but I think we can pull it off."

"What are you talking about?" Butch asked.

Noah Blackwood told Butch what he had in mind.

Marty and Luther roared down the hill and screeched to a stop in front of a metal Quonset hut large enough to store five ships the size of the *Coelacanth*.

"Is this the jet hangar?" Luther asked.

Marty shook his head and pointed back toward the Fort. "The jet hangar's over there next to Lost Lake."

"Oh, yeah," Luther said, grinning. "That's where they keep the dolphins that you thought were sharks."

"It wasn't funny," Marty said. "I almost drowned. And your illustration of the incident was awful."

Luther continued to grin. He and Marty had been swapping insults like this their whole lives. "At least in my drawing they looked like *dolphins*," he said.

"Bo's probably down at the lake," Marty continued, ignoring the retort. "She hates the dolphins and loves to tease them, but I wanted to show you where Ted Bronson lives before we ship out. The building is called the QAQ, the Question and Answer Quonset, which is where eWolfe does all of its research and development."

The boys looked at the armed guard standing outside a little gate built into one of the ginormous sliding doors.

"Is that the only way in?" Luther asked.

"Yep," Marty answered. "I've been around the building a dozen times. No windows to peek through, either. It's like a giant vault."

"And Ted Bronson's never been out?"

Marty shook his head. "Not in years."

"I take it▪he's not going to New Zealand with us, then," Luther said.

"Duh *du jour*," Marty said. "Ted's a total recluse. I don't even know what he looks like. He's not about to sail across the Pacific Ocean."

"So, what kind of things do they research and develop?" Luther asked.

"Amazing things," Marty said. "I was going to wait and show you this later, but it might help us find Bo." He pulled something about the size of a handheld video game player out of his pocket.

"Is that the Gizmo?" Luther burst out. "The way you described it, I thought it'd be smaller."

"The other Gizmos are smaller," Marty said. "This one's a prototype that Ted came up with. It has a function that none of the other Gizmos have."

The regular Gizmo had video conferencing, email, web browsing, an encrypted satellite phone, a global positioning system, and a digital camera, as well as the ability to track people and animals wearing tags, and linkups to the video cameras the animal scouts wore, among dozens of other functions.

"What does yours do that the others don't?" Luther asked.

Marty hit a button on the Gizmo that said WAKE. A little drawer on the top of the Gizmo slid open. Inside was something that looked like it was made of gold.

"What is it?" Luther asked.

"Ted calls it a bot-fly," Marty answered. "But I call it a dragon-spy. It takes a while for the little bug to get moving, but when it gets into gear it can dart around as fast as a bullet."

"Yeah," Luther said impatiently. "But what is it?"

"It's a micro-robot. That's where the word *bot* comes from."

"It flies?" Luther asked.

"It does a lot more than that," Marty answered. "I told you about how Wolfe puts cameras on Bo and the raven, Vid, and the dolphins?"

Luther nodded.

"He lets them go free when he's looking for cryptids," Marty said. "When we were in the Congo, the animal scouts kept an eye on things, including Grace and me when we got in trouble. Bo became our eyes in the trees. Vid was our eyes in the sky. Wolfe's taking the dolphins with us to New Zealand, and they'll be our eyes beneath the sea. The problem is that Wolfe can't control where the animal scouts go or what they look at. So Ted created a robot that will go exactly where we want it to go. There's a micro-camera built into its eyes and it can even pick up audio, but I haven't figured out how to use that yet."

"You're lying," Luther said.

The tiny golden bot started to move—or actually to *unfold*. Its head came out from under a wing and its camera-like eyes blinked. It stretched its right wing out, then its left. The golden wings shuddered, then began vibrating with a buzzing sound. A second pair of wings unfolded behind the first set. The bot stood up and stretched its six legs as if it were getting the kinks out of them.

"I can see why you call it a dragonspy," Luther said. "It looks just like a dragonfly."

"It flies like one, too," Marty said. "It can stop on a dime, fly upside down, hover—"

"Is it made out of gold?" Luther interrupted.

Marty shook his head. "It's a special alloy Ted invented. I don't know what it's made out of, but it's as light as a feather."

"It must have cost millions of dollars to research and develop," Luther said. "No offense, but why would they give it to you?"

"Because no one else can fly it without crashing it. Ted made three bots altogether. They wrecked the first two in the hangar by flying them into walls. I asked Wolfe and a couple of Ted's geeks if I could try my luck with the third. They of course said no way, then Wolfe's Gizmo rang. He listened for a moment then said, 'Are you sure, Ted?' Then he handed me the last bot and the docking Gizmo."

"Ted Bronson was in the hangar?"

Marty shook his head. "He must have been watching the disaster by video from the QAQ. Anyway, at first the dragonspy was a little hard to maneuver, but I managed to fly it for half an hour without squishing it. The controls are pretty touchy. When it gets out of control, the trick is to put it into hover mode until you figure out what to do next."

The bot turned its tiny head toward them. Marty hit a

button on the Gizmo, and Luther and Marty's faces appeared on the Gizmo screen.

"Any chance I can try?" Luther asked.

"Sorry," Marty said. "Wolfe said that I'm the only one who can fly it. If I break the rule, he'll pull my wings. Now let's see what Bo and PD are up to."

The dragonspy took off. Marty had it do a couple of wide 360s, then put it into a hover about a hundred feet above their heads.

Luther looked down at the Gizmo screen and saw a video of himself and Marty standing far below. "What powers it?"

"The wings have solar collectors that charge a series of microscopic batteries. It'll fly all day long outside. Inside it'll fly for an hour or two. If the juice gets low, you have to land it near a lightbulb to recharge." He pointed at a small gauge on the Gizmo screen. It read 4:37. "When we got back from the Congo, Ted took all the Gizmos back and converted the batteries to charge on solar, too. Mine has about four and a half hours left. When we were in the jungle, Wolfe's battery conked out and we lost touch with him, and no one wants that to happen again."

Marty maneuvered the dragonspy toward Lost Lake, then hit the ZOOM button. A four-wheeler came into view. A chimpanzee with a teacup poodle sitting in her lap was driving it along the shore.

"There's the thief and her accomplice. She's trying to bait the dolphins. The problem is, they're not in the lake. Wolfe moved them down to the *Coelacanth* two days ago. We'd better hurry over there and grab her before she figures out her archfoes are gone."

Marty hit a button marked HOME. The dragonspy buzzed back to the Gizmo and climbed into the tiny drawer. Marty slid the drawer closed, and he and Luther jumped onto the four-wheeler and peeled out toward Lost Lake.

The cabins were small, but nicer than Grace had expected. They were equipped with a writing desk, bookshelves, a wardrobe, a bathroom, a comfortable bunk, and in her cabin an African gray parrot that was delighted to see her. Congo jumped from his perch to her shoulder (his injured wing still prevented him from flying), and together they explored their new living quarters.

The walls were paneled in beautiful blond wood. With the setting sun dancing through the portholes, the overall effect was quite cheerful. It was hard to believe that such horrible things had happened aboard this ship.

The only thing Grace hadn't been able to find was her Frankenstein Monkey. She'd been searching for it for days. She knew she was too old for stuffed animals, but she'd had Monkey her entire life. Marty had named Monkey after Dr. Frankenstein's monster because the fabric was covered with patches and stitches that looked like scars. Its mouth and ears were long gone, but they had recovered its left arm in the Congo and Wolfe had stitched it back on. Grace had asked Marty if he'd seen it, and he'd told her it was probably packed away somewhere she hadn't looked yet. Duh *du jour*. He could be so dense sometimes that it was hard to believe they were related. She could not imagine sailing to New Zealand without Monkey, but it looked like she was going to have to.

She put Marty's and Luther's things away, hoping to find Monkey stuffed in one of Marty's bags, but it wasn't there. Disappointed, she unpacked her own gear, saving the Moleskine journals for last. She dragged the heavy suitcase into her cabin and began sorting through the black-covered diaries, placing them on the shelves above the desk one at a time in order, like small slices of her life. The third-to-last Moleskine, #316, looked different from the others. It was swollen and battered from their adventures at Lake Télé, but it was the most important one. It was in that slice of her life that Grace had learned who she really was, who her father was, and who her grandfather was. She glanced over at the trunk with the faded rose painted on the lid, which she still had not opened. *Inside is all that my mother was,* she thought. *Rose . . .*

Grace took a brand-new Moleskine out of the drawer, peeled off the plastic covering, opened it to the first blank page, and began to write with her fountain pen.

> It doesn't seem like my birthday because I thought I had already turned thirteen on Marty's birthday a couple of months ago. Nevertheless, I'm commemorating the day by starting a new Moleskine — my third since we got back to the island. . . .
>
> No word about ~~our~~ Marty's parents. . . . He doesn't talk about them much except to ask me

once in a while if I think they're okay, but I know he thinks about them. I was just unpacking his things and found several drawings of them in his sketchbook. It made me sad to think of him alone in his room, drawing them from memory so he won't forget them. The drawings are beautifully detailed. They look like photographs, almost as if he's willing them back to life (back to us) on paper. If Wolfe doesn't find them soon . . .

But he <u>will</u> find them!

He told me yesterday that he wished he was in Brazil looking for them himself, but without any real leads there's little point in him personally hacking his way through the rain forest. He has a dozen people searching the area where the helicopter crashed and burned. And he's paying them a fortune. This is why this expedition is so important. Most of eWolfe's money is tied up in research and development. He and Ted Bronson are nearly broke. They had to borrow the money for the expedition. If Wolfe doesn't bring in a live giant squid, his company will go bankrupt. They'll lose the island and everything they own. But if they bring one in, Wolfe will get half the gate receipts from NZA for as long as the squid (singular or plural!) survives.

Phil and Bertha Bishop drove our stuff down to the dock in one of the surplus Humvees. We had a hassle with Al Ikes's security guards. They wanted to search everything. This would be fine normally, but there was one item I did not want them to search because I haven't opened it myself — my mother's trunk, which we brought back from the Congo. It took a call to Wolfe to get the guards to back off. He drove down to the dock, ordered them to leave the trunk alone, and helped me bring it into the cabin.

Marty opened the trunk when I was kidnapped by Butch McCall. He was trying to find a clue about where I was. Instead, he found my past. He discovered that I'm his cousin, not his twin sister. That my grandfather is Noah Blackwood, and that my real father is Travis Wolfe. That my real mother's name was Rose — and that she was the only child of Noah Blackwood. I thought about leaving the trunk on Cryptos, but realized that I could no sooner do that than Wolfe could leave the dinosaur eggs on the island. I could not leave my past behind, unprotected. Marty already told me what was inside the trunk: newspaper clippings, research notes, photos of my mother when she was my age, and photos of me when I was a baby in the Congo — before my mother was killed by a Mokélé-mbembé when I was two. And Moleskines, just like the one I'm writing in now. "Stacks of them," Marty said.

I'm looking at the trunk right now. Did my mother paint the rose on the lid? Will I go through the trunk on this voyage? I don't know, but I am glad it's here. My mother is buried beneath a mound of rocks in a small clearing near Lake Télé in the Congo, but her life is in the corner of my little cabin. . . .

BO VOYAGE

Bo had led Marty and Luther completely around the island twice and they hadn't gained a foot on the marauding chimp and her accomplice, PD.

"She's good!" Luther shouted, clutching Marty's waist as they jumped a log.

"Yeah," Marty shouted back. "This is definitely not working. Bo's playing with us. And it's getting dark. If we don't catch her soon, she'll climb a tree, build a nest, and go to sleep with PD cuddled in her hairy arms. The *Coelacanth* will sail without us."

"I can think of worse things than being stranded on Cryptos for three months on our own," Luther said. "But I doubt your uncle will leave without us."

"I wouldn't be so sure," Marty said. "He gets distracted. He might not realize we're not aboard until the ship gets to the South Pacific."

"What about our tracking tags?" Luther asked. "That Ikes guy will certainly check them before the ship sails."

"Yeah," Marty said. "And he'd be delighted if you and me and Bo were left behind."

"We'll catch her," Luther said. "If nothing else, she'll run out of gas."

Gas! Marty thought, glancing at the gauge. The needle was bouncing on EMPTY. He had fueled the thieving Bo's four-wheeler just before he met Luther at the dock. They were going to run out of gas long before Bo.

Marty skidded the four-wheeler to a stop.

"What are you doing?" Luther yelled. "She'll get away."

Marty grinned. "Turning the situation around."

Bo put on the brakes and looked back.

"Just like I thought," Marty said, his smile broadening. "She *wants* us to chase her." He looked at Luther. "We're going to run out of gas, the four-wheeler Bo's on is faster than ours, and we're carrying three times the weight."

"Not to mention she's a better driver than you are," Luther added.

"Very funny," Marty said. "Take your helmet off."

"Why?"

"Bait," Marty answered.

"I don't get it," Luther said, removing his helmet.

Marty laughed. "You *will* if we don't beat Bo down to the dock. Hang on!" He turned the four-wheeler around and twisted the throttle handle forward as far as it would go.

The moment Bo saw Marty reversing—and Luther's orange hair—she roared after them.

Bo caught up to them before they were halfway to the dock and made a grab for Luther's flaming hair. Marty jigged the four-wheeler to the right. Bo missed the hair and nearly flipped her four-wheeler. As she regained control, Marty was able to pull ahead of her again.

"I'm the bait?" Luther shouted.

"Duh *du jour*!" Marty shouted back. "I hope the security gate is open at the dock, or you're going to be bald."

Marty zoomed down the hill. Bo was ten feet behind and gaining. Fortunately, the gate was open. Unfortunately, when the Bullet Heads saw the four-wheelers, they wedged their well-conditioned bodies into the opening like double iron doors.

Marty knew that if he didn't get Bo trapped on the dock, they might never get her onto the ship. And if he stopped, Luther was going to get plucked like a dead Rhode Island Red chicken.

"Halt!" the Bullet Heads shouted.

Marty wasn't about to halt or even slow down, which must have been apparent by the look of alarm on the Bullet Heads' faces. One dove right and the other dove left as Marty zoomed through the narrow opening, followed closely by Bo and the teacup poodle. He turned his head and shouted for the Bullet Heads to shut the gate so Bo could not escape. One of the men slammed the gate closed, then they both sprinted down the dock toward the ship.

"What am I supposed to do when we stop?" Luther shouted.

"Run!" Marty shouted back. "Get onto the ship and find someplace to hide until we can get Bo under control."

Luther was off the four-wheeler before it came to a stop. He sprinted up the gangplank with Bo right behind him, having completely forgotten her fear of ships.

"Snake!" Marty yelled. PD jumped into his cargo pocket just as the two furious guards reached him.

Marty looked at them. "Sorry," he said, not in any hurry to join Luther and Bo aboard the creepy ship.

"Sorry?" Bullet Head #1 growled. "That doesn't quite cut it, does it? You just violated every security rule we have."

"And nearly killed us in the process," Bullet Head #2 added.

"Wolfe told me to get Bo aboard the *Coelacanth*, and this was the only way I could figure out how to do it," Marty explained. "And you guys are like Olympic athletes with lightning reflexes. I knew I couldn't hit you with a four-wheeler if I tried."

The flattery seemed to defuse some of their anger. "We're supposed to search everyone going aboard," Bullet Head #1 said.

"Not much to search on Bo," Marty said. "She's naked and doesn't have pockets. And I can vouch for Luther. He didn't pick up anything on the island." He looked at the Bullet Heads' hands. They were red, as if the men had been scratching them.

"You're welcome to search me again if you want," Marty offered.

"Forget it," Bullet Head #2 said. "You'd better get aboard. You and your friend are the last ones. We're shipping out in half an hour."

"Are you sailing with us?" Marty asked.

Bullet Head #1 smiled. "Duh *du jour*," he said.

Marty smiled back. Maybe they weren't as bad as he had thought.

"What are your names?" he asked.

"I'm Roy," Bullet Head #1 said.

"Joe," Bullet Head #2 said.

Marty looked up the long gangplank to the haunted ship like it was the tongue of a demon. "Do you guys believe in ghosts?"

They shook their bullet heads.

"Why is that chimp chasing your friend?" Roy asked.

"She wants to scalp him," Marty answered. "It's going to be a long cruise."

He started up the gangplank with dread.

Luther was not overly attached to his fluorescent orange hair, but he was not about to have it detached by a deranged chimpanzee.

And he was going to kill Marty for turning him into Bo bait, but first he had to ditch the chimp, which was proving very difficult. Bo was fast and agile. She had already managed to pluck a few orange treasures as they dashed down narrow corridors, up and down companionways, through hatches, knocking down half a dozen startled people. Some cursed, some laughed, but none of them helped. On the bottom deck he came to a dead end and a set of doors marked with a sign:

MOON POOL
AUTHORIZED PERSONNEL ONLY!
ABSOLUTELY NO ENTRY!

A set of pneumatic doors hissed open and Luther ran through. They hissed closed behind him just as Bo arrived. Luther was trapped in what looked like an air lock. In front of him was a second set of pneumatic doors. To his relief, they opened and he ran through, colliding with a woman with a whistle clamped in her mouth and a stainless steel bucket of fish in her hands. She didn't seem at all perturbed that he had just knocked her down and was sprawled on top of her. The collision had almost made him forget why he'd been running in the first place, but he remembered when he heard Bo go absolutely bonkers. She had made it through the air lock and was running on all fours around the largest pool he had ever seen, screaming as if she had lost her mind.

"Excuse me," Luther stammered, untangling himself from the woman. "Sorry. I didn't mean to burst in here, but the chimp was chasing me."

The woman got to her feet, looked at Bo, and smiled. "It's a bonobo chimpanzee," she said. "Very rare, and smarter than your average chimp. Why was she chasing you?"

"Uh . . . ," Luther answered. "My hair."

"Your hair *is* a little unusual," the woman said, helping him to his feet. "Do you dye it?"

"No way," Luther answered. "I was born with it." He'd been asked this question a thousand times before. His science teacher at Omega Prep had told him the orange hue was not a color found in nature. His father, Luther Percival Smyth III (LPS 3), had tried to get Luther (LPS 4) to dye his hair black, saying that no one would ever take him seriously with "that mess" on top of his head. Luther had refused, saying, "If they don't take me seriously as I am, then they aren't going to take me seriously as I am not." (LPS 3 had no idea what his only child meant by this.)

"I like the color," the woman said.

No one had ever told Luther that before.

"My name is Yvonne," the woman said, offering a slender hand sprinkled with silvery fish scales.

He shook her hand. "Luther Smyth."

"Marty O'Hara's friend," Yvonne said.

"You know Marty?"

"No, but I've heard a lot about him and his cousin, Grace. There are no secrets on a ship, or on a small island . . . although I haven't been on the island this trip."

"At all?" Luther asked.

Yvonne shook her head. "Winkin, Blinkin, and Nod were transferred to the Moon Pool before I arrived. I stepped from Phil's seaplane right onto the ship."

"Winkin, Blinkin, and Nod?" Luther asked.

"Wolfe's dolphins," Yvonne said.

Luther looked across the vast pool and realized that there were actually two pools separated by a thick Plexiglas window that went all the way up to the ceiling. The dolphins were in the smaller of the two pools. Bo had stopped circling the smaller pool and was pacing a ten-foot area, back and forth, back and forth, pausing to slap the water every few seconds with her hairy hand. Winkin, Blinkin, and Nod watched her from a safe distance. Then one of them spit out a stream of water, hitting the chimp squarely in the face. Bo shook her head and let out an eardrum-shattering hoot.

Yvonne laughed.

"I guess dolphins are smarter than bonobos," Luther said.

"I wouldn't be so sure," Yvonne said. "And they're not really fighting."

Luther wasn't convinced. Bo looked like she wanted to fillet them.

"We'll have to have her come down here during the voyage and play. It will be good for all of them."

Luther wasn't convinced of that, either. "So, what do you do here?"

"I'm a freelance marine mammal trainer. Wolfe flies me onto Cryptos Island three or four times a year to work with the dolphins. I'm conditioning them for a new camera array Ted Bronson's come up with."

"Wolfe's eyes beneath the sea," Luther said.

"I guess," Yvonne said. "But they're being pretty tight-lipped about how the dolphins are going to be used to catch a giant squid. All I've been told is to get them accustomed to the cameras. I assume they are going to use the larger pool to confine the squid. The two pools are enclosed systems and can be pressurized separately. There's a sealed opening between the pools, so the dolphins can get from the big pool to the smaller pool. There are also separate openings for the pools beneath the ship. What have you heard?"

"Nothing," Luther said, glancing at Bo. "I just got here myself, and I've been a little preoccupied. I know Wolfe used a flashlight to catch the little squid in his library."

Yvonne laughed. "I've seen them. I don't think a flashlight is going to work on *Architeuthis*."

A loud rumbling started.

"It sounds like we're getting under way," Yvonne said. "That means that all the tags have been checked and everyone is aboard."

All the tags *had* been checked by Al Ikes, and everyone was aboard.

But not everyone aboard was wearing a tag.

SHIP'S TOUR

As the *Coelacanth* pulled away from the dock, Marty stood on the deck, using his Gizmo to locate Luther. He found Luther's orange tag in an area called the Moon Pool, along with a white tag belonging to someone named Yvonne. He was about to head down below to see if Bo had given Luther a new haircut when he remembered the dragonspy. He still wasn't ready to enter the bowels of the haunted ship.

He programmed the dragonspy to fly to the orange tag, which negated the need to use controls. A couple of crew members swatted at the bot as it buzzed over their heads, and came pretty close to squishing it. Wolfe would have to issue a *stop swatting the bot* order or the dragonspy would be exterminated before they reached the open ocean. When the dragonspy encountered a closed door, it would hover until someone opened it, or find a different route. Marty was impressed, but not surprised. When Ted Bronson invented something, he didn't cut corners. He had somehow tied the bot's tiny computer brain into the Gizmo tracking program. It knew where everyone on board was and which way they were going.

When the dragonspy reached the closed Moon Pool doors, it

hovered outside for at least five minutes, which Marty took to mean that there was no other way in. Finally, the doors hissed open, and he saw a blurry Bo rush by with what looked like a fish in her mouth. The dragonspy zipped through the first set of doors and barely made it through the second set before they closed.

Marty put the dragonspy into hover over Luther and Yvonne.

Luther looked up and waved. Most of his hair appeared to still be attached to his head. He was talking to Yvonne, but Marty couldn't understand what he was saying—he sounded like an insect. Marty hadn't perfected the dragonspy's audio yet, but he was getting closer to figuring it out.

He switched the dragonspy back to manual control, moving it up to the ceiling. The Moon Pool was too big to see on the little screen, but he could make out the dorsal fins of the three dolphins and an overturned stainless steel fish bucket. Bo had obviously decided that stealing one of her enemies' fish was more important than Luther's hair—temporarily, at least. Marty would have to get Luther a sock cap, or Bo would be after his friend the entire voyage. He called Yvonne on her two-way radio with his Gizmo. Everyone on board was required to carry a two-way. Luther hadn't been aboard long enough to get his yet.

"This is Marty. Can I speak to Luther?"

Yvonne handed her two-way to Luther.

"Thanks for using me as chimp bait," Luther said. "That was a riot."

"Sorry," Marty said, not meaning it. "Could you open the doors so the dragonspy can get out? I want to take a look around the ship."

"I ought to leave it locked in here until its juice dries up and it drowns in the pool," Luther said. "Then you can explain to Wolfe and Ted how you lost their million-dollar bug."

"Whatever," Marty said. "Just open the doors so I can look around."

"You could use your legs to do that," Luther said, walking to the doors. "The ship's interior looks better than the exterior, although I didn't get a chance to see much of it because I was running in terror."

Marty didn't want to admit that his own legs were trembling a little at the prospect of walking below deck. "What are you doing down at the Moon Pool?" he asked. "In fact, what *is* a moon pool?"

Luther repeated what Yvonne had told him.

"Oh," Marty said, not understanding half of his explanation.

"We're going to put on wet suits and swim with the dolphins," Luther told him. "And I won't be wimping out like you did the last time you went for a dip with them. Yvonne's great. She's Wolfe's dolphin trainer."

The dragonspy buzzed back out of the two sets of doors.

Marty looked at the power gauge. He had about forty-five minutes of flying time before he had to call the dragonspy back to its little drawer or land it near an artificial light source to recharge.

He flew it down passageways, through the engine room, then up to the bridge, where Wolfe was standing next to a gnarled old man with a carefully trimmed white beard and white hair battened down by a captain's hat. According to the Gizmo, his name was Cap. He looked old enough to have sailed on the *Titanic*.

The deck below the bridge had a large library that looked very similar to the library on Cryptos, minus the fireplace, aquariums, and high wire. Next to it were a series of laboratories, but the doors were all closed, so Marty couldn't get the dragonspy inside. He caught Al Ikes strutting down a companionway (in a three-piece suit, of course) and followed him. Al slid a card through an electronic lock at the end of a corridor, and a door slid open. Marty flew the dragonspy inside behind him. Joe, a.k.a. Bullet Head #2, sat at a bank of surveillance screens, including one showing Marty standing on the deck maneuvering the dragonspy. He didn't see any of their living quarters on the screens, but he wouldn't be surprised if Al had cameras there as well.

Al paused and looked at a couple of monitors while Marty made some adjustments to the dragonspy's settings. He was rewarded with clear audio for the first time: "Stay diligent, Joe," Al said. "If you see anything unusual, report it to me immediately on the secure radios."

Yes! Marty thought. Now he could not only see people, but he could listen to them as well. Al, Wolfe, and the security force had different radios than the crew did. They were probably military issue and encrypted so no one could monitor their conversations.

Al left the room. Marty followed him back through the door with the dragonspy, then continued his flying tour of the ship.

Their living quarters were on the deck below the laboratories. They were nice. In fact, everything inside the ship looked as if it had been gutted and refurbished. Marty hoped the ghosts and the curse had been thrown out with the old stuff. He flew the dragonspy into his and Luther's cabin, then through the adjoining door into Grace's cabin. She was sitting at a small desk, scribbling in a Moleskine.

Birthday! Marty thought. *I have to make a cake!*

This meant that he was going to have to call the dragonspy back to roost and go below deck. The dragonspy could do a lot of things, but it could not make a cake from scratch.

The dragonspy landed back at the Gizmo two minutes before running out of juice. Marty slipped the Gizmo into a cargo pocket, then took his first steps inside the haunted ship.

CAKE

The kitchen, or galley, was next to a large communal mess hall. There were a lot of people sitting at tables drinking coffee and eating. Marty didn't recognize any of them. The mess was set up buffet style. Men and women in white uniforms scurried back and forth from the galley to the buffet counter, replenishing trays and pans of food.

Marty walked through the swinging doors into the galley, expecting to see Bertha Bishop directing the cooks and servers. Instead, he found a little man standing on a small stool shouting orders at the frenzied staff. He was pudgy, with long greasy black hair, a scraggly beard, crooked yellow teeth, and beady brown eyes.

He glared at Marty and shouted, "What are you doing in here? Serving staff and cooks only!" He pointed an index finger at the doors. "Get out!"

"Where's Bertha?" Marty tried to "Lutherize" him with a goofy grin. It didn't work on this guy.

The man scowled, hopped off his perch, and strode over to Marty like he was going to hit him, but Marty held his ground. He had to bake a cake for Grace, and he wasn't about to get booted out.

"I'm in charge here," the man said. "Bertha's back on Cryptos with Phil."

This was news to Marty. He had just talked to Bertha the day before. She was worried about how she was going to cook for a crew of fifty. Marty had offered to give her a hand whenever he could.

The man swept his hands around the galley. "I don't think she could handle this," he said.

Marty laughed. There wasn't anything Bertha couldn't do — including kill the little man standing in front of him with nothing more than *her* index finger. The noisy galley had gone completely silent. Not a pot or pan clattered as the workers stared at the confrontation.

"I have to make a birthday cake for Grace. I'm Marty O'Hara, and Travis Wolfe is my—" Marty said.

"Yeah, yeah, we know," the man interrupted. "He's your uncle. Big deal. We've heard all about you and your snotty cousin."

It took a lot to make Marty mad, but the man had crossed the line. Marty's fists clenched and his face flushed. Grace *was* a little snotty at times, but with good reason: She was smarter than anyone he knew. And no one was allowed to call her snotty except Marty . . . and maybe Luther. Marty had defended Grace when he thought she was his twin sister, and that wasn't going to stop now that they were only cousins. He glanced at the man's hands to make sure he wasn't holding a butcher knife or a meat cleaver, and took a step forward.

"What's going on here?" Al Ikes shouted as he barged through the swinging doors.

Marty and the man nearly jumped out of their shoes.

Miniature cameras, Marty thought, glancing up at the ceiling. *Just like the ones on the dragonspy.* They'd be invisible unless you knew where to look. Joe or Roy must have called Al and told him there was trouble in the galley.

"Nothin', Mr. Ikes," the chef said. "I was just tellin' the kid that he can't come waltzing in here and push us around just because he's Dr. Wolfe's nephew. We're a little busy making sure the crew gets their grub. He didn't like it and started mouthing off."

This was a blatant lie, of course, but Marty didn't contradict the man. He was curious about the extent of Al Ikes's surveillance capabilities and this might be a good way to find out.

Al stared at the chef. "You and I know that's not what happened, Theo," he said.

So the chef's name is Theo, Marty thought. *And Al can see as well as hear everything we're doing aboard ship.*

"It's exactly what happened," Theo said. "The kid thinks he owns the ship. Wants to bake a cake, for crying out loud." He scowled at Marty. "Like he could bake a cake. We don't have any cake mix. We set sail before all our supplies got here. We'll be lucky if we don't starve to death before we get to New Zealand."

"I've never used cake mix," Marty said. "I make my cakes from scratch."

"Yeah, right," Theo said.

Marty ignored him and turned to Al. "I thought Bertha was going to handle the cooking on board."

"Change of plans," Al said. "She and Phil will be joining us later. They stayed on the island to tie up some loose ends. We have some new caretakers arriving on Cryptos in a couple of days. A Mr. and Mrs. Hickock and their son, Dylan. Phil and Bertha need to brief them before they turn the island over."

Marty looked at Theo. "So you're just the temporary chef until Bertha joins us."

"So what?" Theo said. "Until she gets here, I'm still in charge."

"And I *still* need to make a cake for Grace's birthday," Marty said. "And I've never used a cake mix. I assume you have flour, milk, sugar, eggs, butter?"

"What do you think?" Theo said belligerently.

"Enough!" Al shouted. "Any time Marty comes in here, I want your full cooperation." He paused and looked at everyone in the galley. "That applies to all of you. And it's not because he's Travis Wolfe's nephew. It's because I told you to cooperate." He looked back at Theo and lowered his voice. "And if you lie to me again, Theo, I will personally throw you overboard."

The last person on earth Marty thought would come to his defense was Al Ikes.

"I'm watching you, Theo," Al continued under his breath. "Marty was not rude when he came in here, and Grace is not *snotty*."

Grace actually liked Al Ikes and got along well with him, something Marty did not understand until that moment.

Theo looked confused. He obviously didn't know a thing about the surveillance cameras peppered around the ship. And Marty wasn't about to tell him.

"Go bake your cake," Al said, and left the galley.

Theo got back on his stool — a little shakily — and told everyone to get back to work, but not nearly as loudly or harshly as he had spoken to them before.

And Marty baked a birthday cake — from scratch.

THIRTEEN CANDLES

The party was held in the Captain's Mess.

Wolfe, Luther, Marty, and Grace sat around a teak table picking at the *special* dinner prepared by Theo, which was nothing more than buffet food plopped onto nice china. Each plate featured a different cryptid from around the world. Wolfe explained that Ted had commissioned the set for him and Rose as a wedding present.

Marty kicked himself for not preparing the dinner along with the cake. Theo was no cook. How had he gotten the job as temporary chef?

PD was sound asleep in one of Wolfe's large cargo pockets, exhausted after her day with Bo. And Bo had not been invited to the party, much to Luther's relief. After the chimp and her pint-sized accomplice had battled the dolphins and stolen a fish, Yvonne had found Bo and coaxed her into her comfortable enclosure with a lock of Luther's hair. Luther was happy to have the hair snipped by Yvonne rather than ripped out by Bo.

Grace didn't mind the small party or the bland food. She was with the people she loved, including Luther, who had been like a second brother to her for most of her life.

After Grace blew out her thirteen candles and everyone enjoyed a piece of Marty's delicious cake, Luther showed off his graphic novel. Wolfe got a big kick out of it and called it a masterpiece—an exaggeration, but a compliment that was greatly appreciated by Luther, whose face flushed bright red.

Grace wasn't expecting a gift from Wolfe. He had been very busy the past few days, and they had departed so quickly she was sure he hadn't had time to even think about her birthday. But Wolfe surprised her by placing a large package on the table.

"I didn't get a chance to get over to the mainland to go shopping," he explained. "But this is a one-of-a-kind gift. It belonged to Rose—to your mother. It was her most prized possession. She would have wanted you to have it."

Grace carefully removed the wrapping, already knowing what was underneath. It was an ancient manuscript. The last time she had seen the book it had been in a glass case in the library back on Cryptos. She opened the heavy leather cover.

"It's a graphic novel!" Luther said.

"It's an illuminated manuscript," Grace corrected. "Written and drawn by hand long before there were printing presses or computers."

Luther leaned over for a closer look. The illustration of the dragon on the page Grace had turned to was beautifully rendered. He looked at the text. "What language is it written in?"

"I don't know," Grace said. It wasn't one of the five languages she was fluent in.

"Rose didn't know, either," Wolfe said. "She spent years trying to decipher the text. All we know is that it's a book about cryptids. It's probably the first book on cryptids ever written. Rose thought the text might not be in an unknown language at all, but in code. She had the manuscript copied and took the reproduction to the Congo when we first set out to find Mokélé-mbembé. While we were there she spent hours trying to break the cipher."

Grace turned the page, and they were greeted by a monster with tentacles pulling a ship beneath the sea.

"The giant squid," Luther said.

"From the illustrator's or author's imagination," Wolfe said. "It's unlikely they actually saw all the creatures in the book themselves."

"Where did my mother get this?" Grace asked.

Wolfe shook his head. "She wouldn't tell me. I suspect it might have been something that belonged to Noah Blackwood or his family."

"She stole it?" Marty asked.

"I don't think so," Wolfe answered. "But I didn't want to leave it on Cryptos in case Noah sends someone to poke around the island while we're gone. Which I think he'll do. I didn't want anyone taking it."

"Is Noah Blackwood the reason Al set up surveillance cameras with audio all over the ship?" Marty asked.

Wolfe, Luther, and Grace stared at him.

Luther looked around the Captain's Mess. "I don't see any cameras," he said.

"They're miniaturized," Marty said. "Just like the cameras Ted put in the dragonspy."

"Not exactly like the dragonspy's, but similar," Wolfe said. "And they aren't all over the ship. They are in the common areas, the bridge, and the labs. But we don't have cameras in the private cabins. How did you find out about them?"

Marty didn't want to admit that he had been stalking Al Ikes with the dragonspy. "I had a little problem in the galley with Theo," he said. "Al came to my rescue. The only way he could have known about it is if he or one of his men were watching and listening."

Wolfe nodded. "I heard about that. And yes, someone was watching—and listening. I'm not comfortable with all of this surveillance and extra security. It's just that I don't know what Noah Blackwood is going to do. And I'm not being para-noid. We have nearly forty people on board whom we don't know all that well. They've all been background-checked, of course, but Al believes that some of them are working for Noah Blackwood, and I agree with him. We have the Mokélé-mbembé eggs on board and we're going after a giant squid for Noah's primary competitor." Wolfe lowered his voice. "And then there is Grace . . ."

Wolfe did not need to finish the sentence. They all knew that Noah Blackwood was going to come after his granddaughter.

"So, there are spies on board," Luther said with undisguised glee. "I bet we can figure out who they are."

"This is not a game," Wolfe said sternly. "I don't want any of you looking for so-called spies. Noah Blackwood and his people are dangerous. If you see something out of the ordinary, just tell me or Al about it. We'll decide whether it means anything."

He locked eyes with each of them, one by one. "Is that clear?"

Marty, Luther, and Grace nodded, but Wolfe doubted their sincerity. He knew he would have to keep a close eye on them.

"Do you have a camera in here?" Marty asked.

"Yes, but it isn't on."

"So, you control them?" Luther asked.

Wolfe took his Gizmo out. "I'm the only one who has the on/off code." He punched the code into the Gizmo. A video of them appeared on the small screen, and Luther waved at the camera. Wolfe reentered the code and the screen went blank.

"Al doesn't have the code?" Marty asked.

"No," Wolfe answered. "I wouldn't give it to him."

Marty had another question that he'd been dying to ask. "I thought you were broke," he said. "And that this expedition was a way of making money so you could continue looking for my parents and search for cryptids. Having Al and his crew must be costing a fortune."

"We're not exactly broke," Wolfe said. "But we do have a cash flow problem. Our money is tied up in research and development. Al and his security people are sort of on loan from the federal government. We don't have money, but we are rich in technology. Ted is waiting for the patents on his inventions before he decides who to sell the technology to. He also wants to make sure they've been field-tested. That's another reason for this trip.

"The government doesn't want anyone else to get ahold of this technology, like the miniature cameras, the bot-fly, and some other things. They offered to have the Secret Service or the

Department of Defense provide security. We compromised and hired Al Ikes. Ted and I have known him for . . ." He paused. "Well, for a long time. The government is footing the bill. This way, Al works for us and we don't have the government breathing down our necks."

"And you trust Al?" Luther asked.

"I've known him for years," Wolfe answered. "He's very good at what he does. And we are going to need him to help us deal with the Noah Blackwood problem."

"What do you mean?" Grace asked.

Wolfe shrugged. "I don't know what I mean. All I know is that once we figure out what Blackwood is up to, we're going to have to get him to back off. Al is good at that sort of thing."

"Can anyone use their Gizmo to access the cameras?" Luther asked.

"Not without the code," Wolfe answered. "And no, I'm not going to give Marty the camera code for his Gizmo."

"Of course not," Luther said. "I was just asking how it worked."

Marty glanced at Luther. He knew his friend well enough to know that he was *not* just asking how it worked. Luther was an expert computer hacker.

"What about Theo?" Marty asked, changing the subject.

"What about him?" Wolfe asked.

Marty pointed at the nearly inedible food congealing on their plates. "He can't cook, for one thing."

"I noticed," Wolfe said. "Theo Sonborn is a little rough around the edges, but he's a good guy. He's been on Cryptos since the very beginning. Bertha will join us as soon as she and Phil get things squared away on the island. Just stay clear of the galley until she gets here." Wolfe looked at his watch. "I better get up to the bridge."

"Thank you for the party," Grace said. "And the manuscript. I'll cherish it . . . always."

Wolfe smiled as he stood up from the table. "It wasn't exactly the birthday party I had in mind, but I'm glad you like the manuscript. Oh—and I have another present for you, but it got delayed in shipment. I hope it arrives before we get to New Zealand." He looked at Marty. "And your cake was delicious." He then looked at Luther and said, "Your graphic novel was excellent. I just hope we don't give you any more material for a second volume during this expedition."

"It's not likely that Noah Blackwood is going to be able to snatch Grace from the open sea," Luther said.

"Which is exactly the reason for our abrupt departure," Wolfe said. "But it would be a mistake to underestimate him. Noah Blackwood has a very long reach."

"Tentacles," Grace said.

"Yes," Wolfe agreed. "But the giant squid's tentacles would feel like velvet gloves compared to Noah's. We need to stay out of his grasp." He turned and walked out of the Captain's Mess.

THE DOGHOUSE

One of Noah Blackwood's "tentacles" was lying on a sleeping bag inside a shipping container deep in the cargo hold of the *Coelacanth*. He had emptied the container's contents and redistributed them into other containers, then rigged the door to close and lock from the inside in the unlikely event someone came down into the hold before they reached New Zealand. The container was a perfect hiding place. With its rank smell and noisy engines, the hold was far from comfortable, but it was better than some of the places Butch McCall had slept in during his rough life.

Since sneaking aboard he had made two trips up top, once to get a couple of cases of canned pork and beans, and again to retrieve a stolen Gizmo from one of Noah Blackwood's spies. He needed the Gizmo to keep track of Wolfe and the kids—the only people on board who might recognize him on sight. Although he doubted that even they would recognize him now. He had lost at least fifty pounds making his way back to civilization from the depths of the Congo. Normally, he would have gained the weight back quickly, but Noah had told him, "Butch, you're a shadow of your former self, and I need you to stay that way."

When Butch emerged from Noah's bathroom without his mustache, Noah had exclaimed, "You have teeth!" Then Noah introduced Butch to his personal makeup artist, who finished the job with a brown wig and a pair of glasses.

When Butch looked in the mirror, he barely recognized the man staring back at him.

"There's nothing we can do about the tattoos and muscles on such short notice," the makeup artist had said, pointing at Butch's huge biceps. "They're a dead giveaway. You'll have to wear long baggy sleeves at all times."

Butch had not seen any surveillance cameras when he was up top, but before he'd left the Ark, Noah had pulled up Albert Ikes's dossier on his computer. Noah's database on people was bigger than the Federal Bureau of Investigation's — and he was right: Albert Ikes was ex-CIA.

"Twenty-year veteran," Noah said. "Security and surveillance specialist. You'll have to be careful. He'll have cameras all over the ship, but he can't watch everyone 24/7. I got another call during your makeover. Albert Ikes only brought two men with him on the *Coelacanth*. He left the others to guard Cryptos. You know how to play it."

Butch knew *exactly* how to play it. During the day he would move around when everyone else was moving around. He would hide in the crowd. His new look gave him a scholarly appearance. He had stolen a lab coat and clipboard and would play the role of a research scientist. It would be easy to blend in with so many new people on board. At night he would return to the hold and sleep in his container.

Lying in the container brought back long-forgotten memories to the newly formed Butch McCall. It reminded him of the doghouse he had rigged for his pit bull, Dirk, when he was a kid. It was made out of a metal septic tank. (Dirk had eaten the two wooden doghouses Butch had built before coming up with the tank idea.)

It was Dirk who had first taught Butch how to hunt. He would climb out his bedroom window and he and Dirk would stalk neighborhood cats. The cats weren't as easy to kill as one might think, but they were no match for Dirk — and eventually Butch, who taught himself to shoot a cat in the eye with his BB rifle from fifty feet away.

When Butch's parents got drunk and fought, which was often, he would sometimes sleep with Dirk in the septic tank in the backyard to get away from the violence. Dirk had terrible breath and he snored, but it was preferable to being inside the house, where worse things awaited him when his parents were at each other.

After a couple of years of successful hunts, animal control got wind of Dirk's taste for domestic cats and euthanized him. A week later, Butch, at the age of twelve, left home and joined the circus, which eventually led him to Noah Blackwood.

Butch turned on the Gizmo. A schematic of the entire ship appeared on the screen, along with an array of tiny colored dots representing the locations of everyone on board. The only areas of the ship not specifically identified were the laboratories, which were instead designated by simple numbers, one through thirteen. Butch was certain that the dinosaur eggs, or perhaps by now the hatchlings, were hidden behind one of these doors. The lab doors could only be opened with an electronic key card and each door had a different card. He would first have to find out which lab held the eggs, then get ahold of a card to get inside — no easy task — but he had plenty of time to figure it out. There was nothing he could do with the eggs until he reached Kaikoura Canyon. Noah Blackwood's ships, *Endangered One* and *Endangered Too*, were faster and would arrive several days ahead of the *Coelacanth*. As soon as the *Coelacanth* got to the canyon, or New Zealand — whichever came first — Butch would steal the eggs, kidnap Grace, and stash them all aboard the *Endangered One* or *Too* with Noah Blackwood.

His other mission was to make certain that Travis Wolfe and NZA failed to bring in a live giant squid. If they succeeded, he had to figure out a way to get the squid away from them. If that didn't work, he was to kill the squid. Not only would this put NZA out of business, it would also ensure Travis Wolfe's financial ruin. The thought brought a smile to Butch's clean-shaven face.

He was amazed at the Gizmo's capabilities, and this new version was even better than the one he had taken from Marty in the Congo. He could still feel the bump on his head where Marty had hit him with a log just before taking his Gizmo back, and the memory wiped the smile from his face. Noah had told him he was not to harm Grace in any way, but he had said nothing about Marty O'Hara.

Butch's smile returned with the thought that tragic accidents at sea were common.

He clicked on Marty's name and a moving gray dot appeared on the screen, sandwiched by Grace's blue dot and Luther's orange dot. His smile broadened as he imagined the look of shock on their faces if he were to step out in front of them and pull off his wig. He wouldn't do that, of course. Butch was a lot of things, but he was not impulsive.

Butch McCall had the patience of a spider waiting for a fly.

PART TWO — OPEN SEA

GHOST SHIP

Marty decided that pea green and fluorescent orange were not a good color combination, especially on the face and head of his friend Luther, who had been puking his guts out since their third night aboard the *Coelacanth*. They had encountered gale-force winds and sickeningly deep swells for over twelve hours, and the ship's physician, Dr. Jones, said that Luther's was the worst case of seasickness he had seen in thirty years. After two days and two nights of retching in their cabin, Luther had been moved to the infirmary so Dr. Jones could keep a closer eye on him and administer IV fluids to prevent dehydration. Wolfe offered to divert the ship to the nearest port and fly Luther back to Omega Prep, or home, but Luther stubbornly refused, insisting he would beat this thing and get his sea legs. Dr. Jones sided with Luther, but Marty suspected that the physician's motivation was more personal than professional. Luther was the only patient in the infirmary. His presence gave Dr. Jones someone to play chess with, but even as sick as Luther was, Dr. Jones had yet to win a single match.

Marty was happy to have the retching Luther out of their cabin, but his friend's absence meant he had to sleep there alone, haunted by thoughts of ghouls and ghosts. The rumors about the *Coelacanth*'s history of bad luck had been racing through the converted freighter like a virus, and they did nothing to ease Marty's mind. Crew members complained of seeing apparitions at night, personal items being moved or missing altogether, strange knockings, screams, and whisperings. Luckily Marty had not experienced any of these strange occurrences — yet.

And then there were the accidents — nothing too serious, but over the past couple of days there had been a half dozen of them. A small fire in the galley, and another in a lab. One of the men in the engine room had slipped off a companionway (the rungs had been greased, and he'd broken his wrist). Bo had escaped from her cage the day before and it had taken them three hours to get her back inside. (While she was loose they bolted the infirmary from the inside so she couldn't get her hands on Luther's hair.) But the worst was the loss of the helicopter. The straps had come undone during a storm and it had tumbled into the ocean. These incidents had contributed to the "bad luck" rumors. By their ninth day at sea, it had gotten so bad that Wolfe called the crew into the mess hall for an early morning meeting.

Marty sat at a table in the back with a plate of semi-cooked scrambled eggs and a tray of yogurt and fruit for Grace, who had elected to skip the meeting and stay in her cabin with the illuminated manuscript.

"This ship is not haunted," Wolfe began, a little testily. "Mass hysteria is more like it. And don't be ashamed. We are all vulnerable to it. We've had rough seas, which has caused some of you discomfort. Combine that with lack of sleep and the ship's tragic history, and we're bound to have accidents."

"What tragic history?" someone called out from the crowd.

Right, Marty thought. *Like anyone in the room doesn't know what happened to the previous crew.* It was all everyone had been talking about since they left Cryptos.

"It happened ten years ago," Wolfe began patiently. "Prior to eWolfe's purchasing the ship, it was hijacked by pirates in the South China Sea. As you know, this is not that uncommon these days. The crew resisted. They were all killed and presumably tossed overboard. The freight was off-loaded and the ship was set adrift. The culprits were apprehended a year later and prosecuted. So, you see, the tragedy was caused by criminals — not ghosts."

Marty didn't blame him, but Wolfe had neglected to mention that the captain had been found in his bed minus his body, and that Wolfe had managed to get the ship on the cheap because there were no other bidders for the haunted vessel.

"And if you're worried about the same fate befalling us, get it out of your minds," Wolfe continued. "First, this is a research ship. We are not carrying freight of any value. Second, as you have probably noticed, we have a security force on board. These men are highly trained professionals. We have a contingency plan in place in the unlikely event that we are attacked." He gave them a small smile. "In fact, I feel sorry for any pirate stupid enough to board the *Coelacanth.*"

No one laughed.

Again, Wolfe had left out a couple of important details, such as the two dinosaur eggs they were incubating in one of the labs, which were worth more than the cargo aboard a hundred ships. And that his daughter, Grace, was the granddaughter of Noah Blackwood, who would stop at nothing and spare no expense to get his hands on her and the eggs. And that the security force consisted of three people, one of whom wore three-piece suits and wing tips.

Wolfe dropped his smile. "Sometime this afternoon, we will be rendezvousing with a sailboat to take on supplies and four additional passengers."

Marty knew two of the passengers — Bertha and Phil Bishop — but he didn't know who the third and fourth were. He glanced over at Theo Sonborn, who was standing about twenty feet away. Theo showed no reaction.

"When the sailboat arrives, four of you are free to board her and leave the expedition," Wolfe continued. "We will pay you for the time you've spent and buy you a plane ticket back to wherever you came from. If there are more than four of you wanting to get off, we'll draw lots. Those who remain here on the *Coelacanth* will stop spreading rumors about ghosts, or bad-luck ships, or any other nonsense that might jeopardize this expedition. If I or Al hear another word about these preposterous things, I will put the perpetrator off this ship without pay or a plane ticket home. That's my final word on this. The choice is entirely yours."

Wolfe walked out of the mess hall.

Marty stayed behind, picking at the plate of gooey scrambled eggs, trying to gauge the reaction of the crew. About half of them didn't seem to know what Wolfe was talking about. The majority of these were researchers and scientific staff who were apparently oblivious to all the talk of ghosts and hauntings. The other half, mostly deckhands and galley staff, appeared to know exactly what Wolfe was talking about and left the mess hall talking to each other in quiet but urgent voices.

Wolfe had left out one last detail: The two fires, the greased companionway, and the lost chopper were not accidents. Marty had gotten quite good with the dragonspy over the past few days. Whenever he saw Wolfe and Al together on his Gizmo, he would join them with his little friend to eavesdrop.

"Arson and sabotage," Al had told Wolfe the night before. "There's no doubt about it. We have one or more people on board determined to scuttle this expedition. Those chopper straps were loosened. I checked them myself a couple of hours before the gale. These people are pros. And I have no idea who they are. They've even managed to find and take out several of the miniature cameras. We replaced some of them, but we no longer have full coverage. Ted didn't give us enough spares."

"Ted doesn't have any spares," Wolfe said. "We used the whole inventory to set up the surveillance on the ship."

"One of the reasons I'm here is to make sure that the cameras and technology you and Ted have developed don't get off the ship and into unauthorized hands," Al said. "Noah Blackwood may not be the only person with spies on board. You might have corporate espionage operatives or foreign agents at work here. Ted's inventions have military and intelligence agency uses.

I wish I'd had those cameras when I was in the trade. They would have been very useful."

"Are you saying cameras have been taken?" Wolfe asked.

"Just one," Al answered. "It was torn from the mounting pretty clumsily, so it might not be much use to them. Others have been disabled."

"How?"

"Paper clip," Al said. "They just walk by, find the camera pin hole, insert the straightened clip, and pop the lens. They've done it when it's crowded, and very quickly. All we've been able to see is a hand and the clip. No way to ID who's doing it, and it could be more than one person. It's probably Noah Blackwood's people, but it could also be crew members wise to the fact that we're watching them and they don't like it."

"I can't say I blame them," Wolfe said, looking uncomfortable. "Since we got back from the Congo we've been running eWolfe like a police state. The cameras might be contributing to the bad morale."

"I doubt it," Al said. "There's something else happening on this ship, and I'm going to get to the bottom of it. And you're not going to like this, but those who choose to leave are going to be strip-searched before I let them go."

"You're right," Wolfe said. "I don't like it at all and I don't want you to do it."

Al shook his head. "We're missing a camera, Wolfe. It's small enough to be hidden anywhere. We can't risk someone getting off the ship with it — even if the camera is damaged. Snapping on the latex gloves and doing body cavity searches is not my idea of fun, but we need that camera back, broken or not. We'll be discreet, meaning we'll search them on the sailboat so no one on this ship knows they got the full treatment."

Marty winced at the idea of getting the "full treatment" from Albert Ikes, and he wasn't convinced Al was telling the truth about it not being his idea of fun.

Wolfe let out a resigned sigh and said, "Do what you have to do. But I want the rest of the cameras pulled."

"What?" Al said.

"If they can take one camera, they can take another camera, or all of them, for that matter. We'll be at Kaikoura Canyon in a few days. If it takes a long time to catch a giant squid, we're going to have to give the crew shore leave in New Zealand or they'll mutiny. We can't strip-search them every time they leave the ship. We have enough data to prove that Ted's cameras work except for the lenses. We'll have to harden them on the next upgrade."

"We'll be operating blind!" Al complained.

"You still have those." Wolfe pointed to Al's eyes. "Pull Roy and Joe out of the surveillance room and have them work the ship's security with what God gave them. And you have a Gizmo. You know where everyone is."

"But not what they're doing," Al said.

"Get rid of the cameras," Wolfe insisted.

"All right," Al said. "You're the boss."

Marty was glad to hear this. Up until that moment he'd been worried that Al was the boss, not Wolfe.

"Pull the cameras," Wolfe added. "Tonight, when everyone

is asleep. I guess there's no reason they have to know that they aren't being watched."

"They're going to figure it out," Al warned.

"Of course they are," Wolfe admitted. "But not for a while. When you get the cameras, give them to me and I'll lock them up in the safe in my cabin."

Good! Marty thought. *Luther won't be bugging me about hacking into the Gizmo to access the cameras.*

"What about that flying insect thing?" Al asked.

The flying insect thing (a.k.a. the dragonspy) was currently clinging to the corner of the ceiling. Marty had gotten very adept at landing the dragonspy. And as usual, Ted had thought of everything. The six insectlike legs were equipped with alternating microscopic hooks and suction cups that attached to any surface, including glass. The advantages of having the dragonspy stationary were that the audio was better (no humming wings in the background), the solar battery lasted longer, and no one noticed it was there, including the very observant Al Ikes, who seemed to have eyes in the back of his head.

"You mean Ted's bot-fly?" Wolfe said. "What about it?"

"Without the cameras we could sure use it," Al said.

"Except for the fact that the only person who knows how to fly it is Marty," Wolfe pointed out.

"He could teach Roy or Joe," Al said. "It's not a toy, and that's how Marty uses it."

"You're right, it's not a toy," Wolfe agreed. "But Ted made it very clear before we left that Marty was the only one he would allow to pilot the bot-fly." Wolfe smiled. "I'm sure Marty would be happy to fly it wherever you want. All you have to do is ask him."

Al had scowled and walked off. And he was still scowling as he walked past Marty in the back of the mess hall, on his way out after Wolfe's brief lecture.

Marty picked up his half-eaten plate of eggs and was about to dump them into the garbage when Theo walked up to him. Marty had stayed out of the galley and clear of Theo since their first encounter.

"Tell me about the eggs," Theo said.

"They were almost raw," Marty said. "I guess if I were an egg-eating snake I'd find them absolutely delicious."

Theo gave him a venomous smile. "I'm not talking about the eggs on your plate. I'm talking about the dinosaur eggs your uncle has incubating in one of the labs."

"Huh?" Marty said, stalling for time. Only a handful of people knew about the dinosaur eggs, and he was certain that Theo was not one of the fingers on that hand.

"Dinosaur eggs," Theo repeated. "Mokélé-mbembé eggs. Two of them, to be specific."

Marty laughed. "The ship is old, but it's not sixty-five million years old, which is when the dinosaurs went extinct. Which means you're not only the worst cook I've ever met, you are also crazy."

"I know we got off to a bumpy start," Theo said. "And I'll admit that I'm not the best cook in the world, but you and I both know I'm right about the dinosaur eggs. There are no secrets aboard a ship. Everyone knows there's something cooking in one of those labs."

Theo had just elevated himself to the #1 spot on Marty's spy list. As far as Marty knew, the only people on board who knew about the eggs were Wolfe, Grace, Luther, and himself. He didn't even think that Al Ikes knew about the eggs.

"I haven't heard any such thing," Marty said. "And I'd know about dinosaur eggs if there were any on this ship." He started to walk away.

"One more thing," Theo said, smiling now. "Just so you know, I didn't volunteer for kitchen duty. Wolfe asked me to take the job until Bertha got here. I'll be happy to get out of there."

Marty stopped. "So, what's your regular job?"

"Jack-of-all-trades," Theo said. "Master of none. I just help out where I'm needed."

Wolfe needs to help Theo off the ship, Marty thought as he walked out of the mess hall. *I've got to find him and tell him.*

A few feet down the corridor he took his Gizmo out and tried to locate his uncle, but Wolfe's tracking tag wasn't online. This wasn't the first time he had taken himself off the grid. Marty wasn't sure how or why he did it, but several times a day Wolfe's tag simply disappeared for a while. Not even the dragonspy could find him then.

LAB NINE

Grace had hardly left her cabin since they'd cast off and was all but immune to the ship's gossip. Marty brought her food from the galley when she asked, which wasn't often. She had lost her appetite, and it wasn't because of the rough seas or the awful food. It was because of the illuminated manuscript. She had been poring over the pages day and night since the moment Wolfe had given it to her, and so far she had learned . . . absolutely nothing.

Marty rushed into her cabin and set a tray of fruit and yogurt on her cluttered desk. "Have you seen Wolfe?"

"Not since last night. How did his pep talk go?"

"It was more like an ultimatum. I need to find him."

"Use your Gizmo."

"He's off the grid—again. I'm still not sure why he does that."

"The eggs," Grace said.

"What?"

"When he checks on them he disables his tag. He doesn't want anyone to know where the incubator room is, or that the eggs even exist for that matter."

"That's what I need to talk to him about! Do you know where the incubator is?"

Grace shook her head. "I assume it's in one of the labs, but I don't know which one. What's the problem?"

Before Marty could answer, Luther came wobbling into her cabin with the green mamba jar. He was obviously still a little woozy, but he looked a lot better than he had the night before, when Grace and Marty had visited him in the infirmary.

"I'm okay now," Luther said, setting the jar on Grace's desk. "And I hope to never see another chessboard for as long as I live . . . or a stainless steel bucket." He picked up a banana from the tray and peeled it while he glanced around the cabin. "What happened in here?"

"Rose is back!" Congo screeched. "Rose is back!"

"You didn't tell me the parrot could talk!" Luther broke off a little piece of banana and fed it to him.

"Saying one sentence over and over again is hardly talking," Marty said. "Grace could be her mom's twin. That's why he says it." He pointed at the mess of paper strewn on the floor and desk. "Grace has been trying to translate that book Wolfe gave her and isn't having much luck. Personally, I think the answer is in that trunk over there, along with some other things she's been looking for."

"Well, personally, I hate it when you two act like I'm not in the room when I'm standing right here," Grace retorted.

"We know," Luther said. "Which is exactly why we do it." He took a large bite out of the banana.

"That might not be a good idea," Marty said. "Grace doesn't want her work slimed by regurgitated banana."

"No, Grace doesn't," she agreed.

Luther stuffed the rest of the banana into his mouth, swallowed, belched, then grinned. "Told you I was okay."

"Physically," Grace pointed out, then turned to Marty. "You were about to tell me why you need to find Wolfe."

Marty recounted the conversation he'd had with Theo.

"How could he know about the eggs?" Grace said.

"He's obviously one of Blackwood's spies," Luther said. "And I know where Wolfe is. I saw him just before I got here."

"Where?" Marty asked.

"Lab Nine," Luther answered.

Butch McCall also knew where Wolfe was.

Like Marty, he had noticed Wolfe's disappearances. What Marty hadn't noticed was that Wolfe disappeared pretty regularly every four hours, twenty-four hours a day. And that Wolfe was careful to disable and re-enable his tag in different areas of the ship so no one could pinpoint where he was during the half hour to forty-five minutes he was off the grid. Butch had also noticed that Wolfe always disabled the tag when he was alone. From this, Butch had deduced several things: First, the eggs were aboard the *Coelacanth*, and they had either hatched or Wolfe believed they were viable and were going to hatch. Second, Wolfe was the only one who knew where the eggs were. Everyone else's tags were on 24/7, including the kids'. If they knew where the eggs were, and were helping to monitor them,

Wolfe would have disabled their tags, too. Third, if the pattern persisted, Butch would have four hours to steal the eggs or hatchlings when the time came.

This still left him with the task of finding out where Wolfe disappeared to. It wasn't without risks, but the meeting that morning had provided Butch with the perfect opportunity to solve the mystery.

Over the past few days he had perfected his cover as Dr. Dirk (in honor of his dog) O'Connor, a large but gentle marine biologist under contract to NZA. His false identity had been further established with the help of a fellow researcher named Dr. Seth A. Lepod on their third night out at sea.

They had been hit by a very rough storm. Butch happened by Dr. Lepod's lab just as he was trying to avert complete disaster.

A lot of the crew were up and wandering around the ship because of the storm. Butch took advantage of the situation by joining the worried crowd after loosening the straps holding down the *Coelacanth*'s helicopter and taking out a couple more cameras in the confusion. He was walking down the laboratory corridor just as the ship was broadsided by a vicious wave that was probably the one that cleared the helicopter pad. A panic-stricken Dr. Lepod burst out of his lab yelling for help.

The wave had knocked over one of Dr. Lepod's aquariums, which in turn had torn out the main pump and filtration system for all the other aquariums. Dr. Dirk O'Connor was more than happy to assist a fellow scientist in distress.

Butch McCall, former circus roughneck and zookeeper, could fix anything. Within half an hour he had the system back online and most of the slimy squid back in their tanks with their arms and tentacles intact.

Disaster averted, the squid savior, Dr. O'Connor, sat down with the grateful squid doctor for a fishy-tasting cup of tea and scientific gossip. It turned out that Dr. Lepod was the world's leading authority on squid — in particular *Architeuthis*. He had no idea how Wolfe intended to catch a giant squid, or how he intended to keep it alive.

Butch could not believe his luck. He sat in the lab for more than two hours, in spite of the horrendous stench, as the long-limbed Dr. Lepod (who resembled a terrestrial octopus) laid out what *he* would do to keep a giant squid alive if Wolfe were lucky enough to lure one aboard.

That morning, as Wolfe delivered his rant about the haunted ship, Butch sat with his "friend" Dr. Lepod in the center of the mess hall in plain view. No one paid the slightest attention to him, and no one joined them at their table because of Lepod's odor and unappetizing appearance.

Butch hid his smile as Wolfe went on about the rumors of a haunted ship — all planted by Butch during the past several days. But he wasn't there to gloat. He was there to discover where the eggs were. If Wolfe followed his established pattern, he would go dark right after the meeting and check on the eggs. With most everyone out of their cabins, heading back to their workstations, it would be easy to follow Wolfe to the nest. The meeting was much shorter than Butch had anticipated, and Wolfe left so quickly that Butch nearly lost him in the crowd. As Butch tailed him, he passed within ten feet of Marty O'Hara. Marty didn't even look at him. He was talking to another crew member who looked familiar, but Butch didn't have time to think about where he had seen the man before. Wolfe was on the move.

Butch pushed his way through the crowd and caught a glimpse of Wolfe as he disappeared around a corner. He hurried forward and found him again just as he entered the bridge. He waited in an alcove outside, watching Wolfe's tag on the Gizmo, along with the tags of the captain, chief engineer, and radio operator. Wolfe was a little behind schedule, but the tag blinked off seven and a half minutes after he entered the bridge. A moment later Wolfe stepped out and walked quickly past the alcove without looking in Butch's direction. Butch gave him a ten-second lead. Wolfe walked directly to the lab deck, stopping only once to say something to Marty's friend Luther. Luther continued on his way, then Wolfe slipped into Lab Nine.

"This is it," Luther said.

He and Marty and Grace were standing outside Lab Nine.

"Are you sure?" Grace asked.

"Well, I can't swear he's still in there, but this is where he went after asking if I was feeling okay."

Marty checked his Gizmo. Wolfe was still off the grid. He looked at the electronic lock on the door. "Did he swipe a card to get inside?"

Luther shook his head. "Nope. He just held up his Gizmo and hit a button. I think it has Bluetooth and so do the locks, which means you can probably use your Gizmo to get into any of the labs, including number nine . . ." Luther grinned. ". . . among other things . . . like accessing the cameras, or turning off your tracking tag, or mine, or Grace's—"

"Or we could just knock on the door," Grace said. "Instead of loitering outside the lab attracting attention Wolfe obviously doesn't want."

She knocked. The lab doors all had peepholes. A few moments later the door swung open. They all expected to find a frowning Travis Wolfe. Instead, he was grinning.

"I wondered how long it would take you to find the incubator room," he said. He was dressed in disposable green scrubs from head to toe, including a mask and surgical gloves. "Come on in. I was about to call you anyway."

They slipped in and Wolfe closed the door behind them. There was an air lock similar to but much smaller than the one at the Moon Pool.

"You'll all need to shower and put on scrubs," Wolfe said. "There are men's and women's showers. The eggs are being incubated in a sterile room. I don't know what viruses and germs Mokélé-mbembé is susceptible to, but I'm not taking any chances. When you're all scrubbed, come through the second set of doors. I'll be waiting for you inside."

Fifteen minutes later the trio stepped into the incubator room looking like a surgical team.

"One of the eggs is pipping," Wolfe said.

"You mean *peeping*," Luther said.

"No," Wolfe said. "I mean *pipping*." He led them over to the incubator.

Inside the sealed Plexiglas were two white eggs the size of small soccer balls, half-buried in rich brown mulch that Wolfe had brought in from the Mokélé-mbembé nest in the Congo.

Luther could barely believe his eyes. He'd heard about the eggs, but this was the first time he had actually seen them.

"Before a chick, or in this case a dinosaur, can hatch, it has to break through the shell. That's called pipping." Wolfe pointed to the egg on the right. "See that little hole on the top of the egg?"

They all nodded.

"Four hours ago it wasn't there," Wolfe continued. "Birds and reptiles, and even some spiders and frogs, have an egg tooth to help them break through the shell. I don't know about dinosaurs, but I assume they have something similar. This one has punctured the shell."

"How long before it hatches?" Grace asked.

Wolfe shook his head. "I have no idea. It could be hours or days. That's out of my area of expertise."

"I'd say that's out of everyone's area of expertise," Luther said.

The egg shuddered and something from inside pushed against the tiny opening.

"I think the hole just got bigger," Marty said.

Wolfe bent down for closer look. "Maybe," he said.

"Can't we help it out of the shell?" Luther asked.

"Not yet," Wolfe answered. "It's best to let nature take its course. The hatchling is still adhered to the inside of the egg.

It's feeding off of it. If we remove it prematurely, we might kill it."

"What do we do?" Grace asked.

"We watch," Wolfe said. "Let me see your Gizmo."

Marty handed it to him.

"I've noticed you've gotten pretty good with the bot."

"I haven't crashed it," Marty said.

Wolfe laughed. "You've done better than that. Like yesterday, when you made a perfect six-legged landing and eavesdropped on Al's and my conversation about pulling the cameras and the sabotage."

"You pulled the cameras?" Luther said.

"Sabotage?" Grace asked.

"I'll tell you later," Marty said. "You knew the bot was there?"

"Kind of hard to miss a gold dragonfly hanging on a ceiling pipe."

"Did Al see it?"

"I don't think so," Wolfe said, typing something on the Gizmo. "Okay, your Gizmo is now fully operational." He showed them the screen. There was a live video of the eggs. "As you can see, I didn't have all the cameras removed. This one has been recording the incubation 24/7 since we brought the eggs to Cryptos. You can zoom in by hitting this button." He demonstrated. "I think we'll keep it right there for now." He gave the Gizmo back to Marty.

"What do you mean by fully operational?" Luther asked.

"It means that Marty's Gizmo will now do everything my Gizmo does."

"Including turning tracking tags on and off?" Marty asked.

"Yes."

"And opening electronic locks?" Luther asked.

Wolfe nodded.

"Bluetooth, right?" Luther said.

Wolfe gave another nod.

"I knew it!" Luther said.

"All you have to do is type in the number or name of the room and hit the SEND button," Wolfe explained. "But I don't want you to abuse this ability—meaning I don't want you to go into any unauthorized areas without permission. The only reason I unlocked your Gizmo is that I'm going to need your help with the eggs now that they're hatching. I'm going to be busy trying to capture a giant squid, and we're the only ones who know about the eggs."

"We're not exactly the only people who know about the eggs," Marty said.

"What do you mean?"

Marty told him about his conversation with Theo.

"What did you tell him?" Wolfe asked.

"I told him he was crazy," Marty said. "Which I think he is. And if I were you I would get him off the ship."

"Theo is fine," Wolfe said. "He was just messing with you. I'll talk to him."

"But—"

"Don't worry about Theo Sonborn," Wolfe interrupted. "We have procedures to discuss. I'm going to need one of you in here twenty-four hours a day on four-hour shifts. We'll add Phil to the rotation when he comes on board and maybe some other trusted people as well, but it's going to be a short list. We'll need to keep this quiet. If word gets out that we have a couple of dinosaurs aboard, the media will be all over us. They'll surround the *Coelacanth* with anything that floats or flies and that'll compromise our capture of a giant squid." He looked at Marty. "You're going to be the gatekeeper. The only way into this lab is with the new Gizmo. That means if someone needs to be let in, they'll have to call you. It shouldn't happen very often because someone should always be inside to open the door. But you are the gatekeeper."

Marty liked the sound of that.

"I've switched your tags off. Blackwood and the people he has on board aren't the only ones we need to worry about. I trust the crew, but if one of them gets wind of this, the temptation to leak it to the media might be too much. The press would pay a lot of money to know there are dinosaurs still on earth."

"What are you going to tell Al about our tags being off?"

"I'll tell him the truth. Al knows about the eggs and so do Joe and Roy. You don't have to worry about them. They have been keeping secrets their whole lives."

The engines rumbled and they felt the ship slow. Wolfe looked at his watch. "Right on time," he said. "Phil and Bertha are here."

"Who are the third and fourth passengers?" Marty asked.

"Another scientist and a journalist," Wolfe answered, looking at Grace. "Do you want to take the first shift?"

"Sure," Grace said. "But I'd like to get my Moleskine and maybe a book to read."

"Go ahead," Wolfe said. "But hurry. We need to get topside and meet the sailboat."

Grace rushed out of the lab and was back a few minutes later with a book, her Moleskine, and her fountain pen.

Wolfe, Marty, and Luther left her to meet the sailboat.

PASSENGERS

The sailboat looked like a rowboat next to the giant *Coelacanth*.

By the time Marty, Luther, and Wolfe reached the deck, the sailboat's crew had disembarked. Phil and Bertha Bishop were talking to Al Ikes. With them were a man, a woman, a boy and a girl a few years older than Marty and Luther, and a very old dog.

Marty was disappointed to see that crazy Theo Sonborn was not waiting with his gear to leave the *Coelacanth* and undergo a cavity search by Al Ikes. In fact, none of the crew members had lined up to abandon ship. Al's disposable gloves would have to wait for another day.

Bertha walked over and gave Marty a bone-crunching hug and Luther's weird hair a pat. "Are you boys staying out of trouble?"

"More or less," Marty said.

"Less, I suspect," Phil said, joining them. "Come on over and meet our ride."

Al walked away without a word as Marty and Luther joined the group. Wolfe was talking to the foursome and appeared to be excited about something the boy was telling him.

". . . as the toucan flies," the boy was saying. "I think that's pretty close to the preserve."

"This is my nephew, Marty," Wolfe said. "And his friend, Luther."

"Rand McKenzie," the man said with an Australian accent. "But you can call me Mac. This is my wife, Sandra, my daughter, Nicole, and this—" He pointed to the dark-haired boy who had been talking. "— is Jake Lansa, the son of a friend of mine, Dr. Robert Lansa, who just happens to be establishing a jaguar preserve in Brazil not far from where your parents' helicopter went down."

"Sorry to hear about the accident," Jake said with an American accent.

"Thanks," Marty said. "Have you been to the preserve?"

"I was there a few months ago," Jake said. "And I'm going back to help my father as soon as we get the sailboat to Australia." He looked at Wolfe. "The preserve is in the middle of nowhere, and communication is slow, but if I can use your radio room, I can start the process of getting word to my father about the crash."

"That would be great," Wolfe said. "We need all the help we can get."

"What's it like there?" Marty asked, excited to talk to someone who knew the area.

"It's an unexplored rain forest," Jake answered. "But if your parents survived the crash, which it sounds like they did, they could live there indefinitely. There's plenty of food and water if they know what they're doing."

"They know what they're doing," Wolfe affirmed. He looked at Marty and Luther. "Do you two want to take Jake up to the radio room?"

"Sure," Marty said.

"I'll go, too," Nicole said. "It'd be nice to stretch my legs on something bigger than our little sailboat."

"I bet it would," Marty said. The sailboat looked like a bathtub toy compared to the *Coelacanth*. "Come on."

"You'll have to make it quick," Mac warned. "There's a storm coming up behind us and I'd like to stay in front of it if I can."

Wolfe nodded and looked at Marty. "Give Jake all of our contact information, including the Gizmo numbers and email." Then he looked at Jake. "Does your dad have a satellite phone?"

"Yeah," Jake said. "But it's a little hard to get a signal through the canopy."

"Give the number to our radio operator. We'll have him try to reach your dad at regular intervals."

"Will do," Jake said.

Marty and Luther led Jake and Nicole up to the bridge, where the radio room was located. The dog followed.

"What's the dog's name?" Luther asked.

"Dyna," Jake said. "Short for Dynamite."

"Without a fuse," Nicole added.

"I thought you were bringing two more people besides Bertha and Phil," Marty said.

"We did." Jake pointed through the bridge window.

Two women were walking very slowly up the gangway. One of them was someone Marty knew very well. "I'll be right back!" He ran out and reached the deck just as the woman stepped on. "Laurel Lee!"

"Hi, Marty!" Laurel gave him a big hug.

"Grace is sure going to be happy to see you."

"I'll be happy to see her, too. I've missed both of you."

Marty looked at the woman with her and saw that she wasn't doing well.

"This is Ana—"

Before Laurel could get the last name out, Ana threw up on Marty's sneakers.

Butch McCall was leaning on the upper deck railing with a dozen other crew members watching the transfer. He recognized *both* women, but at the moment he was more concerned about the kids' tracking tags going offline than he was about Laurel Lee and her friend. Without the tags, it was going to be difficult to avoid bumping into them and impossible to track them. Why did Wolfe switch them off? And where was Grace? He thought for sure she would be with Marty and Luther to meet the sailboat.

Wolfe swept Laurel Lee off her feet. When he put her down the tiny poodle jumped out of his pocket and into Laurel's arms. She and Wolfe spoke for a few moments, then he showed her something on his Gizmo. Laurel stared at the Gizmo in wide-eyed surprise, gave Wolfe a quick kiss on the cheek, then hurried away.

What's the rush? Butch thought as he started to follow her. He didn't get very far. A frantic Dr. Lepod intercepted him.

"Dr. O'Connor, I'm glad I found you," Lepod sputtered breathlessly. "I'm having another filtration problem in the lab. I need your help."

"Sure," Butch said, watching Laurel rapidly increase her lead. "I'll try to stop by later."

"I was hoping you could do it now," Dr. Lepod persisted. "It's serious."

At that point the real Butch McCall would have grabbed Dr. Lepod by his white lab coat and used the scientist to troll for sharks. But gentle Dr. Dirk O'Connor would never think of such a thing. Butch watched Laurel trot down a companionway to a lower deck and disappear, then turned to the squidlike scientist.

"If it's serious," Butch said, "let's take a hook."

"Hook?" Dr. Lepod asked.

Butch smiled. "I meant look."

The crack had not gotten any bigger, but Grace had seen the egg shudder a couple of times as the hatchling shifted inside its leathery shell. She was acutely aware of the miracle she was observing, but she couldn't help remembering that one of the hatchling's relatives had killed her mother and bitten off her father's leg. She was dealing with these mixed feelings (as she did with all conflicts) by writing in her Moleskine when she heard a light tapping on the laboratory door. She got up, looked through the peephole, and nearly tore the door off the hinges opening it.

"Laurel Lee!"

With tears running down her face, Grace threw her arms around the small, birdlike scientist and pulled her into the laboratory.

"Sorry I missed your birthday," Laurel said, setting PD on the ground.

"I didn't even know you were coming at all!" Grace said. "Wolfe told me that you might stay in the Congo indefinitely."

"That was a fib," Laurel said. "We wanted to surprise you for your birthday. But it took me a couple of days longer than I expected to get out of the Congo. By the time I got to Cryptos you had already left. I flew out with Bertha, Phil, and a journalist named Ana Mika to meet the sailboat."

"How's Masalito?" Grace asked, smiling at the thought of the trusted friend who had helped save them at Lake Télé.

"He's fine," Laurel answered. "I invited him to come with me, but when I told him that we would have to fly on an airplane and sail across an ocean, he turned around and headed back into the jungle."

"I'll bet," Grace said. "Did Wolfe tell you about the sterile room?"

"He sure did." Laurel looked down at PD. "Sorry, but your master said no dogs allowed." She opened the lab door and scooted the tiny poodle into the hall.

Grace waited happily for Laurel to get into her scrubs. They entered the incubator room together.

"I don't believe it!" Grace said.

A small dinosaur head and neck were sticking out of the egg that had pipped.

• • •

"Thanks again for your help," Marty said. He was walking Jake and Nicole back to the sailboat. Luther had taken Ana down to the infirmary after asking her if she liked to play chess.

"No problem," Jake said. "As soon as my dad gets the message, he'll put the word out and start looking for your parents. And I meant what I said. They're probably just lost. It's easy to get disoriented down there. But there's plenty of food up in the canopy and it sounds like they've had a lot of field experience. There's a good chance that they're holed up someplace, figuring out a way to *get* out."

Marty knew that Jake might be mistaken, but the other boy's confident tone made him feel better. They stepped aboard the sailboat just as Wolfe and Mac were coming up the gangplank.

"All set?" Wolfe asked.

"Yes, sir," Jake said. "Your radio man will probably make contact with my dad before I do, but I sent him a message anyway."

"Thanks."

"We better push off," Mac said.

Marty and Wolfe untied the lines. The little sailboat motored a safe distance away, then unfurled the sheets.

"That was a good bit of luck running into Jake Lansa," Wolfe said. "I met his father at a conference once. He's one of the best field biologists in the world. If I'd known he was working in that area of the Amazon, I would have tried to get in touch with him when I was down there looking for your mom and dad."

"Doesn't sound like it's easy to get in touch with anybody down there," Marty said.

"That's part of the problem." Wolfe's Gizmo buzzed. He put it to his ear and listened. "We'll be right down!"

"What's up?" Marty said.

"Looks like we have a couple of dinosaurs," Wolfe said, grinning. "One's almost all the way out and the other egg is pipping. We'll pick up Luther from the infirmary on the way."

Butch stepped out of Lepod's lab just as Wolfe, Marty, and Luther rounded the corner with foolishly eager grins on their faces. He managed to dart back inside just as the ecstatic trio barreled past him.

Dr. Lepod was surprised at his abrupt turnaround.

"I need to check one more thing," Butch told him. "We can't have your filter breaking down in the middle of the night when you're not here." *And I can't have Wolfe throwing me into the brig or dumping me on a deserted island if he recognizes me,* he thought. He faked a tiny adjustment and turned to his colleague. "That does it. It should be good for the rest of the voyage."

"Dr. O'Connor, you're a godsend," Dr. Lepod said. "If you ever find yourself looking for another research position, I would be honored to have you join me."

"That's very kind of you," Butch said, peeking out the doorway. There was no sign of the Cryptos crew, which could mean only one thing: History was being made — or hatched — in Lab Nine.

Having Wolfe and the kids off the grid was going to be a bigger challenge than Butch had anticipated. One thing he could not disguise was his size. Aside from Wolfe, he was the tallest person aboard the ship. And now there were even more people on board who might recognize him. The only solution was to eliminate a few of them.

The only one among them who was safe was Grace.

ONE AND TWO

"We can't call them One and Two," Grace said. "Those aren't proper names for a miracle."

"Maybe not," Wolfe said. "But the numbers will help us keep track of which one hatched first. And we don't know their sex. We can't give them proper names until after we figure that out."

They were all crowded around the incubator, unable to take their eyes off the baby dinosaurs. The hatchlings were miniatures of the adult Mokélé-mbembés, with the same smooth, dark purplish skin, long tails, snakelike necks, alert golden eyes, and rows of tiny, sharp white teeth in their mouths.

"I think we should call them Marty and Grace," Laurel suggested. "After all, they're the ones who found the eggs."

"But which is which?" Wolfe said.

"We can call the first one Marty," Grace said. "He's older than me." She looked at Marty. "At least chronologically."

"Very funny," Marty said. "But I see what Wolfe means. They're virtually identical except One has a small dark spot on its head that Two doesn't have. They could be a boy and a girl, two girls, or two boys."

"I think Luther is a good name," Luther said.

"If they're both girls, we'll call one Luther and one Grace," Marty said.

"You're hilarious," Luther said.

"I guess One and Two are fine for now," Grace said.

"Then that's decided," Wolfe announced. "We'll wait to name them later."

"They look hungry," Grace said. "What are you going to feed them?"

"They're probably still absorbing nutrients from the egg sac," Wolfe said. "But yes, I think we should try to feed them. The question is, what? Are they carnivores, herbivores, or omnivores like humans, eating a little bit of both? Another question is, are dinosaurs birds, reptiles, mammals, or a combination? If they're reptiles, they would forage for food on their own. If they're more like birds, their mother would feed them regurgitated food."

"That woman Ana might be good for that," Marty said, deciding he'd keep the disposable booties on until he washed his sneakers.

"Or maybe Luther could help," Grace suggested. "He's had a lot of practice on this voyage."

"I liked you better when you were Marty's twin sister," Luther said.

Wolfe ignored the banter. "If they're mammals, their mother would feed them milk, which means we would have to come up with a formula and bottle, or tube feed them. I've developed three feeding regimes. We'll try all of them and see which one they respond to. But before we get to that I need to lay out the husbandry routine, which everyone needs to absolutely adhere to without exception.

"As I've already mentioned, we need to maintain a strict sterile environment. If any of you aren't feeling well — sore throat, cough, temperature — we'll take you out of the care rotation until you feel better. We can't risk cross-contamination. The hatchlings look alert and healthy, but that can change in an instant if they contract a virus. I can't emphasize this enough. When you're in here you need to pretend that you're doing open heart surgery until we determine the cross-contamination factor."

There was a different tone to Wolfe's voice and manner. He was clearly excited, but at the same time, dead serious. Even Luther was paying attention.

"All of us have risked our lives for these two and I would hate to lose one because someone sneezed without a mask on."

He locked his eyes on each of them in turn, then said, "I guess it's time to crack the incubator open and find out what dinosaurs eat for breakfast."

He pushed a button on the front of the incubator and the top slid back. The hatchlings looked up through the opening with eager golden eyes.

Butch McCall sat on his sleeping bag, leaning against the cold metal wall of his container. He scraped the can he was eating from for the last spoonful of pork and beans. He wished his old dog Dirk was with him. It was time to go hunting.

WHAT DINOSAURS EAT FOR BREAKFAST

"Ouch!" Luther said, shaking his latex-gloved finger, which One had just bitten. "Why does everything aboard want to bite me?"

"It might be a good idea not to wave your finger right in front of its mouth," Wolfe said.

"Yeah," Luther said.

"And Bo hasn't bitten you," Marty pointed out. "She just yanked your hair out, which your own father has been trying to do for years."

"Strip your gloves off," Wolfe said. "Disinfect your hands, bandage your finger, then put on fresh gloves."

"Look at One," Laurel said. "It looks like it's enjoying the taste of Luther's blood."

"I think you're right," Wolfe said.

One was licking its tiny teeth with its purple tongue.

"Do you think there's enough of Luther to feed them until we get back to Cryptos?" Marty asked.

"I think so," Grace said. "If we feed him to them slowly, a bit at a time."

"Oh, you two are really funny," Luther said from the sink.

"You should tour comedy clubs. A Mokélé-mbembé bite might be venomous. Did you ever think of that?"

"You might be right," Marty said. "You should probably go to the infirmary."

"No, thanks. Dr. Jones has his hands full — or stainless steel bucket full — with that woman who puked all over your shoes, which by the way *was* funny."

"How is Ana?" Laurel asked.

"Not nearly as seasick as I was, much to Dr. Jones's disappointment. He asked if she played chess and she said no. Poker's her game. He lost interest in her immediately, gave her some pills, and sent her to her cabin to rest."

Wolfe — intense as always — didn't appear to be listening to their conversation. He was totally focused on the hatchlings, scribbling something on a clipboard. He handed the clipboard to Grace.

"I've made up a temporary feeding chart. I'll make up an official chart and make copies when I get back to my quarters. We'll need to mark down everything we feed them to the very last gram. When they're not eating I need all of you to write down exactly what they are doing, every five minutes."

"I thought that's why we had the video camera," Luther said. "Can't you just review the tape?"

Wolfe shook his head. "We need to learn everything we can about these animals, and the only way to do that is through direct observation." He smiled. "And jotting down what you see will also keep you awake. Right now the hatchlings are curiosities. We're all excited about them. After a couple of days of watching them 24/7, they'll be about as interesting as chickens in a barnyard. Trust me. I know what I'm talking about. I've spent most of my life observing animals. In no time you'll start taking them for granted. And we aren't saving the video on tape. It will be stored on a hard drive. When you note something unusual, we'll be able to find the video instantly by searching the time log." He pointed to a digital clock above the incubator. "The clock is tied into the computer. Note the exact time whenever you record an observation."

Grace and Laurel understood the scientific necessity of what Wolfe was saying perfectly.

Luther and Marty glanced at each other and stifled groans. Raising dinosaur babies didn't sound half as fun as it had five seconds earlier.

Wolfe took a container out of a refrigerator and dumped its gooey red contents on the stainless steel counter.

"What's that?" Marty asked.

"Pulverized organic chicken livers mixed with fish."

Wolfe pinched the red goo with a pair of forceps and put it on a digital scale, carefully removing stringy bits and pieces until the scale read exactly sixty grams, or a little over two ounces.

"Note the time and the amount of food," he said to Grace. "We'll try feeding One first."

He dangled the slimy red hunk over the opening and both One and Two lunged violently for the morsel. One beat Two, nearly pulling the forceps out of Wolfe's hand. The group watched in shock as the lump worked its way down One's throat. Both hatchlings began mewing and jumping.

"They like meat," Wolfe said, stating the obvious.

"Carnivores," Grace said. "I thought sauropods were vegetarians."

"I guess they're not sauropods," Wolfe said. "I suspected as much when Rose and I were . . ." He looked at Grace uncomfortably.

Grace finished the sentence for him. "Attacked."

"Right. When you were in the nest, did you see any bones?"

"There could have been bones," Marty answered. "But I didn't notice any. We were a little distracted by the rotting Mokélé-mbembé carcass, the eggs, the vultures—"

"And the explosion when Marty blew up the Mokélé-mbembé, the resulting fire, and Butch McCall waiting outside the entrance to the nest," Grace interrupted.

"I didn't mean to blow it up," Marty said defensively. "And the fire was minor. But you're right about Butch. I was a little worried about him."

"I saw a few bones in the nest," Laurel said. She had stayed behind at Lake Télé to monitor the nest's environmental conditions. The data she gathered had been transmitted to the incubator's controls to help duplicate the conditions of the real nest. "Perhaps Mokélé-mbembé ate the animal's meat and bones."

"We'll stick with meat for now," Wolfe said. "We can sprinkle it with calcium powder in case that's an essential part of their diet. Their teeth are sharp, but not big enough at this point to masticate bone."

He handed two pairs of forceps to Luther and Grace. "Try to feed them at the exact same time at opposite ends of the incubator," Wolfe said. "That way there's less of a chance they'll bite each other. Their skin looks thin. I don't want to have to treat them for lacerations."

An hour later, with everyone having taken turns feeding them, the hatchlings were finally satiated. They lay down with bulging bellies and fell asleep with their long necks entwined around each other.

Wolfe looked at the chart and did some calculations. "They each ate nearly a pound of meat. That's incredible for their first meal. Who knows how much they'll be eating in a couple of weeks."

"Or how big they'll be," Luther added.

"Good point," Wolfe said. "They could outgrow the incubator in a few days. We'll put a floor pen in the lab, but they might outgrow that, too, before we get back to Cryptos. We may have to move them out of the lab. The question is, where? And how, without anyone seeing them?"

"How about the cargo hold?" Marty said.

"That might work. All we have down there are a few shipping containers. I'll get in touch with Ted and have him come up with a design." He looked at Laurel. "I'm going to be a little busy trying to catch a giant squid. You've spent more time in the nest than anyone. Do you want to head up the dinosaur nursery construction?"

"I'd be happy to."

"I'll get Phil to help, along with a couple of the crew members I know we can trust. Grace and Luther can help, too, when they're not taking care of the hatchlings."

"What about me?" Marty asked.

"You're going to be busy," Wolfe answered.

"Doing what?"

"Bertha needs your help in the galley."

"Let me get this straight," Marty said. "While you're catching a giant squid, and Laurel and Phil are building dinoland, and Grace and Luther are taking care of the two rarest animals on earth, I have kitchen patrol?"

"I'm afraid so," Wolfe answered. "We've all got to do our part."

Marty had no problem doing his part, but he didn't expect to have such a *small* part. He wasn't happy about it.

"I'm sorry, Marty, but Bertha needs you down there. If we don't improve the grub, we'll have a revolt on our hands."

Marty thought, *It's a miracle we don't have one already from the revolting food.* Wolfe had made a mistake putting Theo in charge of the galley, even temporarily. Al Ikes was probably a better cook than Theo.

"Are you all right with that?" Wolfe asked.

"Fine," Marty answered curtly.

"Good." Wolfe looked at his watch. "Grace and Luther will take the next shift in here. If the hatchlings wake up and look hungry, feed them, and record the amount. Dip the meat in water before you offer it to them. We need to keep them hydrated."

"What about the calcium powder?" Grace asked.

"I think we'll skip it for the first couple of feedings. I don't want them getting constipated. I need to examine their stools and see where we're at before we go overboard with supplements. When they poop, scoop it up and put it in one of these specimen containers with the time and which one the stool belongs to.

"I need to check on some things, then I'll call Ted and get him started on the nursery design." He looked at Laurel. "Can you track Phil down? He's probably on the bridge swapping war stories with Cap. Fill him in on what's going on. Maybe you and he can look around the cargo hold and figure out where to put the nursery."

Wolfe and Laurel walked out, with Marty trailing behind dejectedly.

"Have fun on KP," Luther said.

Marty turned around before the air lock door slid closed. "Have fun scooping dinosaur doo-doo," he said.

KITCHEN PATROL

Bertha Bishop stood in the middle of the galley with her hands on her wide hips, looking like a grizzly bear wearing a tent. Standing next to her was Theo Sonborn, looking like her pugnacious cub.

"Thank goodness you're here," Bertha said to Marty as he walked up. "This might be the most inept group of people that I have ever seen gathered in one room."

"Tell me about it," Theo said.

Oh, please, Marty thought. *Theo's the one who's inept . . . and on top of that, he's a spy.* Marty still didn't understand why Wolfe wasn't concerned about Theo.

"We need to come up with a system to keep the crew fed and healthy," Bertha continued. "Having hungry troops is a recipe for disaster. Any ideas?"

"Yeah," Marty said, glaring at Theo. "Actually cooking the food before feeding it to the troops would be helpful."

"Good idea," Theo said, completely undisturbed by the direct insult.

Something beeped inside Theo's pocket and Marty was shocked to see him pull out a Gizmo.

"How'd you get a Gizmo?"

"The same way you did," Theo said. "Wolfe gave it to me."

"Wolfe didn't give me my Gizmo," Marty said. "Ted Bronson did."

"Ted Bronson's an idiot, then, giving a kid a Gizmo like it's a toy."

"Ten Bronson is not an —"

"Save it," Theo said. He looked at Bertha. "Looks like I have another assignment. The galley's all yours."

They watched Theo strut out through the swinging doors.

"About ninety percent of your problem is solved," Marty said.

"How so?" Bertha asked.

"Theo is gone." He told her everything that had happened between them.

"Theo is not a spy," Bertha said when he finished. "He's been on Cryptos from the start. He's just been messing with you."

"That's what Wolfe said, more or less, but I don't believe it. There's something not right about Theo. How did he know about the eggs?"

"Scuttlebutt," Bertha said. "There are virtually no secrets on an island, and even fewer on a ship. Subordinates watch their bosses very carefully. They're like a dog watching its owner. The dog knows more about its owner than the owner knows about the dog."

"Well, Wolfe better start watching that dog or he's going to get bitten in the butt."

Bertha laughed. "Don't count on it. Theo Sonborn's bark is bigger than his bite. Now, let's whip this galley into shape."

THE CARGO HOLD

Butch McCall, ever alert, heard the cargo hold door creak open before the lights came on. He put down his third can of pork and beans, turned off his flashlight, closed the container door, and locked it from the inside before whoever was coming took their first step down the companionway.

He'd chosen his doghouse well. It was one of the few containers with small holes cut into it. He could hear and see everything.

When he first saw Laurel and Phil, he could hardly contain his excitement. Even if they screamed, no one would hear them this deep in the ship. Then cold, quick logic took over.

Butch checked the Gizmo. Pros and cons fired through his brain like bullets: Unlike the others on his "to do away with" list, Phil's and Laurel's tracking tags were still active. This meant Al Ikes and Wolfe knew exactly where they were, and it would be the first place they'd search. It would be hard to make their deaths look like an accident in the cargo hold. Plus he'd have to kill both of them at the same time in the same place, then loosen one of the straps on one of the containers, setting it up to look like it had shifted at the exact moment they walked past it. Stranger accidents had happened at sea, but Al and Wolfe would investigate the deaths thoroughly. They would certainly open the other containers and discover evidence of a stowaway. Where would Butch go? Killing Laurel and Phil, then throwing them overboard, was out of the question. He would have to wait for night to haul their bodies up to the deck. They'd be missed long before then. But what if he killed them, threw their tags overboard, and got rid of their bodies at his leisure? With both tags in Butch's hands it would look as if Laurel and Phil had gone up to the deck together. But at the moment the sea was dead calm. It would be hard for anyone to believe that two people had fallen overboard in a flat sea.

All of this flashed through Butch's mind in the time it took for Laurel and Phil to reach the bottom of the companionway.

"Wolfe missed you while you were gone," Phil said.

"I missed him, too," Laurel said. "And Grace and Marty."

"But you missed Wolfe in a different way."

"You're fishing, Phil."

"No, I'm not. I've known Wolfe for more than twenty years and this is the happiest he's been since he was with Rose."

"And that wouldn't have anything to do with Grace being back in his life and two freshly hatched dinosaurs up in the lab."

"Of course he's happy about that, but when he saw you step off that sailboat he lit up like a Roman candle and so did you. All I'm saying is that you and he make a good couple . . . a good team. Those kids need a mom in their lives."

"Good grief, Phil. Now I'm a wife and a mom? Let's just concentrate on where to build this dinosaur nursery."

"Okay, I'll drop the subject—for now. But you know I'm right. How big is this nursery supposed to be?"

"I don't know. Ted Bronson is coming up with the parameters. I guess it has to be big enough to house two juvenile dinosaurs, lab equipment, a clean room, a couple of cots. . . . It's noisy down here."

"We can make the room soundproof. We'll have to rearrange these containers. The calmest place will be right in the center of the hold where this container is . . ."

Phil slapped the container where Butch was hidden, standing perfectly still and listening to every word they were saying, his mind still racing. The dinosaurs had hatched. Butch was losing his hiding place to make room for them.

"All we can do now is some preliminary work," Phil continued. "We'll need supplies to actually build the room."

"We'll pick them up when we get to New Zealand."

"We're not going to New Zealand."

"What are you talking about?"

"We aren't going any farther than Kaikoura Canyon. We're not making landfall. We're staying in international waters where Blackwood's legal eagles can't touch us. I'll have to have the supplies freighted out to us."

"I didn't know that."

"Only a handful of people do. I'm sure Wolfe would have told you if you'd been here. He's not even going into port to refuel. We'll have to do that with a tanker at sea. In fact, maybe I can get the tanker to haul in the supplies for us."

"He hasn't told the crew yet?"

"They'll learn soon enough. We'll be at Kaikoura in less than forty-eight hours."

"When we get back to Cryptos, what's to prevent Blackwood's legal team from going after Grace?"

"Jurisdiction. Officially, Cryptos doesn't exist. Unofficially, it's a country unto itself. A protectorate of the United States, but not subject to its laws—except taxes. Wolfe and Ted couldn't talk them out of that one."

"How did they end up with an island all to themselves?" Laurel asked.

"Not even I know the answer to that, except that it had to do with something they did for the government years ago. As payment, at their request, they were given a hundred-year lease for the island."

"Whatever they did must have been huge."

"You're right about that. But they didn't want money. They wanted the island and to be left alone."

"This happened after they caught the great white shark for Blackwood?"

"No. They had the island before that. They hired on with Noah to get the seed money to start eWolfe, and that's another reason Noah has it in for Wolfe. After they brought the great white in, he expected them to stay on with him. But they had other plans, which in Wolfe's case included eloping with Blackwood's only child, Rose—ensuring that Noah would be his enemy forever. And Butch McCall isn't far behind Noah in his hatred of Wolfe. Butch had been eyeing Rose for years, figuring that he would become Noah's son-in-law and the heir apparent to Blackwood's fortune. It's been a bitter history, and now with Grace as Blackwood's only living relative, it's gotten even more convoluted. Noah has declared all-out war, and Wolfe and Ted are going to protect their den like tigers with cubs. They . . ."

Phil and Laurel walked to the far side of the hold out of Butch's hearing range, then a few minutes later wandered back past his container.

"So much for the history lesson," Phil was saying. "I'll send a crew down tomorrow to move some of the containers. As soon as Ted gives us the design I'll order the material and we'll have it up in no time."

"This place kind of gives me the willies. I sense danger."

"Wolfe told me that you were . . . uh . . . sensitive."

"In what way?"

"Nothing negative. He just said that he thought that sometimes you see and feel things others don't. Maybe what you're feeling down here is the ship's violent past. I'm not saying that the ship is haunted, but I do think that horrors can linger. I've never felt it myself, but when I was in the military I knew soldiers who could tell you where bad things had happened long after the fact."

"I think it's more immediate than that, but we'll let it go for now."

Butch didn't move until the lights went out and the door clicked closed at the top of the companionway.

Up to this point he had maintained strict radio silence, but with these new developments he was going to have to risk breaking it. He composed a long, detailed email to Noah Blackwood on the Gizmo, read it over twice, then hit the SEND button.

With the email sent, he quickly gathered his meager belongings. He was going to have to find new living quarters. And he knew just where to look.

PART THREE — THE ABYSS

OVERBOARD

It took two days and nights for Marty and Bertha to get the mess squared away. During that time, Marty did not leave the galley once, preferring to take short naps on the cot Wolfe brought in for him to sleep on.

Bertha was uncharacteristically passive, leaving every decision to Marty as if she were his lieutenant and Marty was the general.

Marty watched all of the cooks, figured out their culinary strengths and weaknesses, and assigned prep stations accordingly. At first they were resentful about taking orders from a kid, but that quickly passed when they saw that the *kid* knew exactly what he was doing. All those years Marty had spent in the kitchen at Omega Prep with some of Europe's great chefs were paying off. The compliments from the crew over the delicious food energized not only Marty but the entire galley staff. The good food put smiles on everyone's faces.

Those same smiles faded a bit when Wolfe announced that they had arrived at Kaikoura Canyon and would be going no farther — that they would be anchored above the canyon and stay there until they caught a giant squid, then head straight back to Seattle without shore leave in New Zealand. But even with this news the crew was still happier than they had been on the voyage from Cryptos. There had been no more accidents and only a couple of reports of things missing or being mysteriously moved.

Late in the evening of his second day as galley supervisor, Marty told Bertha he needed to go up to the deck for some fresh air.

"We have it under control down here," Bertha said. "Take your time. In fact, why don't you spend the night in your own cabin? Let's see how the cooks do on their own."

"Deal," Marty said. "I'll see you tomorrow morning."

On his way up he was tempted to stop at Lab Nine and check on the hatchlings, but he was too desperate for fresh air. Forty-eight hours of butter, olive oil, garlic, onions, fish, dough, and meat had been enough. He didn't want to add dinosaur poop to the mix before he filled his lungs with brisk sea air.

Grace, Luther, Wolfe, and Laurel had all been in the mess to eat and had told him about what was happening with the hatchlings. They had outgrown the incubator and had been moved to a pen on the floor of the lab. They were walking now and had taken a shine to Luther, following him around like chicks following a mother hen. Grace was a little jealous of their obvious affection for Luther. She said the only reason they liked him better was that he had given them their first taste of blood.

Marty reached the deck and took in a deep breath of fresh

sea air, which smelled like perfume compared to the greasy galley. The dark sky was moonless, lit by millions of stars. The *Coelacanth* was anchored. He walked over to the rail and looked down at the water. Somewhere beneath the dark water a giant squid awaited.

Tomorrow, if things are going well in the galley, I'll spend the day on deck getting some sun, he thought. *I can fly the dragonspy and goof a—*

Something slammed into his back and he was falling over the wrong side of the rail. One of his flailing hands managed to snag the edge of the scupper and he came to a shoulder-wrenching stop. He managed to get his other hand onto the scupper, but his position was still precarious. His first thought was that Bo was loose again. She loved sneaking up behind people and pushing them, but the push had been too hard. Something a lot bigger than Bo had hit him. He tried to pull himself up, but he didn't have enough strength. He began to yell his head off. The sharp edge of the scupper was cutting off the circulation to his fingers. If someone didn't hear him in a minute or so, he was going to drop into the dark sea and never be heard from again.

He looked up as he continued to shout for help. The bottom rung of the rail was a good two feet above his head, impossible to grab, even if his shoulder wasn't killing him. It was a miracle that he had caught the scupper, but all the miracle was going to do was delay a watery death.

"Someone help me!"

Marty felt for some kind of purchase with his toes to help

relieve his aching arms and fingers. There was nothing but the slick metal skin of the old ship. He wished Wolfe had reactivated his tracking tag when he'd sentenced Marty to kitchen patrol. If it were active, he could tear it off and Roy or Joe would come running. The Gizmo was in his pocket, but he was afraid to pull it out. He'd never be able to hang on with one arm. He wondered if Ted had thought to make the Gizmo waterproof. There was a good chance it was. Ted had thought of everything else. He might be able to make a call after he hit the water, if a shark didn't get him first.

"Help! Man overboard! Boy overboard! Help!"

"Grab the line."

A rope flew over the rail and slapped the hull right next to him.

Marty grabbed it with tears of relief flowing down his face.

"I'm alone!" a voice shouted above him. "I can't pull you up. Can you climb on your own?"

"I think so!" Marty shouted back. The rough rope felt like soft leather compared to the edge of the scupper. He ignored the pain in his shoulder and fingers and started up the rope like a monkey, desperate to get the deck under his feet. When he reached the bottom rail, a pair of hands reached out and pulled him over the top.

The hands belonged to Theo Sonborn.

"I thought I lost you," Theo said. "You gotta be more careful."

Marty's grateful grin turned into a sour frown as he got to his feet.

"I was pushed."

"Pushed? Why would someone push you?"

"That's a good question, Theo. But here's a better one. Where were you when I was pushed?"

"You don't think *I* pushed you?"

Marty didn't answer.

"Why would I push you overboard, then save you?"

"Maybe because I managed to save myself and I was screaming my head off and you thought someone else might hear me. If I happened to see you before I went over and someone else saved me, it would be all over for you—I know you're one of Noah Blackwood's spies."

"I didn't push you. I saved you. And I'm not one of Noah Blackwood's spies. But I would still like to know more about those dinosaur eggs you were telling me about the other day."

"*You* were talking about dinosaur eggs and I told you that it was the most ridiculous thing I had ever heard. There are no dinosaur eggs." *Which is true,* Marty thought. *At least it is now.*

Theo smiled. "Come on, Marty. I didn't push you. If it weren't for me, you'd be swimming with the fishes. The very least you can do is tell me about those eggs. And I ain't working for Blackwood on the sly. I just want to know to satisfy my own curiosity."

"I'll tell you what, Theo. How about you and I go find Wolfe and you can ask *him* about the dinosaur eggs?"

"Okay," Theo said.

This wasn't the answer Marty was expecting. "You really want to ask Wolfe about the eggs?"

"Why not?"

"All right," Marty said, rubbing his sore shoulder. "Let's go."

THE TRUNK

Grace and Laurel were heading to Grace's cabin. They had just finished their shift, feeding the hatchlings more than two pounds of meat each—their third meal that day. The hatchlings would sleep for three or four hours now. Luther was keeping an eye on them.

As soon as they walked into the cabin, Congo screeched and flew to Laurel's shoulder.

"I see you're feeling better," Laurel said.

"That's the first time he's flown since Wolfe set his broken wing," Grace said.

Congo nibbled Laurel's earlobe.

"That tickles."

"I'm sure he feels neglected. I've hardly been in here since the eggs hatched."

"That's not all that's been neglected," Laurel said, pointing to the paper and books strewn all around the cabin. "What is all this?"

"The illuminated manuscript that belonged to my mother. Wolfe gave it to me for my birthday."

"You're trying to translate it," Laurel said.

"Yes, but I haven't gotten very far. My mother was trying to translate it, too."

"How far did she get?"

"I don't know."

Laurel glanced at the trunk in the corner of the cabin. For the first time, Grace regretted bringing the trunk on board, because she knew what Laurel's next question would be.

"Why haven't you opened the trunk?"

"I'm not sure."

"Are you afraid?"

"Yes," Grace said, so quietly she wasn't certain she had said it out loud.

"I completely understand," Laurel said. "I think I would be nervous, too."

"But you would open it anyway," Grace said.

"Probably."

"I've gotten over so many of my fears since you taught me how to focus on the high wire, but I haven't been able to look inside the trunk."

"You brought the trunk aboard," Laurel said. "At least you're trying to overcome that fear."

"Marty doesn't think so. He's asked me a dozen times if I've opened it."

"That's because it's the essence of *your* mother that's inside, not his. It's full of her thoughts and dreams and memories—and what are we without those? Sometimes the simplest fears are the most difficult to conquer. As simple as opening a trunk." Laurel walked over to the illuminated manuscript. "Do you know why you're trying to decipher this?"

"Curiosity," Grace answered.

"That might be. But here's another reason to consider: Perhaps you're trying to translate the manuscript because you know you can't."

"What?"

"Think about it, Grace. You brought both the manuscript and the trunk with you on the voyage, when you knew you'd be going back to Cryptos. Why?"

"Because Wolfe thought my grandfather would send people to Cryptos and I didn't want them to steal the trunk. And I didn't bring the manuscript with me. Wolfe brought it and gave it to me here on the *Coelacanth* on my birthday. We were at sea."

"But you knew the manuscript had been removed from the display case in the library on Cryptos."

"Yes."

"And you weren't surprised when Wolfe gave it to you for your birthday."

"No."

"I think you brought the trunk because of the manuscript. You're hoping your frustration over the translation will make you open the trunk. Your mother was a brilliant woman. Wolfe told me she spent years trying to decipher the manuscript. Everything she knows about it is in the trunk. But there are a lot of other things in that trunk as well. Things that you are afraid to learn."

"What if my mother wasn't the woman I think she was?" Grace asked.

"You didn't even know she was your mother until a few

weeks ago. What if your mother is more remarkable than you think?"

"It's ridiculous, I know," Grace said. "Will you open it with me?"

"I wish I could, but you know as well as I do that I can't help you conquer your fears any more than you can help me conquer mine."

Laurel put out her index finger and Congo climbed onto it. She moved him back over to his perch.

"I guess we'd better check on our two friends and Luther," she said, smiling. "Make sure they haven't eaten him."

Grace looked at the trunk. "If you don't mind, I think I'll stay here for a while."

Laurel gave her a kiss on the forehead and left her alone in the cabin.

DESSERT

Butch McCall was stretched out on his new cot with his hands behind his head, a satisfied grin on his face, surrounded by his new friends, all of which had eight arms and two tentacles.

One down, he thought, *a few more to go.* Wolfe, Laurel, that obnoxious reporter Ana, Bertha, and maybe even Luther Smyth and Phil, if the opportunity presented itself.

Marty O'Hara had been so easy to dispatch. . . .

Butch had just finished a perfectly broiled rib-eye steak (rare) in the mess and had been thinking about getting some dessert when a haggard-looking Marty O'Hara pushed through the galley doors. Dessert could wait.

He'd followed Marty up to the abandoned deck, watched him lean over the rail, and hit him squarely in the back with both hands.

Butch hadn't even waited to hear the splash. He'd strolled back to his new home—Lepod's lab. He'd told Lepod that he'd had a falling-out with his supervisor, and Lepod had been delighted to take the gentle Dr. O'Connor on as his assistant. Butch had suggested they move a cot into the lab so he could monitor the filtration system 24/7.

If it weren't for the rotten fish smell, the lab would have been perfect. Butch found the bluish light from the aquariums and the squid jetting through the salt water relaxing. He was growing quite fond of squid and was thinking about removing calamari from his diet entirely. It seemed a shame to eat such an efficient predator. They were opportunistic — just like Butch had been when he'd caught Marty leaning over the rail. By now the sharks were gulping the boy down, or perhaps a giant squid had found him, pulled him into the deep, and was tearing him apart with its beak.

With that pleasant picture in his mind, Butch closed his eyes and fell asleep.

THEO SONBORN

"Come in," Wolfe said from behind his heavy teak door.

Marty and Theo walked in.

It was the first time Marty had been inside Wolfe's cabin. It was at least twice the size of his and Luther's. And Wolfe needed the room. The cabin was crammed with electronic equipment: monitors, computers, radios, and other stuff Marty couldn't even name. The cabin looked like the "Wolfe Den" back on Cryptos, the room that was the heart of Wolfe's cryptid search — and the search for Marty's parents in South America. *Luther would love this room,* Marty thought.

"What's up?" Wolfe asked from behind a large desk cluttered with nautical maps. His prosthetic leg was leaning against the desk with its size-fifteen deck shoe attached.

"I need to use the head," Theo said, and walked into the bathroom as if he had used it a dozen times before. He closed the door.

Wolfe looked at Marty. "Is there a problem?"

"I'll wait for Theo," Marty said. "He has an interesting question to ask you."

"Theo always has interesting questions," Wolfe said.

"He also has homicidal tendencies," Marty said. "He just tried to kill me by pushing me overboard."

A look of alarm crossed Wolfe's face. "Are you sure you were pushed?"

"Duh *du jour*, and I would have been in Davy Jones's locker if I hadn't managed to grab the scupper on my way down."

"Tell me everything," Wolfe said.

Marty did.

"It does sound like you were pushed," Wolfe said when he finished. "Which is very bad news. It also sounds like you were very lucky that Theo happened by when you fell."

"I have a different theory," Marty said. "Like I said, I think Theo was the pusher. When he saw that he had blown it, he pulled me back up to make it look good."

The bathroom door opened.

The man who had walked into the bathroom was not the man who walked out. He looked like a model who had just finished a photo shoot for a men's sporting magazine. He had short blond hair, blue eyes, no facial hair, and he wore a crisp polo shirt, jeans, and Birkenstock sandals.

"What the—"

The man cut Marty off, looking at Wolfe. "I assume Marty filled you in on what happened." Smiling with perfectly white teeth, he glanced at the flabbergasted Marty. "Or what he *thinks* happened."

Theo Sonborn must still be in the bathroom, Marty thought.

"He told me," Wolfe answered. "Did you see anyone?"

"No, I was—"

"What's going on?" Marty shouted. "Who is this?"

"I'm sorry," Wolfe said. "I'd like you to meet my partner, Ted Bronson."

Marty stared at the man. He'd expected Ted Bronson to be a geek in a stained lab coat and thick glasses held together with duct tape. The man in front of him looked like a movie star action hero.

"You're joking."

"No joke," Ted said.

"What's with the Theo disguise?"

"I've used it for years. It's a good way to get out of the QAQ and see what's going on in the real world. Theo is short for Theodore, my given name. And Sonborn is an anagram — my last name scrambled around. Not very clever, but no one's ever figured it out. The disguise helps."

"Do Phil and Bertha know about the disguise?"

"Yes, and so does Al, but they're the only ones."

This explained why Bertha and Wolfe hadn't been concerned about Theo and the eggs, but it didn't explain everything.

"Why were you such a jerk in the galley? Why did you ask me about the dinosaur eggs?"

"We'd better sit down," Ted said. He cleared maps and papers from a couple of chairs. "I've been watching you ever since you arrived on Cryptos, Marty . . . well, off and on when I could."

"Why?"

"At first I was just curious. But then I noticed that you have something that few people have."

"What?"

"For lack of a better word, audacity. A visceral, or gutlike, intelligence. I've never seen it in someone your age. In fact, I started to doubt my observations. I decided to subject you to a rigorous scientific inquiry to test my observations."

Marty was flattered by the comment about his gutlike intelligence, but he wasn't sure if he liked being part of Ted's rigorous scientific inquiry without being asked.

"Grace is the genius," Marty said. "Not me."

"I didn't say you were a genius," Ted pointed out. "And there's no doubt that Grace is brilliant. But she's smart in a different way than you are. Your intelligence is more physical, driven by lightning-quick thought processes. For instance, when you fell out of the jet over the Congo you saved yourself, Grace, and even PD in a free fall. Ninety-nine point nine percent of humans would have either passed out from fear or their minds would have simply shut down in terror."

"I was scared to death," Marty said. "When I landed I puked my guts out."

"Most people's guts would have been smeared all over the jungle floor," Ted said. "Here's another example: You figured out how to lure Bo onto the *Coelacanth*. Impressive."

"It wouldn't have worked without Luther, and he sure didn't think it was impressive."

"If Luther hadn't been there you would have thought of some other way to get her on board. And then there's the most recent example: Somebody pushed you overboard. Most people would not have caught that scupper. They would have hit the water hard and been sucked underneath the ship."

"Did you push me as part of your experiment?" Marty asked sharply. He wasn't sure that he liked Ted Bronson any better than he liked Theo Sonborn. And he was absolutely sure that he didn't like being a guinea pig.

"I did not push you," Ted said. "But you *were* pushed. I just sent a video of the incident to our mainframe computer. But we won't be able to see much because of the light and the angle."

Wolfe hit a few keys and a bird's-eye view of the deck appeared on a monitor. Ted was right; it wasn't very clear. The camera caught a shadow of Marty walking across the deck. He looked up at the sky for a moment, then he leaned over the rail. A couple of seconds later something large, dark, and blurry rushed up behind him, then hurried off as quickly as it had appeared.

All Marty could tell from the video was that whoever had pushed him was bigger than Ted Bronson and Bo. "Wait a second," he said. "I thought you pulled all the cameras?"

"Not all of them," Ted said. "And I've already taken a look at the tracking tags. You were alone up there until I showed up." He looked at Wolfe. "Right now the only people without active tags besides you and Marty are Grace, Luther, Ana, and Laurel. None of them pushed Marty over the rail." He looked back at Marty. "I would have gotten to you sooner, but I was down at the Moon Pool. I was too afraid to even slow down and make a radio call. To tell you the truth, I thought you'd drop before I got there."

Wolfe picked up his encrypted radio and keyed the mic. "Al?"

"Go ahead."

"Do we have anyone on board who's taken off their tag in the past half hour or so?"

"Negative. We haven't had anyone take off their tag since we left Cryptos. Why?"

"I'll get back to you." Wolfe cut the connection and looked at Ted. "Looks like we have a stowaway."

"A nasty one," Ted said. "One of Blackwood's."

"Probably."

"How do you want to play it?"

"Quietly," Wolfe answered. "If he knows we've discovered him, he'll go to ground and we'll never find him. And I suspect he's had some help aboard."

"He might even have a Gizmo," Ted said. "We lost one of them a few weeks ago."

Wolfe swore, then got on the radio. "Al? Have you been monitoring Gizmo email?"

"Negative. I didn't think it was necessary since everyone with a Gizmo is on our side, and no one else aboard has email access."

"Not anymore," Wolfe said. "I'll explain later. Start monitoring all incoming and outgoing Gizmo email."

"Done," Al said.

Wolfe looked at Marty. "New rules. You, Grace, and Luther are not to go anywhere without a guard until we find this guy. I'll go down to tell them personally. If he doesn't have a Gizmo, he certainly has a two-way like everyone else aboard. Who knows, he might even have an encrypted radio like Al and his crew and I are carrying, although it wouldn't do him much good without the code."

"What do you want me to do?" Marty asked.

"Stick with Ted. You have a lot to discuss."

Wolfe strapped on his leg and hurried out of the cabin.

"What do we have to discuss?" Marty asked, still a little annoyed with Ted for experimenting with him.

"For one, you asked about the cameras. . . ." Ted pulled a Gizmo out of his pocket and quickly released a bot-fly, which he proceeded to pilot expertly around Wolfe's cabin before landing it on the ceiling. Ted's bot was translucent, making it almost invisible as he flew it around the room. It blended in with every color and would be nearly impossible to spot.

"Obviously I'm not the only one who can navigate the bot-fly," Marty said.

"You don't think I'd invent something I couldn't operate, do you?"

"I guess not."

"If it makes you feel any better, you and I are the only ones who can fly it. And I actually like *dragonspy* better than *bot-fly*. If you don't mind, I'd like to use your name for it when we apply for the patent."

"Fine," Marty said. "But why did you give me the dragonspy in the first place?"

"To see how you'd do with a million-dollar bug. I had no doubt you would figure out how to fly it, but what I really wanted to know was if you'd follow the rules. No pun intended, but you passed with flying colors when Luther asked if he could fly it and you told him no."

"You overheard that conversation?" Marty asked.

Ted nodded. "My dragonspy has been with you since you got back to the island."

"Any other tests?"

"The galley," Ted said. "Two dinosaurs hatch, and instead of being allowed to take care of them you get KP. Not only didn't you complain, you turned around the terrible food situation I had intentionally created."

"You *are* a lousy cook."

"Actually, I'm a better cook than Theo Sonborn, but not by much."

"Where's all this going? Why have you been testing me?"

"I'll show you," Ted said. "Let's go down to the Moon Pool."

ROSE

Grace undid the two latches on the old trunk, then paused.

"You are being ridiculous!" she whispered. "Do you expect a skeleton to jump out? Open the trunk!"

She lifted the lid.

Inside was a jumble of manila envelopes, file folders, and dozens of Moleskine journals just like the ones Grace used. Buried beneath the mess was the Frankenstein Monkey. She remembered what Marty had said: "It's probably packed away somewhere you haven't looked yet." She untangled Monkey and pulled him out, happy to have him aboard, but mad at Marty for hiding him in the place she was least likely to look.

With Monkey in her lap, she picked up the top envelope and carefully undid the clasp. Inside were photographs of her mother when she was young. Marty had told her about the photos, but she hadn't really believed him until now. Her mother, Rose Blackwood, looked exactly like Grace had when she was that age. The same robin's-egg-blue eyes, the same curly black hair . . . It was true: She and her mother could have been twins.

There were photos of her mother holding tiger cubs, riding a zebra, feeding an ostrich . . . And in every photo was a beaming, younger Noah Blackwood. He didn't look at all like the evil person she knew him to be. He looked like a happy, doting father. But there was something very important missing from every photograph. . . . A wife. Rose's mother. Grace's grandmother.

Where was she?

Who was she?

What happened to her?

There was a knock on the door.

"Come in," Grace said, trying to get the photos back into the envelope, but not before Wolfe walked in with a worried look.

"Thank God you're all right," he said. "I was just down at the lab, and Laurel and Luther said you were in here alone."

"I spend a lot of time in here alone," Grace said.

"Not anymore. I'm having Laurel move in with you."

"Why?"

Wolfe filled her in on his conversation with Marty.

"Is Marty okay?"

"He's fine."

"Do you have any idea who the stowaway is?"

"No, but it's certainly one of Blackwood's men, and whoever he is, he had help getting onto the *Coelacanth*, so we're dealing with more than one person. I think the stowaway is operating in the open, posing as someone he isn't. Hopefully Al will be able to figure out who he is and who's helping him. Until he does, you, Marty, and Luther aren't to go anywhere alone. The only people you can trust are me, Bertha, Phil, Al and his men, Laurel, and Ana Mika, whom I don't think you've met yet, but you will. As soon as she's feeling better she's going to help with the hatchlings. Everyone else aboard is suspect. I thought our quick departure would keep us a step ahead of Blackwood, but it looks like he's caught up with us. After what happened to Marty tonight, we know he's coming at us hard." Wolfe paused. "Ted and I knew it would come down to this one day."

"What really went on between you and my grandfather?" Grace asked.

"It's been going on for so many years," Wolfe said. "It's hard to know where to start. Your grandfather was a friend of my father's. I've known him since I was a kid. My father and Noah had a falling-out, but not before I learned more about him than I ever wanted to."

"Then why did you catch the great white shark for him?"

"You've heard the saying, 'Keep your friends close, but keep your enemies closer.'"

Grace nodded.

"It works both ways. Ted and I needed money to fund his inventions. I needed money to start eWolfe and to get Rose away from Blackwood. Noah hired us because we were the only people with the technology to get the job done, but that wasn't the only reason. He wanted to keep me close so he could keep an eye on me. I knew a lot more about him than he wanted me to know. And he recognized Ted's genius. He wanted that, too. Ted and I knew this going in, so we took precautions. Noah has met Ted, but he really doesn't even know what Ted looks like.

"When we caught the great white, Ted disguised himself as an absentminded geek." Wolfe smiled. "Believe me, Ted is anything but a geek. He did it because we knew from the very beginning that Noah Blackwood was going to come after us eventually. When you don't trust someone and consider them a future adversary, it's best to have them underestimate your capabilities. This way they'll base their decision to hurt you on who they *think* you are. In other words, underestimating you weakens their attack."

Grace was confused. This was a side of Wolfe she'd never seen. He didn't sound like a biologist. He sounded like a general waging a war, or a spy. "How do you know all this?"

"That's a long and very complicated story, which I'd prefer to save for another time. For now let me tell you about the great white shark."

"All right," Grace said. "But only if you promise to tell me the long, complicated story soon."

"Cross my heart," Wolfe said, sounding more like the father she knew.

"I've told you what Ted and I knew before we caught the great white. After we caught it, we knew we weren't going to give Noah the shark box we'd built, no matter how much money he offered to pay us for it. We also knew that we weren't going to catch a second great white for him after it died, which of course it eventually did. We knew that as soon as we had the money in hand for catching the shark, I was going to marry Rose and take her away from Noah. Rose and I knew that we were going to find every cryptid we could and protect them from her father and stop him from adding them to his ghoulish collection." Wolfe paused and tears came to his eyes. "Then I got Rose killed."

"That wasn't your fault," Grace said.

"In Noah Blackwood's eyes it was totally my fault. And there's something else. . . ."

"What?" Grace asked quietly.

"After my father died, Noah took me under his wing. He didn't do it out of affection. He did it because I was very good at finding things that were supposed to be impossible to find, but that doesn't matter. In his eyes I betrayed his trust. Ted and I are the only two people on earth who have survived that sin. The time has come to pay the devil his due."

Wolfe looked at the manila envelope in Grace's hands. "You opened the trunk."

"Just before you came in," Grace said. "These are old photographs. Mom and I look just like each other."

"You certainly do."

"There don't seem to be any photos of my grandmother . . . at least that I've seen yet."

"I don't think you'll find any."

"Why?"

"That's another question Rose was trying to find an answer to. Blackwood told her that her mother had died when she was a year old, but Rose didn't believe him. There are photos of her when she was just hours old. Her mother isn't in them. Rose didn't even know her mother's name. Blackwood refused to tell her. He told her that her mother's loss was too painful for him and that she was never to bring it up."

"She didn't even know her mother's first name?" Grace asked.

Wolfe shook his head. "The only person who knows who

your grandmother was is Noah Blackwood. Rose was convinced that Noah kept it a secret because her mother was still alive. With a name, even just a first name, Rose might have been able to track her down."

"Have you ever looked through the trunk?"

"Rose showed me some of the photos, but I never went through it on my own. She never said that I couldn't, but I considered the trunk her private domain. There was an unspoken agreement that I shouldn't. After she was killed and I lost my leg, the trunk was the least of my concerns. I needed to get you back to the States and situated with my sister so Blackwood couldn't get his hands on you. I thought about the trunk from time to time. I could have gone back for it, or had Masalito ship it to me."

"Why didn't you?"

"I didn't want to dredge up old memories. I was afraid."

THE ORB

"You're not claustrophobic, are you?" Ted asked Marty as they walked through the air lock to the Moon Pool. He had changed back into Theo Sonborn in case anyone saw him on their way down.

"No," Marty said.

"I didn't think so." Ted locked the doors behind them and started stripping out of his Theo disguise. "Your first week on Cryptos, I watched you explore the volcano on the east side of the island. You went through some pretty tight places."

"I didn't get very far," Marty said.

"When we get back I'll take you on a little tour. There's more to that volcano than meets the eye."

"It must be a pain in the butt getting in and out of that disguise," Marty said.

"It is, but as you can see I've had a lot of practice and it doesn't take long."

"It must be hot."

Ted nodded. "But that just adds to the sweaty, nervous demeanor of Theo Sonborn. It's not so bad on Cryptos because I spend most of my time inside the QAQ working. Aboard the *Coelacanth*, I'm in and out of this thing a half dozen times a day."

"How do you get out of the QAQ building without being seen? The entrance is always guarded."

Ted laughed. "I watched you circling the building trying to find a way inside. And I have to say that you let me down on that one. There's a secret tunnel leading from my private lab to the outside. When I'm in the lab there are strict orders that I am not to be disturbed under any circumstances. I've been known to stay holed up in the lab for weeks at a time. No one can be sure if I'm in the lab or not. Sometimes I'm not."

"Where is this tunnel?" Marty asked.

"Nice try," Ted said. "You were close a couple of times. You'll figure it out."

Marty was certainly going to try when they got back to Cryptos. "Why did you ask if I was claustrophobic?"

"I haven't been watching you solely for my own amusement. There is a method to my madness."

Ted went over to a keypad on the wall and punched in a code. A hidden door slid open on the far side of the pool, revealing what looked like an elaborate control room. He hit another button, and bubbles started coming up from the bottom of the Moon Pool. The dolphins started chattering. A moment later something started to rise from the bottom. It was glowing.

"What is that?" Marty asked.

"That is the Orb."

It broke the surface and bobbed in the center of the pool, still glowing. For a moment Marty was speechless as he stared at the giant golden ball. It was the size of a small car, and a humming noise came from within it.

"I'll bring it over for a closer look," Ted said. He took out his Gizmo and used it to maneuver the ball toward the edge of the pool.

"Where did it come from?" Marty asked. The water in the pool was crystal clear and something that big and bright couldn't be missed.

"Secret door on the side of the pool," Ted said.

"What does it do?" Marty asked.

"It's an Oceanic Reconnaissance Bot."

"O-R-B for short," Marty said.

"Exactly," Ted said.

Marty noticed the numbers on the side: *007.* "Like in James Bond?" he asked.

Ted shook his head. "More like an ironic coincidence."

"What does it do?"

"It's a miniature nuclear submarine," Ted answered.

It didn't look like any submarine Marty had ever seen. "Unmanned?"

"No. Three people will fit inside."

Three small people, Marty thought. "How did you get permission to build a nuclear sub? I thought nuclear power was regulated."

"It is, but Wolfe and I have friends in high places. It's the fastest sub in the world and it will dive deeper than any other sub ever has." Ted hesitated. "I hope."

"What do you mean you hope?"

"It's only been field-tested off the coast of Cryptos Island. The real test will come tomorrow morning in Kaikoura Canyon."

"What happens if it doesn't work?"

"The Orb will crumple like a soda can being stepped on by an elephant."

Marty ran his hand over the golden surface and felt a tingling sensation like static electricity. "It's soft . . . pliable."

"The Orb is my pride and joy. I've been working on it for years. It's made out of a special synthetic alloy. The same material the dragonspies are made from, but they're just trinkets compared to the Orb. There's only one man I would trust in the copilot's seat and that was Travis Wolfe."

"What do you mean *was*?" Marty asked.

"Travis is too big for the seat. And then there's the fact that he only has one leg. There are foot controls. He has a prosthetic leg, but after about an hour in the same position his thigh starts to cramp. He has to stretch his leg to get rid of the cramp. There's no room in the Orb to stretch, especially for someone his size."

Marty didn't see a hatch or a porthole. In fact, he didn't see a seam. "So, it has a design flaw," Marty said.

"Not a flaw. A structural necessity. The speed and maneuverability of the Orb is directly related to its size, which leaves your uncle out of the equation. He'll be directing our dive from the control room."

Marty walked over to the room and looked inside. It looked like a set from a science fiction movie.

He turned to Ted. "What do you mean *our dive*?" he asked.

"This is why I've been watching you," Ted answered. "And, yes, testing you. I want you to be my copilot. If you can fly the dragonspy, you can pilot the Orb."

At that moment, every negative feeling Marty had felt toward Ted Bronson vanished behind a grin of sheer joy.

"I take that as a yes," Ted said.

"Duh *du jour*," Marty said.

"It's not without risk," Ted warned. "The Orb is completely experimental. I've only taken *007* beneath once. She performed perfectly, but I wasn't nearly as deep as we're going tomorrow. The difference between the two depths is the difference between walking on Mars and walking on Earth. It took a lot of persuasion to talk Wolfe into making you my copilot. The only reason he gave in was because there's no other choice. And you have Noah Blackwood to thank for that. If he hadn't arrived back at the Ark sooner than expected, Wolfe would have found another copilot. He was talking to NASA to see if one of their astronauts was interested. You'd still be in the galley on KP or feeding those hatchlings."

The truth was that Marty hadn't minded working in the galley. It didn't compare with copiloting the Orb, but he was proud of what he had accomplished in the galley even though it had taken him away from the hatchlings and his friends.

"How's the Orb going to help us catch a giant squid?" Marty asked.

"Cat and mouse," Ted answered. "The squid is the cat. The Orb is the mouse. We'll use it like a fishing lure. If the squid isn't interested in eating the Orb, we'll use it to irritate the beast.

One way or the other we'll get a giant squid to come after us. What we want to do is entice it to chase us right up through the Moon Pool and trap it. Of course, that's easier said than done. The horseshoe-shaped canyon is a thousand miles long and pitch-dark. Finding a giant squid to chase us is going to be difficult."

Marty looked at the three dolphins. They were keeping their distance from the Orb but were obviously very curious about it.

"What role do the dolphins play in catching the giant squid?"

"None," Ted answered. "Winkin, Blinkin, and Nod are decoys. We'll put cameras on them and let them loose, but the only reason they were brought aboard was to make everyone think that our plan was to use them to catch the squid. We needed a way of diverting attention from the Orb, which only a handful of people know about. The Orb is the main reason Al Ikes and his men are here."

"Not the miniature cameras?"

"Those, too," Ted said. "And the hatchlings, and the dragon-spy, and Blackwood, and Grace . . . but mostly the Orb. We haven't decided what to do with this new technology. Until we figure that out, we want to keep it quiet, which reminds me . . . Can Luther keep a secret?"

"Absolutely," Marty said. He and Luther had shared secrets for years.

"Good. Because he and Grace and a couple of others are about to be brought into the inner circle along with you. No one can know about the Orb. Loose lips sink ships."

"Luther will keep his mouth shut," Marty promised, looking back at the Orb. "What if the cat catches this mouse?" The Orb looked more like a golden egg than a rodent.

"I don't know," Ted said. "The Orb hasn't been field-tested for that possibility, which is why I warned you, there are some risks involved. We aren't completely defenseless, but it would be best if we didn't get snagged by a giant squid."

Marty continued to stare at the Orb in awe and a tiny bit of fear. "There aren't any portholes. How do we see out?"

"Cameras," Ted answered. "Similar to what we have on the dragonspies. We can access the cameras while we're in our aquasuits."

"What's an aquasuit?"

"Let's go into the control room."

As they started around the pool to the control room, they were interrupted by the sound of the Moon Pool door hissing open.

It was Ana Mika. She looked very different than she had the last time Marty had seen her. Her black hair was curled, she was wearing makeup, and she was dressed in stylish pants and a blouse, with enough jewelry to buy the *Coelacanth*.

She walked straight over to Ted without smiling and kissed him on the lips, long and hard enough to make Marty stare at his sneakers as if they were the most interesting two objects he had ever seen.

When they finally broke apart, Ana said, "Wolfe told me I would find you two down here."

"How are you feeling?" Ted asked.

"Thanks for asking," Ana said. "But you're about two days late . . . as usual."

"I did check on you," Ted said. "Twice. Both times you were sound asleep."

"Dr. Jones must have given me knockout drugs, but I do feel better. I got up a couple of hours ago, showered, dressed, and ran down to the galley to get something to eat. The food was wonderful."

"Here's the chef," Ted said, nodding at Marty. "Or I should say former chef, Marty O'Hara."

"Ana," she said, extending an elegant hand with three gold rings.

Marty shook her hand and said, "We met when you came aboard the *Coelacanth*. You barfed on my shoes."

"Those were your shoes? Sorry about that. Your parents will get a big kick out of that when you tell them."

"My parents are—"

"Your parents are *lost*," Ana interrupted. "I'm sure Sylvia and Timothy are fine. Wolfe will find them, or they'll stumble out of the jungle on their own. They've been in much worse situations than that."

"You know them?"

"I've known them for years. Your mother introduced me to Ted, but I'm not holding that against her. She is the best field photographer who ever lived. And Timothy could always write circles around me. *That* I do hold against him."

"So, you really are a reporter?"

"I prefer the moniker *investigative journalist,* but yes, I'm a reporter."

"Speaking of which," Ted said, "how did the press conference go?"

"You mean the Noah Blackwood show?" Ana said. "Divisive as usual. When I popped the giant squid question, he acted like he knew all about the expedition, but I could tell he was lying through his artificially whitened teeth. We tipped him off. I told you it was a bad idea for me to go to the press conference and ask him what he thought."

Marty noticed that she was paying absolutely no attention to the golden orb in the pool, which could only mean that she had seen it before.

"He would have found out anyway," Ted said. "Your telling him might have lost us an hour at the most. And it accomplished one of the things we wanted to do. He lied on camera about our involvement in catching the great white, and we'll be able to use that against him one of these days. Wolfe and I watched the clip on the news." Ted straightened up and gave them a big fake smile and a pretty good imitation of Noah Blackwood: "Travis and Ted were deckhands, and not very good ones at that."

Marty and Ana laughed.

"Noah wasn't even there when we reeled in the great white," Ted continued. "And we have a dozen witnesses to corroborate that fact. You rattled him at his own press conference, and that's exactly what we wanted you to do."

"That's exactly what your partner just told me," Ana said. "He also told me about the hatchlings and the stowaway — exciting times aboard the *Coelacanth*. I could win a Pulitzer prize if you'd let me tell the story, but of course that's out of the question . . . right?"

"Right," Ted said. "But I love you, Ana."

"Humph," Ana said.

"Noah lied on camera. The more we get of that in the public record, the better off we'll be."

"I still don't understand how that's going to help us," Ana said.

"Because at this moment Noah Blackwood's *Endangered One* and *Endangered Too* are twenty miles away. He'll anchor the ships at Kaikoura Canyon, uninvited, waiting for us to pull a giant squid out of the abyss, and—"

"Correction," Ana interrupted. "His ships showed up when I was in Wolfe's cabin. They're anchored half a mile away."

"It doesn't matter," Ted said. "My point is that Noah just got back from a harrowing experience in the Congo, and within hours he jumps on his yacht and sails to the exact spot his main competitor is going fishing. Does that sound like someone who doesn't care about what the Northwest Aquarium is doing?"

"No, it doesn't, but I have another correction," Ana said. "Noah didn't sail here. He took his private jet to New Zealand and just landed on the *Endangered One*'s helipad in his private helicopter."

"Noted, Ms. Stickler for Details," Ted said.

"Blackwood isn't being very subtle," Marty said.

"There's no reason for him to hide," Ted said. "Up to this point we've been fighting a cold war with Noah Blackwood. But after what happened in the Congo, it's a *hot* war. We need everything in our arsenal to defend ourselves. One shield we can use, which Noah has hidden behind his entire life, is his mastery of public relations and public perception. We need to start chipping away at his cover." He looked at Ana. "And you just struck the first blow."

"It was a very weak blow," Ana said. "Butch looked like an angry stag frozen in the headlights of an oncoming truck, but the reporters only had eyes for Blackwood. When I popped the squid question, Noah whispered something to Butch, and he did the worst I'm-going-to-collapse-from-disease routine I've ever seen. Of course the reporters gulped down the alleged collapse like hungry vultures."

Ted laughed.

"Have you given Marty the chicken-and-egg question yet?" Ana asked.

"I was just about to when you came in."

"What are you talking about?" Marty asked.

"You'll see," Ana answered. "I'd better get going, but before I do, Wolfe asked me to tell you that he just talked to Dr. Robert Lansa in Brazil. He's going to do everything he can to find your parents. Oddly, I interviewed Dr. Lansa a few years ago for an article I was writing on field biologists, and he was the best of the bunch. If your parents are within a hundred miles of his jaguar preserve, he'll pick up their trail and track them down. He's a bit abrupt and rude, but he is very good at what he does."

"That's great." Marty was happy to hear this, but he didn't want to get his hopes up, nor did he want to think about what his parents were going through if they were still alive. He changed the subject. "So, you're here to write about catching the giant squid."

"Indirectly," Ana said. "What I'm really doing here is adding material to an investigative piece I've been working on for years about the *real* Noah Blackwood. Up till this point I've been able to stay beneath his radar, but after showing up at the press conference I'm officially a blip on Blackwood's screen." She looked at Ted. "As Butch and Blackwood were heading back to the mansion, Butch recovered enough from his so-called illness to ask me who I was and who I worked for. I lied. But by now they've figured out who I am and they've probably connected me with you and Wolfe. I'll bet Blackwood's probably on *Endangered One* right now, thumbing through a thick dossier his people have gathered on me."

"You're probably right," Ted admitted.

"I'll leave you two alone," Ana said. "I'm going to poke around the ship and talk to the crew. I don't agree with Wolfe and Al's idea of quietly looking for the stowaway. If you want to find someone, you need to talk to people. There are dozens of people who have seen this guy and spoken to him. I just have to find the right crew member and ask the right question."

She gave Ted another kiss (not as long as the one she had given him earlier, to Marty's relief) and walked out through the air lock.

ENDANGERED ONE

Noah Blackwood sat in a leather chair behind a huge rosewood desk in his well-appointed cabin. The *Endangered One*, like the *Endangered Too*, was considered a research ship by his adoring fans, but in reality it was a two-hundred-and-seventy-three-foot luxury yacht Noah used almost exclusively for entertaining influential guests and smuggling rare animals into the United States.

But this voyage is a little different, he thought, and smiled for the first time in an hour, which was how long it had taken him to read Ana Mika's dossier, emailed to him by his very private and well-paid investigators. Thinking about his investigators caused a frown to reappear. He was going to have to do some reorganization when this was all over. It was his investigators' job to make certain that people like Ana stayed away from him. He was surprised they'd had the gall to attach the dossier. The document was a testimony to their complete incompetence.

Ana was friends with Sylvia and Timothy O'Hara, Wolfe, and Ted, a fact that had not appeared in any of *their* dossiers. And she had been stalking Noah for — not days, not weeks, not months — but *years*.

Like Butch, Noah also had a "to do away with" list, but his was much, much longer. On the bright side, a number of the people on his list were together aboard the *Coelacanth*, and he had enlisted some professional help to cross them off it.

He switched on the computer's webcam and a live, high-definition picture of his famous face appeared on the flat screen. Except for the scowl, he liked what he saw.

The fact that eWolfe and NZA were on a secret expedition for a giant squid was perfect for Noah's purposes. The only reporter within a hundred miles was aboard the *Coelacanth*, and since she was on his list, she would be taking the information for her article to the bottom of the sea with her hysterical lungs filling with salt water. By the time anyone figured out that the *Coelacanth* had disappeared from the face of the earth with all hands on board, Noah would be back at the Seattle Ark holding a press conference about the tragic loss of his dear colleagues. It was a low priority, but if they succeeded in catching a giant squid before he scuttled their ship, he might try to put the leviathan in the Moon Pool on *Endangered Too*, then make the ultimate sacrifice of giving it back to NZA — thus removing all suspicion of his having anything to do with the loss of the ship and crew they'd hired. When NZA went bankrupt — which he would make certain happened — he would get the giant squid back and put it on exhibit in his own park.

"Come see *Architeuthis* at the Ark," he whispered.

That's good, he thought.

The smile returned.

He clicked the webcam RECORD icon.

"Wildlife first," he said in his melodic, hypnotic voice. "This was Northwest Aquarium's expedition, not mine. I was only there in a support role in the event that they needed my expertise. I am giving them the giant squid because, frankly, their facility is better suited for this amazing creature than the aquarium I currently have at the Ark. We are, and always will be, on the same team. Wildlife first."

Noah knew that the competition would be short-lived. A few weeks after the squid splash at NZA, the Ark would make a splash of its own in the form of two baby dinosaurs, which would cause the fickle public to forget all about *Architeuthis*.

He replayed the sound bite and liked what he saw and heard. He walked over to the window and looked at the *Endangered Too*, twice as big as *Endangered One*, anchored a few hundred yards away. Unlike the *Coelacanth*, both of his vessels were beautiful inside and out.

Butch still didn't know how Wolfe was going to catch a giant squid, but in his email he'd said that the rumor was that they were going to somehow lure it into the Moon Pool with the dolphins. Butch had learned a great deal about how to keep a giant squid alive from one of the scientists aboard the *Coelacanth*. Right now, Noah's technicians were retrofitting their Moon Pool to accommodate this denizen of the deep.

Travis Wolfe and Ted Bronson would not spend the money or time to go after a giant squid unless they were reasonably confident they could bring one in. They had no doubt come up with some brilliant yet simple capture method that Noah hadn't thought of—meaning that Ted Bronson had come up with the method. When this was all over, with Travis dead and eWolfe in ruins, Noah was going to go after Ted Bronson. Ted was not on his "to do away with" list. Noah wanted Ted alive and well and working for him—like his taxidermist, Henrico.

Noah hadn't seen Ted since he and Wolfe brought in the great white and kept it alive in Ted's shark box. He was a painfully shy, distracted geek, and totally dependent upon Travis Wolfe. Noah had heard from his spies on Cryptos that Ted had turned into a complete recluse, never leaving the Quonset hut where he came up with his marvelous inventions.

Without Wolfe, Ted was just another mad scientist. Without Ted, Wolfe was another twisted cryptid hunter.

But together . . .

And this was yet one more thing that irritated him about the self-righteous Travis Wolfe. If he knew about Henrico, Wolfe would be outraged. He would probably try to free him from the basement. And yet Wolfe had his own Henrico in the form of Ted Bronson. Henrico was happy in the basement creating works of art for Noah. Ted Bronson was happy in his Quonset hut inventing things for Wolfe. There was absolutely no difference in Noah's mind, except that Wolfe was too much of a coward to admit that he used people to benefit himself.

Noah decided he would fly to Cryptos with Grace immediately after the *Coelacanth* went down. He would collect her things and make Ted Bronson an offer he could not refuse. With Wolfe dead, Noah Blackwood, as Grace's grandfather and legal guardian, would own Travis's half of eWolfe's assets, including

Cryptos Island and every invention Ted Bronson had ever come up with. Ted would have to come over to Blackwood's side or lose everything.

Noah could hardly contain his glee at this prospect. In a few days he would have a pair of dinosaurs, an island, the most brilliant inventor since Leonardo da Vinci, and his granddaughter.

He strolled over to the other window and looked out at the broken-down *Coelacanth*, knowing full well they were in turn staring at his two ships. His smile broadened. What they didn't know was that soon there would be a third vessel. And it was this third vessel that would take them down.

History was going to repeat itself.

The *Coelacanth* was indeed a bad-luck ship.

THE CHICKEN AND THE EGG

"So," Marty said. "Ana is like . . . uh . . . your girlfriend?"

He and Ted were standing exactly where Ana had left them, staring at the Moon Pool door.

"Yep," Ted answered.

"She's something," Marty said.

"A force of nature," Ted said with a grin. "We've been together for years—whenever we can be together, that is. We're both pretty focused on our work, which makes it a pretty good match."

"I like her," Marty said.

"So do your parents. I don't know if Wolfe told you this, but Ana flew down to Brazil with him when they crashed in the jungle."

The way Ana was dressed, it was hard for Marty to imagine her hacking her way through a sweaty tangle of leaves and vines.

"So, you think my parents are okay?" Marty asked.

"I don't know," Ted answered. "But I do know Ana. If she thinks there's a chance they're alive, there's a chance. You probably noticed, but she doesn't mince words. She says what she means and means what she says. If she thought they were dead, she would tell you."

Ted looked at his diver's watch. "We don't have a lot of time, but I suppose I should take a couple of minutes to talk to you about the chicken and the egg. It will give you some insight into how I think, and how Wolfe thinks as well. In a few hours you and I will be exploring unknown territory in very tight quarters. I know something about how you think. It would be best for both of us if you know something about how I think. Ready?"

"Sure."

"Which came first, the chicken or the egg?"

"I don't know," Marty said. "Why is that important?"

"Because it's the foundation of my theory of invention," Ted answered. "And you have to know the answer if you are going to be my copilot."

"Fine," Marty said. "Which came first?"

Ted shook his head. "First I need to explain some things to you." He patted the side of the Orb. "I came up with this new alloy by studying the exoskeleton of a dragonfly Wolfe found in the Congo when he was there with Rose. He was looking for a dinosaur and stumbled across a very unusual dragonfly, previously unknown to science, and sent it back to Cryptos. If Wolfe had not gone to Lake Télé to find Mokélé-mbembé, he would not have found that dragonfly. I would not have been able to synthesize the alloy and invent the bot-fly—or dragonspy, as you call it—or the Orb, or the aquasuits, which I'm going to show you in a moment—all of which are made out of the same material.

"There is nothing new under the sun," Ted continued. "All great inventions are a synthesis of things that already exist in nature. A lot of people think that Travis Wolfe is a lunatic, risking his life and fortune pursuing animals that are not supposed to exist. But you see, finding these animals is secondary to searching for them. You can't discover anything unless you're out looking. Hunting cryptids is an excuse for looking.

"The two hatchlings gulping down pounds of meat in Lab Nine are interesting, but their discovery doesn't matter unless we ask the right questions about why they still exist when every other dinosaur disappeared tens of millions of years ago. What makes the hatchlings different from all the other dinosaurs that went extinct? The answer to this might lead to dozens of new technologies . . . or it may lead to nothing . . . but that doesn't matter. Which leads me back to my original question: Which came first, the chicken or the egg?"

Marty shrugged his shoulders. "I don't know."

"That's close," Ted said. "But the real answer is: *It doesn't matter.* The important thing is the question. Do you understand what I'm getting at?"

"Maybe," Marty said. "Let me give it a shot."

"Go ahead."

"If you hadn't gotten the contract to go after the giant squid, you might not have invented the Orb. Without the alloy, you wouldn't have been able to come up with the Orb. Without the Orb, you wouldn't be able to explore Kaikoura Canyon. If you couldn't go into the canyon, you'd never know what's down there. We may not catch a giant squid, but what we find in the canyon might lead to something that could help us up here."

"I knew you'd get this!" Ted said enthusiastically. "And if we're lucky enough to capture a squid and get it back to Washington alive, we'll learn from the creature."

"And make money," Marty added.

Ted laughed. "Money has never meant much to me, or to Wolfe. If you find your passion and pursue it, the money will follow. Wolfe and I use money to keep the gas tank full so we can look around. Speaking of which, do you want to see the aquasuit?"

"Yeah."

Marty followed Ted into the control room, which looked even more elaborate up close than it had from a distance.

"Wolfe, or whoever is manning the room, will be able to see and hear everything we see and hear in the Orb. Another set of eyes in case we miss something in the deep."

Opposite the screens and computers, hanging on a rack, were three golden suits with attached hoods. On a shelf above them were three black high-tech-looking helmets with black visors.

"The suits aren't as scratchy as they appear," Ted said. "Yours is the one on the left. While you were in the Congo trying to kill yourself, I used a pair of your jeans and a T-shirt for the measurements."

"Correction," Marty said, imitating Ana. "While I was in the Congo with Butch McCall trying to kill me."

"Noted," Ted said. "My point is that the suit should fit pretty well. The alloy stretches and contracts like spandex."

Marty felt the suit. "It *does* feel like the stuff the Orb is made out of."

"Same alloy," Ted said. "But a lighter version. It's sort of like an exoskeleton that's molecularly adaptive to any environment. It's cold in the abyss. The aquasuit will keep you at a comfortable seventy degrees, or whatever temperature you choose."

"You make it sound like the suits are alive," Marty said.

"In a way they are, and so is the Orb. It's a bit complicated to explain, but the Orb and the aquasuits are actually organic body armor impervious to just about everything, and they will adapt instantly to any environment. Why don't you slip into your suit? You'll have to strip down to your underwear. Once I have you zipped in, I'll get into my suit."

"I don't see a zipper," Marty said. "How am I supposed to get into it? Through the neck?"

"With this." Ted pulled what looked like a glass knife out of a pocket in Marty's aquasuit. He pushed a green button on the handle. The blade started to hum and turned green.

"What is that?"

"You probably noticed there is no hatch in the Orb. This is the key to the Orb and the zipper to the aquasuits. It's a molecular particle disrupter. Green opens the zipper. Red closes the zipper." He ran the key down Marty's aquasuit, ripping it open from the neck to the crotch. "Step inside."

Marty took off his jeans and T-shirt and pulled on the aquasuit.

Ted hit the red button and the key glowed red. "You're going to feel a tingling sensation like static electricity." He ran the key along the tear and it came together like it had never been torn.

"Amazing!" Marty said. "We just rip a hole in the side of the Orb to get inside."

"That's right. Once it's sealed, it's a completely enclosed environment. And with the helmets attached and functioning, the aquasuits are also completely enclosed."

"Who does the third suit belong to?" Marty asked.

"One of the scientists aboard. For security reasons we haven't told him that he's going into the canyon yet. We'll let him know tomorrow morning just before we leave."

"What if he doesn't want to go?"

"Don't worry," Ted said. "He'll go. He wouldn't miss this opportunity for anything in the world. Go ahead and put your helmet on."

Marty took it from the shelf and put it on his head. As soon as the helmet touched the fabric around his neck he felt another burst of static.

"The helmet is adhering to the suit," Ted explained. "Leave the visor up for a moment while I get into my suit."

Marty did a few stretches. The suit, helmet included, was featherlight, comfortable, and covered every inch of his body down to his fingertips and toes. Ted zipped himself into his suit and put on his helmet.

"You look like you're ready for a moon walk," Marty said.

"With this suit I *could* walk on the moon. Flip down your visor."

Marty reached up to pull it down, but Ted stopped him.

"No," Ted said. "It's computer-controlled. There's a button on the right side of the helmet, but before you push it I should tell you that it's going to be a little disorienting. I nearly fell over the first time I buttoned up. As soon as the visor comes down, the environmental systems, video, and audio are going to kick in. You're going to feel a little pressure in your ears and sinuses for a few seconds while the system adjusts to your physiology and the suit seals. Oh, and it will be pitch-black. The visor is actually a video screen. You won't be able to see anything until we activate it."

Ted's description of what it would feel like was not even close to what Marty experienced when he hit the button. He felt like he was falling into a black, bottomless pit. His eyes burned, his ears popped, and his knees buckled—at least he thought they buckled. He wasn't sure if he was standing on his feet or his head.

"Close your eyes." Ted's voice came through speakers in the helmet.

"How do I know they're open?" Marty said.

Ted laughed. "I told you it was disorienting. Just close your eyes. On the left side of the helmet is another button that turns on the onboard computer. The reason you need to close your eyes is that it's a little bright as it boots up."

Marty pushed the left button.

"It should look like someone is shining a flashlight into your closed eyes."

"Yeah, I see red."

"Good. Your eyes are closed. Give it a few seconds, then open your eyes."

Marty counted to ten silently, then opened his eyes. "Whoa!"

"Cool, huh?"

"It's awesome! It's like I'm seeing through the visor, not looking at a screen. And everything is so clear. I have hawk eyes, not human eyes."

"High definition and you have a three-hundred-and-sixty-degree view. Turn your head."

Marty did. When he put on the suit, he'd been facing opposite the Moon Pool. He was pretty sure he hadn't moved, but he could see the Moon Pool, the Orb, and the dolphins as if he were facing in that direction.

Marty looked back at Ted, who had put his visor down. "Where's the power for this thing? With all this high-def video and audio, it has to be burning a lot of juice."

"There's a battery built into the helmet. If you look up in the left-hand corner you'll see a digital countdown timer. What's it read?"

"Thirty-seven minutes."

"That's because you have all the bells and whistles turned on. If you shut down everything except the oxygen and pressurization, you'd have about an hour of battery left. When we hook the suits up to the Orb, the components will run indefinitely. Wolfe told me you know how to scuba."

"Yeah."

"About thirty miles west of Cryptos there's a small trench approximately a thousand meters deep. I made it all the way to the bottom in the aquasuit."

"That's more than three times deeper than the world record!" Marty said.

"I know," Ted said. "I could have gone much deeper. And I came straight back up without pausing for decompression. No bends, no ill effects whatsoever."

"Incredible," Marty said. "So what's the suit's limit?"

"I have no idea," Ted answered. "And I hope we won't have to test the limits on this trip. That would mean the Orb got crunched and we had to eject. The suits are kind of a fail-safe system, an Orb within the Orb. And now it's time to get into the Orb and familiarize you with the controls."

PORK AND BEANS

Phil Bishop walked into Wolfe's cabin holding a can of pork and beans with a spoon sticking out of it.

Wolfe looked away from the computer screen, where he'd been staring at a crude sonar map of Kaikoura Canyon, wishing there were more details so they would have some idea of where to hunt for a giant squid.

"I'm not hungry, Phil. And if I were, I wouldn't be interested in sharing a can of pork and beans with you."

Phil set the can on Wolfe's desk. "I was just down in the cargo hold with a couple of guys, rearranging the shipping containers for your dinosaur playroom. One of the containers seemed lighter than the others, so we opened it up to see what was inside."

"And you found a half-eaten can of pork and beans," Wolfe said, wondering why Phil was bothering him with this.

"Nope," Phil said. "We found *cases* of pork and beans. Dozens of empty cans, a sleeping bag, flashlight batteries, disposable razors, dirty socks, underwear —"

"The stowaway," Wolfe said.

"His hideout, anyway. He wasn't home. He moved the stuff

from the container to the other containers and rigged a way of locking the door from the inside."

"Did you tell Al?"

"He's down there right now with his forensic kit, lifting finger-prints. After he finishes, he's going to stake it out and see if the guy comes back, but I don't think he will. No clothes except for the socks and shorts. No toiletry stuff. He's moved up in the world and it might have been me and Laurel who tipped him off. When we were scouting the hold, we weren't exactly whispering. We talked about Grace, Blackwood, Cryptos, and — I hate to admit it — baby dinosaurs."

Wolfe frowned.

"Laurel said that she thought something was wrong down there. Said that she felt something. I thought she might be thinking about what happened on the ship before you bought it. But it looks like she was right."

Wolfe's frown turned into a scowl.

"Sorry," Phil said.

"I'm not mad at you. I wouldn't have been whispering down there, either. Maybe he wasn't there."

Phil shook his head. "He was there all right. The only way he could have figured out we were relocating anything to the cargo hold was if he overheard us."

Wolfe's phone rang. He hit the SPEAKER button.

"Are you sitting down?" Al asked.

"Yeah. I'm sitting at my desk looking at a can of pork and beans with a spoon in it. Phil's with me."

"Anyone else within earshot?"

"No, we're alone."

"The prints belong to Butch McCall."

"Butch McCall is on my ship!" Wolfe shouted, jumping up from his chair. "How'd he get aboard so fast?"

"He had to have help."

"We have to get guards on Grace, Marty, and even Luther. Anyone who can identify him is a target."

"I've already taken care of that. We're a little shorthanded, so we'll have to keep the targets together as much as possible. Ana is another potential target. She's in my office right now and we're going over the footage from the press conference, downloading stills into a computer program and trying to figure out how he might have disguised himself. He can change his face, but he can't change his size. We'll find him."

Wolfe wasn't so sure. He and Butch had been adversaries for years, and Butch had come out on top more than once.

"I'd better get down to the galley and tell Bertha," Phil said.

"Tell her that I want her to personally guard Grace," Wolfe said. "I want her with Grace 24/7. I assume she came aboard armed?"

"Not that she needs a weapon to take someone out," Phil said. "But yeah, as always, she showed up with a small arsenal. Any idea who might be helping Butch?"

"It has to be one of the old-timers," Wolfe said. "And there's only about fifteen aboard, including you and Bertha. Let's have a little get-together with our old friends and see if we can get one of them to crack."

"I'm on it," Phil said, and left the cabin.

SPECIAL DELIVERY

"I don't think it's a good idea for us to meet out in the open on deck like this, Butch. We shouldn't be seen together."

"We'll be fine," Butch said to the little man who had gotten him onto the *Coelacanth*. "By the way, I never did catch your name."

"Mitch," the man said.

Snitch, Butch thought. "We're alone up here, Mitch," Butch said. "If someone comes along, it's just two crew members getting some fresh air and shooting the breeze."

"I'm serious," Mitch insisted. "Something's up. Phil just called a bunch of us to meet with him and Wolfe. Everyone on the list has been on Cryptos from almost the beginning. I think they know there's a stowaway and one of us helped him get aboard."

Butch snorted. "You're way behind them. By now they know the stowaway is me."

Mitch looked like he was going to be sick. "What are you going to do?"

Butch pointed across the water toward Blackwood's ships. "See those lights?"

"*Endangered One* and *Too*. That's all anyone's been talking about since they anchored. Do you think Noah's aboard?"

"He's aboard," Butch said, although he didn't know for certain.

"I might be able to get you a life raft," Mitch said. "You could reach him in no time."

"And leave you here alone?" Butch said.

"I'll be okay. I've been feeding Noah information for years and they haven't caught me yet."

Noah, Butch thought and almost laughed. *Like this little snitch is on a first-name basis with Noah Blackwood!* Butch himself wasn't even on a first-name basis with Dr. Blackwood. In fact, the only person he knew who was on a first-name basis with Noah Blackwood was Travis Wolfe, which annoyed Butch to no end.

Butch took out the Gizmo and thumbed in a message to Dr. Blackwood.

"Are you telling Noah you're coming?"

"Something like that. I don't have time to get a raft and I might get caught. I guess I'm going to have to swim."

"It's not that far," Mitch said. "And the sea's calm."

"So, you're a pretty good swimmer?"

"I swim like a fish."

Butch nodded and took a waterproof bag out of his pocket. Inside were several folded sheets of paper. He slipped the Gizmo in with the papers and resealed the bag.

"I won't be needing this anymore," he said, and shoved the bag deep into the snitch's pocket.

"Noah might want it," Mitch said.

"You're right," Butch said. "And you'd better make sure he gets it."

"What?"

Butch answered by pushing Mitch the Snitch over the rail.

Mitch was not nearly as fast or lucky as Marty O'Hara. He hit the cold water two seconds after the push.

Butch walked away from the railing, whistling, hoping for Mitch's sake that Blackwood was checking his email.

Noah Blackwood was in the middle of typing a press release to his public relations firm.

TENTACLES

Even though exhausted from my recent ordeal in the Congo, I have decided to join my good friends, the Northwest Zoo and Aquarium, in their pursuit of the giant squid. I am participating in a completely voluntary and supportive role. This is their expedition. I am simply here to lend a hand and offer my experience should they need and ask for it. Should they be successful, and I hope they are, I will be the first in line to see this magnificent creature of the deep at their wonderful aquarium.

He smiled and hit the SEND button. Within hours the article would appear in every major newspaper around the world, setting the stage for Noah Blackwood to save the day once again.

Noah stood and stretched, debating whether he should order

a late-night snack from his personal chef or just go to sleep in his luxurious bedroom.

A snack before bed, he thought, and was about to call the galley and order it up when his computer indicated that he had an incoming email.

> Subject: We've been found out
> From: gizmo4@ewolfe.com
> To: nbPhd@ark.org
>
> Unfortunately, we have worn out our welcome here. As you read this we are swimming your way. If possible could you please send a boat to pick us up and assure our safe arrival? Butch

We? Noah thought. *Our safe arrival?* Had Butch lost his mind? Without him and his spies aboard the *Coelacanth*, Noah's plan would fall completely apart. In the last email, Butch had indicated that there was a slight problem, but he hadn't even hinted that the situation was this dire. What could have changed in such a short period of time? He hadn't heard any gunshots, and he couldn't imagine Butch jumping ship for anything less than a barrage of bullets.

Noah punched a button on the intercom and told the captain to launch the tender to pick up the unexpected and unwelcome passengers. If Butch didn't have an excellent excuse for abandoning the *Coelacanth*, Noah would personally toss him off the *Endangered One* and never think of him again.

Al Ikes walked into Wolfe's cabin carrying a single sheet of paper.

"This better be good news," Wolfe said.

"Depends on how you look at it," Al said, handing him the page.

Wolfe read the printout of Butch's last email.

"Good news, bad news," Al said. "Good news, it looks like Butch is off the ship. Bad news, he does have a Gizmo, and in a few minutes Noah Blackwood is going to have that Gizmo and he's going to know where everyone aboard is located."

"Who jumped ship with Butch?"

"Mitch Merton."

"Are you sure? Mitch has been our head maintenance chief for years. He would be the last person I'd suspect."

"We're tracking his tag and it's headed directly toward *Endangered One*."

"Can we pick them up before they get there?"

"Joe jumped into a Zodiac as soon as we intercepted the email, but Blackwood got his tender in the water before we did. We can track directly to the tag; they can't. So there's a chance we might reach Butch first."

Al's radio beeped. "Al here."

"Sorry, boss," Joe said. "They got lucky. Grabbed them before I was even close."

"Were you close enough to see them haul them in?"

"Negative."

Wolfe looked at his Gizmo and saw Mitch's tag speeding toward the *Endangered One*.

"Do a sweep, Joe," Al said. "Only one of them had a tag. The one we want might have gotten separated."

"It's not likely they got separated," Wolfe said. "They wouldn't be heading back to the *Endangered One* without Butch aboard."

"I'm just trying to be thorough," Al said. "I'll call Joe back in a few minutes. We need him back on board. Roy is handling security all on his own. Can we turn the Gizmo off remotely from here so Blackwood can't use it?"

Wolfe shook his head. "No. If we could, we would have done it when Ted told us he thought Butch had the Gizmo. Ted can give you the technical details, but the Gizmos are linked in a chain. If you take one offline, they all go offline. I should have had you monitoring the emails as soon we found out one had been stolen. That was a huge blunder. We can turn off all the tags, making Butch's Gizmo virtually useless. I guess with Butch and Mitch off the ship we don't need the tags anyway."

"That's if Mitch was the only one helping Butch," Al said. "And if Butch actually went overboard. We don't have concrete proof that he did."

"Why would Butch give Mitch the Gizmo? It wouldn't be much help aboard the *Endangered One*."

"You know Butch better than anybody here," Al said. "How smart is he?"

"He's pretty bright in a predatory way, with incredible survival instincts, meaning he knows when to cut and run, or in this case jump and swim. If you're asking me whether he's smart enough to fake leaving the *Coelacanth*, the answer is: maybe.

That kind of clever thinking is in Noah Blackwood's realm. But Butch has been with Blackwood a long time. I'm sure he's learned a few things from the master."

The master sat behind his rosewood desk with his steely eyes fixed on a wet and shivering Mitch Merton.

"Where's Butch?"

"He threw me overboard!" Mitch shouted. "I could have drowned."

"Well, you didn't, so shut up. Is Butch still aboard the *Coelacanth*?"

"As far as I know," Mitch said bitterly. "He's probably sitting in the galley having a hot cup of coffee and a slice of pie. Just before he tossed me, he gave me this." Mitch dropped the wet waterproof bag on Blackwood's desk.

Noah opened it and skimmed the papers. He stopped skimming when he got to the paragraph about dinosaur hatchlings in Lab Nine that were growing so fast they were building a bigger place for them in the cargo hold. He read the paragraph twice, then looked up at the shivering Mitch Merton.

"This is excellent," Noah said, setting the papers on his desk and picking up the Gizmo. "Show me how this thing works."

Mitch demonstrated how to use the Gizmo.

In his note, Butch said that the kids' tags and those of the others taking care of the dinosaurs had been turned off. Noah typed in Albert Ikes's name and saw that he was in Wolfe's cabin, no doubt talking about what they were going to do. This little invention would come in very handy tomorrow morning.

"What's going to happen to me now?" Mitch asked.

Noah looked up crossly.

"I mean, I can't go back to Cryptos," Mitch continued. "Thanks to Butch, my cover's completely blown."

Noah looked at him for a moment, then smiled. "Are you good with your hands, Mitch?"

"Are you kidding? I've been making my living with my hands my whole life. They're like precision instruments. I could have been a brain surgeon if I'd wanted to. What do you have in mind?"

"Taxidermy," Noah said pleasantly.

"You mean stuffing dead animals?"

"No, I mean fine art. The ability to make the dead come back to life. I have the perfect position for you at the Ark. You'll like it."

"How much does it pay?" Mitch asked.

"Don't worry," Noah said. "You'll have all the money you need."

Noah looked back down at the Gizmo, scanned the names with active tags, and selected one of them.

"Who's Theo Sonborn?" He was in the Moon Pool area.

"One of the old-timers," Mitch answered. "He's an idiot and lazy. I'm not sure why Wolfe has kept him on all these years. I guess he's a charity case. And he's a miserable cook. He ran the galley when we set sail and we all thought we were going to be poisoned."

"According to Butch's notes the Moon Pool is restricted," Noah said.

"It is," Mitch confirmed. "I've only been down there once, when I helped haul the dolphins down. There's a keypad at the entrance and you have to have a code, which I hear they change from time to time."

"Why do you think Theo Sonborn is down there right now?" Noah asked.

Mitch shrugged his shoulders. "I don't know. He seems to have access to everything. He pops up all over the place, but I've never seen him do a lick of work. The guy's a loser. Like I said, Wolfe is crazy to keep him on."

Noah picked up Butch's notes and looked for Theo Sonborn's name. It wasn't there. Why would Travis Wolfe give a *loser* access to a restricted area?

The Gizmo flickered and a tired-looking Travis Wolfe appeared on the tiny screen.

"Hello, Noah."

"Travis. How wonderful to see you!"

"Don't even start, Noah. I need to talk to Butch."

"What are you talking about, Travis? You know as well as I do that Butch is recuperating from a bout of malaria back in Seattle. He is in no condition to travel."

Noah had no doubt that Wolfe was taping this miniature video conference, and he had no intention of saying anything self-incriminating.

"And please thank Ted again for giving me this Gizmo," Noah continued.

"Ted did not give you the Gizmo," Wolfe said.

"I stand corrected," Noah said cheerfully. "He *loaned* it to me. Regardless, it's a wonderful invention and I do hope you've recorded our other conversation for posterity. It will really add to the public record of your momentous expedition."

"What are you doing here, Noah?"

Noah laughed. "As we agreed, my presence here is completely supportive and subordinate. I'm here to help only if you need me, which I doubt you will with the wonderful crew you've put together."

"We don't have any agreement," Wolfe said. "And we never had an agreement."

"Certainly not in writing, Travis. But your phone call to me asking for help is all I needed. As we discussed, old colleagues like us don't need lawyers and contracts. Our word to each other is the only contract we need. I'm simply here because you requested it."

"That's a lie," Wolfe said. "There was no phone call. We didn't ask you to come here."

Noah lowered his voice and became serious. "Travis, you haven't been drinking again, have you? I warned you and Ted about that all those years ago. I told you then that drinking would be your downfall if you didn't stop it. Remember the last time?"

"There was no last time," Wolfe said.

"Not that you and Ted could possibly remember," Noah said. "You and he were passed out on your bunks when I captured the great white shark. I don't hold it against you and Ted for taking credit for catching that great white, but I did think with all the success you two have had the past few years it meant that you had given up the bottle."

Noah was now enjoying himself immensely. He, too, had seen the video of the press conference and knew he had lied on camera about the great white. He looked at the Gizmo screen and saw that it was recording his and Wolfe's conversation. When he finished the call, he would give the Gizmo to his video technicians and have them edit it to make Travis look like an idiot.

Aboard the *Coelacanth*, a completely frustrated Travis Wolfe glanced up at Al Ikes, who was shaking his head. Wolfe looked back at the Gizmo screen and the calm but deeply concerned face of Noah Blackwood.

"We're shutting down all the tracking tags," Wolfe said. "You might as well toss the Gizmo into the ocean for all the good it will do you."

"I wouldn't think of throwing Ted's brilliant invention into the sea. By the way, is Ted aboard? I would love to talk to him."

Finally catching on to what Noah was doing, Wolfe said, "You know as well as I do that Ted hasn't left Cryptos in years. And he certainly wouldn't travel all the way out here. He hates the ocean and doesn't even know how to swim."

"That's right," Noah said. "I forgot. Tell him I'd like to drop by Cryptos when we get back to the States and talk to him face-to-face. I'd love to see him again."

Wolfe cut the connection and killed the tags.

"That went well," Al said sarcastically. "Noah Blackwood could sell venom to a rattlesnake."

"He probably has," Wolfe said glumly.

"Joe is still out there," Al said. "He could be on and off the *Endangered One* in ten minutes with the Gizmo in hand."

"Blackwood has men aboard both ships." Wolfe held his hand up. "And don't start, Al. I know that Joe is better than Blackwood's men. But we're not in the covert ops business anymore. Right now, we're playing defense all the way. Get Joe back on board, and guard the perimeter the best you can."

Al spoke into his radio. "Party's over, Joe. Come back to base."

PREHISTORIC GAS

Theo Sonborn left Marty outside the door to Lab Nine, where Roy was standing guard disguised as a research scientist. The bulge of his pistol under the white lab coat was a dead giveaway.

"The kid can go in," Roy said to Theo. "But you can't."

Belligerent Theo puffed out his chest. "Oh, yeah? Who says?"

"I say," Roy answered.

"And who are you?"

"I'm a guy over a foot taller than you." Roy opened his lab coat. "With a gun."

Very subtle, Marty thought. *And mature.*

"Big deal," Theo said.

Ted took his idiot Theo role seriously, but Marty thought he was pushing it a little too far with Roy.

"Go on, Theo," Marty said. "I'm just going into the lab to check in on Grace and Luther and see what they're cooking up."

"Yeah, okay," Theo said. "I got things to do. But try to get some sleep tonight. You and me are going fishing at o'dawn-thirty tomorrow."

Marty and Roy watched him swagger down the hall.

"What's going on?" Marty asked.

"I guess someone's trying to kill you and kidnap your cousin, so now you're under twenty-four-hour security watch. Where'd you come from?"

"From the Moon Pool."

"And they let that moron escort you up here?" Roy said. "You'd be safer by yourself."

"He's tougher than he looks," Marty said. "And smarter."

"Whatever," Roy said. "What's his name?"

"Te—" Marty stopped himself. "Theo Sonborn."

Roy took a three-by-five card out of his pocket and read it. "He isn't on the safe list. Who said he could bring you up from the Moon Pool?"

"I don't know," Marty answered. "Wolfe, I guess."

"I'm going to have to call Al on this. It's a breach of security."

"Fine. While you're taking care of that, can I squeeze by you and go inside?"

"Yeah. You're on the cleared list for Lab Nine."

"Thank goodness," Marty said.

Marty stepped into the clean room, showered, and put on a set of disposable scrubs.

The nursery was crowded with Grace, Luther, Laurel, and two hungry dinosaurs. The hatchlings were gulping down fist-sized hunks of raw meat as fast as Luther and Laurel could get them to their snapping mouths.

Bertha was there, too. She was standing in the corner in XXL scrubs, cradling a twelve-gauge shotgun. Clipped to her belt was a military radio like the ones Al and his men carried, and she had a throat mic around her neck and an earpiece stuck in her ear. Marty wondered how she'd managed to disinfect the weapon and the radio.

The lab reeked.

"What is that smell?" Marty asked, trying not to gag into his disposable mask.

"Dinosaur poop," Luther said, with a ball of meat in his hand. "And don't worry, you won't get used to the smell. At least it's clear now why dinosaurs went extinct — and where that term comes from. It must be a derivative of the word *stink*. The dinosaurs gassed themselves to death. Guaranteed."

"*Extinct* does not come from the word *stink*," Grace said.

"Well, it should have," Luther said, holding out the lump of meat to One. "This is what they mean by *greenhouse gas*."

Snap!

The meat disappeared down One's long neck.

"Jeez, that was close," Luther said, checking to see if he still had all of his fingers.

"Are you all right, Marty?" Grace asked with concern, ignoring Luther. She was holding a clipboard, presumably trying to keep track of the amount of meat going into the hatchlings' gaping purple maws. "Wolfe told me what happened to you up on deck."

"The deck was fine," Marty said. "Being flipped over the rail was the problem."

Luther went over to grab another handful of meat. "I hear it was ol' Butch McCall that tried to give you the heave-ho. That will make a good panel in our next graphic novel."

"Wrong hemisphere," Marty said. "Different story. Butch isn't here."

"He's the one who pushed you," Bertha said.

"Butch is on the *Coelacanth*?"

Snap!

"Not anymore," Luther said. "Bertha just got word that he and another guy did their own header over the side and stroked out to Grandpa's yacht."

"We think there were two of them," Bertha clarified. "And we think that one of them was Butch. But he might still be on board, which is why Roy is at the door and I'm armed." She proceeded to summarize everything that had happened in the past few hours with a half-dozen crystal clear sentences that only an ex–Army general could compose.

Snap!

Snap!

"So, where the heck have you been?" Luther asked Marty.

"Copiloting a nuclear sub," Marty answered.

"Right."

Snap!

Marty had not seen the hatchlings since he'd been banished to the galley. They looked like they had doubled in size, and they'd been moved out of the incubator to a makeshift cage on the floor of the lab.

Snap!

Snap!

"I think they're done," Luther said, wiping his bloody gloves on his scrubs. "Get ready."

"Get ready for what?" Marty asked.

Everyone but Marty had already backed away from the cage and were covering their masks with both hands, including Bertha, who had set her shotgun down.

"Ohhh . . . ," Marty said, staggering backward.

"Goes through them as fast as it goes into them," Luther said.

"We need gas masks." Marty gagged. "These disposable surgical masks are worthless."

When the hatchlings finished their business, which seemed to take an impossibly long time, they plopped down and promptly fell asleep.

Laurel turned the exhaust fan to full blast, which had little effect.

If Ted had really wanted to test me, he should have left me in the nursery, Marty thought.

"When we write our next graphic novel, it's going to be hard to illustrate that olfactory sensation," Luther said.

"Maybe we can put in a scratch-and-sniff panel," Marty suggested.

"Yeah," Luther said. "But what do you put under the scratch? There's nothing in nature that smells like that. At least not anymore."

MONKEY BUSINESS

Laurel volunteered to watch the dinosaurs while Marty, Grace, and Luther returned to their cabins to get some sleep. None of them offered to stay with her.

Bertha exchanged the shotgun for an automatic pistol in a shoulder holster and a knife, big enough to gut a *Tyrannosaurus rex,* hanging in a sheath next to her radio. Outside their cabin doors she gave each of them a hug, wished them sweet dreams, then took up a position between the two doors, ready to kill anybody who tried to enter.

Inside they opened the connecting doors between the cabins, and Marty caught up Luther and Grace on what had happened since Butch had tried to toss him overboard. He also revealed the real identity of Theo Sonborn, who had given him permission to tell them.

"You're lying," Luther said. "There is no way that Theo is Ted Bronson."

"You'll believe me when you see him," Marty said. "The disguise is real Hollywood stuff, and as soon as he puts it on he becomes Theo. It's kind of creepy. Wolfe, Bertha, Phil, and us are the only ones who know—oh, and Al Ikes and Ana Mika."

"The reporter who puked on your shoes?" Luther asked.

"Yep." Marty told them about the long Moon Pool kiss.

"That sounds awkward," Luther said.

"It was," Marty admitted.

"Okay," Luther said. "I'll buy that Theo is actually Ted and I'll buy the sickening lip-lock, but the nuclear squid bobber is a bit much. Even if it were true, why would Ted pick you as his copilot? No offense, but you're only thirteen years old."

"Because Wolfe's too big to fit into the Orb. Ted is small. He's been testing me ever since I got to Cryptos."

Marty went on to explain the test, ending with the chicken-and-egg question.

"I totally get that," Grace said when he finished.

"I totally *don't* get that," Luther said.

"You can ask Ted about it yourself tomorrow morning," Marty said. "You're both invited to the launch of the Orb at dawn."

Marty took his Gizmo out of his pocket and handed it to Luther.

"I think you're going to make it," Luther said. "If you survived Butch McCall twice, you should have no problem with a giant squid."

"That's not why I'm giving it to you," Marty said. "I asked Ted if you could pilot the dragonspy. He said yes, as long as your parents pay for it if you crash it."

"Of course they'll pay for it," Luther said.

"I'm just kidding. Ted didn't say that. He just said yes."

"Thanks for asking," Luther said, punching in the code and bringing the dragonspy to life.

There were actually a couple of reasons Marty had asked Ted. He knew that when Luther saw him in the gold suit and black helmet going where no man had gone before, his best friend was going to feel left out. (And now that Marty had seen—and smelled—what raising baby dinosaurs was really like, he was *really* happy he'd asked.) The second reason Marty had asked was to test Ted's test. If the point of letting Marty fly the dragon-spy was to see if Marty would obey the rules, then there was no reason for Ted to say no. Marty had passed the rule test with flying colors. Not only had Ted said yes, he'd offered to loan his transparent dragonspy to them whenever they wanted so they could fly them in tandem.

Right out of the drawer, Luther had the dragonspy in a perfect hover in the center of the cabin. He had been play-ing video games since he was two years old. His parents and nannies had used the games to pacify the wild-haired child. He circled the dragonspy around the small cabin without even looking at the controls, as if his thumbs had brains of their own.

Marty was a much better artist than Luther, and certainly a better cook, but Luther was the Michelangelo of video games. Marty realized that if Ted had seen Luther's natural ability, it would have been Luther in the aquasuit and Marty in scrubs scooping up dino poop.

"I can't understand how anyone could crash this thing," Luther said. "It's a lot more stable than those RC helicopters I have back at Omega Prep that you were always wrecking."

"I didn't always wreck them," Marty said. "And the controls

should be easy to use, considering the dragonspy costs about as much to produce as a corporate jet."

Marty looked over to the chair where Grace had been sitting and saw she was no longer there. He walked into her cabin and found her on her bed next to the Frankenstein Monkey.

"I see you found Monkey," Marty said.

"No thanks to you," Grace said.

"I all but told you where he was."

"It was mean to hide him in the last place I wanted to look."

"It was one of those 'which came first, the chicken or the egg' things."

"You hadn't had that conversation with Ted when you hid Monkey in the trunk."

"I must have intuitively understood the theory before he mentioned it to me. That's why I didn't think he was completely crazy when he brought it up. What else did you find in there?"

"A mess." Grace got up and opened the trunk.

"Whoa," Marty said. "It didn't look that way when I put Monkey inside. I guess it all got mixed up in the move to the ship. You'll get it untangled. You're good at that."

"If I have time," Grace said, closing the lid. "I've barely been in my cabin since the dinosaurs hatched. All I've looked at are a few old photos."

"Pretty weird, aren't they? When I saw them I thought they were photos of you when you were little."

"I know," Grace said. "But what's even stranger are the photos of Noah Blackwood as a father. Looking at them, it's hard to believe that he's the same man Wolfe's portrayed. When you were rummaging through it, did you happen to see any photographs of my grandmother?"

Marty had to think about it for a moment. He did have a photographic memory, particularly for visual images, but when he'd gone through the trunk back in the Congo he'd been in a panic over Grace and his mental camera lens was a little out of focus.

"I don't think I saw her," he finally answered. "I would have noticed that."

"But you didn't notice the lack of a grandmother," Grace said.

Marty shook his head. "You're right. I was thinking about what was there, not what was missing. That might be another one of those chicken-and-egg things. There are a lot more photos at the bottom of the trunk, and memory sticks with either photos, video, or maybe digital recordings on them. And then there are the Moleskines. I bet they have stuff in them about Wolfe."

"At this point, I'm more interested in who my grandmother was, or *is*," Grace said. "She might still be alive. We know all about Wolfe."

Marty shook his head again. "I think we know what Wolfe wants us to know, and one thing we *don't* know is how he and Ted ended up with their own personal island that's so secret it doesn't show up on a map."

"The government gave it to them," Grace said.

"Right, but *why* did they give it to them? What did they

do for the government that would make them hand over an island?"

"Something important, I suppose," Grace said, walking over to the porthole.

She looked out at the lights of her grandfather's ships, then turned back to Marty with an expression on her face that he hadn't seen since they were in the Congo — an expression he'd hoped to never see again. He'd thought that after she discovered her night terrors were actually memories of her forgotten past, Grace wouldn't have any more premonitions; they were about eighty percent accurate, and they creeped Marty out.

"Promise me something," Grace said.

"What?"

"If something should happen to me, I want you to go through this trunk and find out whatever else is inside."

"What do you think is going to happen to you?" Marty asked, alarmed.

"I don't know. I just feel something big is coming my way. Something unpleasant."

"You're probably just tired from dino duty," Marty said, trying to reassure his cousin.

Grace shook her head and picked up Monkey. "Promise," she repeated.

Marty felt like there were ants crawling up the back of his neck. He shuddered, and gave Monkey's arm a squeeze.

BLACKWOOD THE PIRATE

Noah Blackwood was making sure that every detail of his plan was in place. His helicopter had just landed on the helipad of the *Endangered Too*. The captain was there to greet him. He shook the captain's hand, thanked him for his speedy crossing on such short notice, and promised that he would be amply rewarded for his diligence.

"I have everyone you requested gathered down in the mess," the captain said.

"And you know what to do tomorrow," Blackwood said.

The captain nodded. "Those not directly involved will be confined to their quarters with windows sealed."

"Was there any grousing?" Blackwood asked.

"Negative. They've been through this before and know the routine. And of course the cash bonus helped."

Blackwood smiled. "It always does. And our other friends?"

"The trawler just arrived. It sailed without lights or communication. I doubt Wolfe's radar or satellite would have picked it up. And even if they did, they'd only think it was a harmless fishing boat, which in fact it is, though the men on board are not fishermen. We tied it to our portside. Even in daylight the *Coelacanth* won't be able to see it. Butch is still aboard?"

Blackwood nodded. "And we have another person aboard as well. They've done an outstanding job."

Blackwood meant this. He was close to forgiving Butch for losing Grace and the eggs in the Congo. In a way it had worked out better for Blackwood. Instead of having two dinosaur eggs, he was going to have two living dinosaurs. Wolfe and Ted had incubated and hatched the eggs for him.

And the Gizmo? Wolfe might have turned the tracking tags off, but he couldn't destroy the wealth of information inside the device. Blackwood's technicians had hacked it within minutes, and it had turned into a tiny treasure chest. Between the data from the Gizmo and Butch's notes, Blackwood had everything he needed.

"Do you have the digital projector and laptop set up?" Blackwood asked.

"It's all ready to go," the captain answered.

Blackwood handed him a flash drive. "Open the PowerPoint called *Coelacanth* and cue it up."

"Yes, sir."

Blackwood and the captain walked into the mess, where a half-dozen men were waiting for them. Blackwood had worked with all of them before and had paid them several small fortunes over the years. But what ensured their loyalty was that he knew things about their pasts that they would prefer stay there. They all knew that if they betrayed him, they'd end up in prison—or worse. Blackwood would hunt them down and kill them along with their families, girlfriends, and anyone else they cared about. There was not a place in the world they could hide from Noah Blackwood. They all sat up a little straighter as the man strode confidently to the front of the mess.

"Let me begin by saying that upon the successful completion of this mission, I will be depositing one hundred thousand dollars into each of your accounts."

This announcement was met with loud cheers. He let the men go on for a moment, then held up his hand for them to stop.

"Not a bad wage for a few hours' work," Blackwood continued. "But of course there are risks involved, something you're all used to. This mission is of a personal nature—a very personal nature. Travis Wolfe has kidnapped my granddaughter and is holding her hostage aboard the *Coelacanth*. Years ago, he also kidnapped my daughter, Rose, and murdered her. Unfortunately, there wasn't enough legal evidence to prove this, so he's been a free man all these years.

"I know what you're all thinking: Why didn't I just have him killed? Believe me, I have tried, but Travis and his partner Ted Bronson have powerful friends in our government and elsewhere, and this has protected him from the retribution he so richly deserves. Tomorrow, with your help, he'll get what's coming to him, and I'll get my grandchild back."

He showed the first slide.

"This is my granddaughter, Grace."

In fact, it was a photograph of Rose at about the same age. Blackwood didn't have a photograph of Grace, but it didn't matter because she and Rose looked nearly identical. Blackwood managed to squeeze out a single tear from his left eye and allowed it to run down his tanned face and disappear into his perfectly cropped white beard. The single tear produced the desired effect on the tough men sitting in front of him: shock. None of them had ever seen Dr. Noah Blackwood cry. None of them thought him capable of shedding a tear. At that moment they would have done anything for him. And by the day's end, they would have to do more than they knew.

Noah wiped the tear away. "Sorry," he said, as if he were struggling to regain his composure, which had never left. "You will be happy to hear that Butch McCall has been aboard the *Coelacanth* since it left Cryptos Island, making arrangements for your arrival. What you don't know is that he is in disguise."

Noah clicked to the next slide, showing the new Butch McCall. The men laughed.

"Butch took this digital photo of himself a few hours ago. I wouldn't laugh. Inside, he is the same Butch McCall. He's included a note for you, which I will read." Noah took a sheet of paper out of his pocket and cleared his throat. "'If any of you even point a weapon at me or the other person we have aboard, I will put a bullet through your eye.'"

The men were not laughing now. They all knew Butch McCall.

Noah put another picture on the screen. "This is the other person Butch is referring to. To help you distinguish between hostiles and friendlies, Butch, his partner, and all of you will be wearing green armbands on your left arms. Lose them or remove them, and you will become targets."

Noah put up pictures of Al Ikes, Roy, and Joe. "This is their security force."

"Three guys?" the leader of the group asked. His name was Pepper.

"Three extremely dangerous guys," Noah said. "They need to be taken out as soon as you board. The man in the suit is ex–CIA. The other two are ex–Navy SEALs. A verified kill on any one of them is worth an extra ten thousand to whoever takes them down. And they're not alone." He brought up another slide. "Bertha Bishop is on board. I know she looks like a fat old woman, but she's a former Army Ranger. She could kill everyone in this room in the time it just took me to utter this sentence."

"I served under her," one of the men said. "She got me thrown out of my unit and court-martialed. I'll put her lights out for free."

The men laughed.

"It would be a life-ending mistake to underestimate her," Noah warned. "She got the drop on Butch in the Congo and put him down like he was a child. I wouldn't underestimate her husband, Phil, either." He showed a photo of Phil Bishop. "He's nearly as skilled as she is."

Next, Noah showed them photos of Marty O'Hara and Luther Smyth.

"Kids?" one of the men said.

Noah gave them a solemn nod. "I'm afraid so. I know that all of you are going to have a hard time with this. I'm not comfortable with it, either. But there will be no survivors aboard the *Coelacanth*. Youngsters, everyone, will go down with the ship. If they don't, you are going to have to kill them up close after the ship sinks. If you're uncomfortable with this, you better make sure the kids are locked up or incapacitated before the explosives you set go off."

"Dead men tell no tales," Pepper said.

Noah nodded gravely. "If there are any survivors, we'll all be dead."

He showed another photo of Rose. "Needless to say, if any of you harm Grace in any way, all of your contracts are canceled." He paused. "Along with your lives. Your job is to protect Grace—with your own life if necessary. Is that understood?"

The men nodded.

"Butch and our other person on board will be responsible for getting Grace off the *Coelacanth* safely. But if something should happen to either of them, it will be your responsibility to bring Grace to me. I need to warn you, though, she is not going to come willingly. Travis Wolfe and the others have poisoned her mind with malicious lies about me.

"I'll get into specific assignments in a moment, but this is essentially a chaos-and-grab mission. Some of you have seen the fishing trawler tied up to our portside, out of view of the *Coelacanth*. There are a group of pirates aboard. Scum. Whom I have hired to attack the *Coelacanth*. That's the chaos, and if another ship happens along at the wrong moment, the pirates will be our cover story. We're going to make this look like a rescue mission. But our goals will remain the same. Needless to say, the pirates will also have to be killed, and we will scuttle their boat along with the *Coelacanth*.

"I've told their captain that the *Coelacanth* has salvaged a sunken payroll ship that was filled with gold and silver coins and headed from Britain to Australia back when it was a British colony. If we're lucky, and his men are as good as he says, they might end up doing your work for you, but I doubt it. They're well armed and experienced, but they are not professionals.

"And we have a little poetic justice here. The pirates' leader was on the original crew that hijacked the *Coelacanth* before it became the *Coelacanth*. He managed to avoid conviction, which I suspect is how he became their leader. This time, though, he will be caught, convicted, and executed for the same crime on the same ship."

Noah smiled and let the irony of the situation sink in; then he turned serious again.

"You'll have to be very careful that none of the pirates harm Grace."

"May I make a suggestion, Dr. Blackwood?" Pepper asked. "It seems to me that the best way to protect your granddaughter is for us to go aboard tonight, take her, then attack the ship."

Noah had already thought of this, and so had Butch. They had both agreed that this wouldn't work because Grace was not the only prize they were after. And the entrance to the *Coelacanth* wasn't open yet. Noah trusted the men in front of him, but only to a point. He was not about to tell them that the other prize was two baby dinosaurs.

"Grace is under twenty-four-hour guard," Noah said.

"We can get past her guards," another man said.

"I'm sure you can," Noah said, but he didn't believe it. "If you took Grace tonight, they would pull their anchor and head to the nearest port and we would lose our cover story. We need to have them and the pirates go down exactly where they are. The canyon we're sitting over is one of the deepest in the world. Even if someone wanted to investigate, they'd never be able to reach the wreckage. It's a good idea, but it won't work."

He moved on to another subject by showing schematics and photos of the *Coelacanth* and pointing out how the men would board and attack the ship. When he finished, he gave them the Blackwood smile.

"So, that's our target," he concluded. "Half of you will be securing the ship. The other half will be setting charges. With some luck we'll be in and out in ten minutes, which is ten thousand dollars a minute for each of you. But remember, if things go sour, we're the good guys. I want the headlines to read: *Dr. Noah Blackwood Saves NZA from Pirates on the High Seas.*"

THE PARTNER

Butch McCall was back on deck watching Blackwood's chopper land on the helipad of *Endangered One*, and he knew the old man had just briefed the troops on *Endangered Too*.

It looked like Mitch Merton had made it and passed the Gizmo and Butch's message to Blackwood, but tossing Mitch overboard hadn't worked out as well as Butch would have liked. Al and his men were still looking for him aboard the *Coelacanth*.

Butch corrected himself. Al and his *man* were looking for him. He had just bumped into Roy. While Roy grilled "Dr. O'Connor" about who he was and what he was doing up on deck, Butch let his telescoping baton drop from his sleeve into his hand, extended it, and in one fluid motion hit Roy squarely on his left temple, dropping him to the deck like an anchor.

Butch took Roy's gun and, more important, his encrypted military radio. He also discovered that Roy was not wearing a tracking tag around his neck. This told him that Wolfe might have deactivated the tags, which is exactly what Butch had wanted him to do. With the tags off, Butch could toss anyone he liked over the side and no one would know. He put the theory to the test by tossing Roy, then plugged the earpiece into his ear and listened. It wasn't long before Al came on the radio and asked for Roy. When Roy didn't answer, Joe cut in and said that Roy had gone to his cabin to get some shut-eye.

Permanent shut-eye, Butch thought. *Or maybe his eyes are open.* One thing was for sure: Opened or closed, Roy's eyes were no longer capable of seeing.

"Why would he turn his radio off?" Al asked, irritated.

"Probably because he wanted to get some sleep," Joe said. "Where are you?"

"Outside Lab Nine," Al said. "I want you guys to keep your radios on at all times. I don't care if the radio traffic bothers you or not."

"We should have brought more people," Joe said.

"I would have if Wolfe had let me," Al said.

"Want me to go down and turn on his radio?" Joe asked.

Al thought about it for a moment. "Nah, let him sleep. One of us needs to be rested for tomorrow. I think that's when Blackwood is going to make his move."

The tags are off, Butch thought. *If they were active, they would know that Roy was not in his bunk.*

Through his free ear Butch heard a quiet footfall coming up behind him. The baton was back up his sleeve. He prided himself on his hearing ability. Years ago, in Tanzania, a leopard had skulked up behind him while he sat in front of a crackling campfire. The cat was dead before it felt the warmth of the flames. He judged the oncoming footfalls to be about fifteen paces away and debated whether he should drop the baton at three feet and hit a homer, or whether he should turn and play the befuddled and kindly Dr. O'Connor.

"It's cold up here," his partner said. "Couldn't you have picked a better place to meet? And what about my tracking tag? They'll know I'm up here."

Looks like I get to play myself, Butch thought. He turned around. "The best place to hide is in the open or in a crowd," he said. "When you lurk around like you were just doing, people notice. You and I can't afford to be noticed. And the tracking tags are offline, which means no one knows where you are or anyone else is."

His partner was a little inexperienced but a lot smarter than Mitch Merton, always thinking, and asked the right questions. He was glad he had chosen Mitch for the swim team.

"What have you learned?" Butch asked.

"Wolfe is on the bridge with Cap and Al. Laurel Lee is in Lab Nine, and I think Phil is with her, which is why they don't have anyone manning the door. The kids are in their cabins, sleeping, with Bertha standing guard outside their doors like the Rock of Gibraltar."

"Is Bertha alone?"

"Yep."

"How'd they take the loss of Marty?"

"What?"

"Marty," Butch repeated. "Grace's obnoxious cousin."

"Marty's in the cabin with Luther."

"That's impossible!"

"I saw him walk into the cabin myself."

"That kid has nine lives," Butch said in disgust.

He was tempted to march down there and put that *theory* to the test. But he would have to get through Bertha, and that could be a problem. She was one of the few people on board who might recognize him from a distance by the way he moved, because of her Ranger training. Her brain would go into high alert no matter who she saw walking past the kids' cabins, especially now after he had tried, and obviously failed, to get rid of Marty O'Hara.

Butch discarded the idea. The only thing that made it easier was knowing that in a few hours he'd get another shot at the little brat, and this time he wouldn't fail.

"What's going on, Butch?"

"Never mind," Butch growled. "Did you find out any more about how and when they're going after the giant squid?"

"I still don't know how, but I do have an idea when. I think they're going to release the dolphins tomorrow at dawn."

"That means the Moon Pool will be opened then."

"Right."

"What else?"

"Something strange is going on down at the Moon Pool. They changed the entrance code. Wolfe said they were doing some kind of maintenance."

"And?"

"I walked right down there to see what they were doing. Someone was inside, but I couldn't see through the door. I hid in a mop closet and watched, hoping Al or one of his men wouldn't show up to ask me what I was doing in there. But with the tags off I—"

"Whatever," Butch interrupted impatiently. "Get to the point."

"About a half hour passed and Ana walked by dressed like she was going to a cocktail party. She punched in the code and walked right through. I couldn't believe it and thought maybe I'd punched in the code wrong. So I left the closet and put in the old code slowly. The doors didn't open."

"Back up a second," Butch said. "Who's Ana?"

"That reporter who showed up on the sailboat."

Liar, liar, Butch thought, and wondered if Blackwood had found out who the woman really was.

"Why would they give a reporter the code?" Butch asked. "And why would she be down at the Moon Pool?"

"I have no idea. She came back out after about fifteen minutes, smiling. I tried the old code again. No luck."

"Who was in there with her?"

"That's the strangest part. I stayed in the closet for at least another hour. Finally, the Moon Pool doors slid open and out walked Theo Sonborn and Marty O'Hara."

"You're kidding me," Butch said. "I heard they hated each other."

"I heard the same thing. They weren't talking when they walked by, but they looked like they were getting along just fine."

Marty again, Butch thought. The kid seemed to be everywhere and involved in everything. "Did you follow them?"

"I was going to, but I wanted to check the code one last time. It worked. The doors opened."

"What'd you find inside?"

"Winkin, Blinkin, and Nod swimming around the Moon Pool."

"There's something we don't know," Butch said.

"I think there are a lot of things we don't know."

"As soon as you let the dolphins go, cut the power like I showed you. I'll jam the two-ways, the satellite phones, and the ship-to-shore radio. They'll still have their secure radios and Gizmos, but there are only a few of those."

"What's the plan after that?"

Butch had no idea what he was going to do after that. All he knew was that out of chaos came opportunity and that he and his partner would have to be ready to exploit any and every opening. "We wing it," he said. "Our job is to create as much confusion as we can."

"I have just the thing for that," his partner said, smiling.

"Good," Butch continued. "We wait for our chance, grab Grace and the dinosaurs, and get them to Blackwood. I'll try to get you a radio so we can stay in touch. Do you know how to use one of these things?"

"No."

Butch demonstrated all the components. "It's not going to be easy getting ahold of another one of these until Blackwood's people get onboard. Have you ever killed anyone?"

"No."

"Knocked anyone out?"

"No."

"You may have to." Butch flipped out his collapsible baton. "Stick this up your sleeve. If you see someone with a radio by themselves, hit 'em in the head as hard as you can, but don't let them see who you are in case you don't kill them with the whack. You're my secret weapon and I want to keep it that way." He pulled a green armband out of his pocket. "When it all starts, put this on your left arm and don't take it off."

"What's it for?"

"It's your bulletproof vest."

Butch got back to the squid lab just as Dr. Lepod was leaving.

"Big day tomorrow, Dr. O'Connor!" Lepod said enthusiastically. "Perhaps a giant day! I just talked with Dr. Wolfe. Tomorrow morning they go after *Architeuthis*."

"That is wonderful news," Butch said. "But who are *they*?"

"Dr. Wolfe didn't say."

"And he didn't mention how they were going to catch it?"

Dr. Lepod shook his head. "They're still playing that hand close to their chest. All he said was that I should try to get plenty of sleep and be ready if they brought one in. If they succeed, it will be the catch of the century."

You wouldn't be saying that if you knew what they had up in Lab Nine, Butch thought. He faked a yawn.

"If you're going to be busy, I'm going to be busy," Butch said. "I better try to get some sleep myself."

"Of course," Lepod said.

As soon as Lepod left, Butch unclipped Roy's radio from his belt. It was identical to the radios Noah Blackwood and half the military forces around the world used, but it would only work if Blackwood's encrypted signal was the same as it had been two months ago.

"And if I can remember the nine-digit code correctly . . . ," Butch said out loud.

He wrote down the current code. He would need it in a few hours so he could monitor what was going on. Then he counted out how many people on board had encrypted radios. It was important to know because it was the only communication that he wouldn't be able to disrupt. Al, Joe, Wolfe, Bertha, Phil, probably Cap, and maybe even that reporter, Ana. There was probably another one in Lab Nine. He was sure that Al and Joe knew about the hatchlings. And they could talk on those Gizmos, too. There were another three or four of those.

Too many ways to stay in touch, Butch thought. *I'll need to do something about that. But first I need to talk to Blackwood.*

After several tries Butch finally picked up some chatter. He listened for a few moments and was pleased to realize that he recognized some of the people talking. Normally, Butch worked alone and preferred it that way. But playing Dr. O'Connor was getting on his nerves. He missed being Butch McCall.

He keyed the mic. "This is Butch."

"As in Butch McCall?"

"That's right, Pepper. As in the guy who's doing all your work for you."

"We're deeply appreciative of all your effort, mate," Pepper said sarcastically. "We saw a self-portrait of you tonight with hair on your head. You need to lose it and grow that 'stache back. With that white lab coat and the retro glasses you're geek-ugly, man."

Butch now remembered why he liked to work alone.

"Patch me over to the old man on a scrambled line."

"Right," Pepper said. "Make sure you have that green armband on tomorrow."

"Yeah," Butch said. "You, too."

There was a burst of static and clicks, then Noah Blackwood came on the line.

"Butch?"

"Are we secure?" Butch asked.

"On this end, but I'm more worried about your end."

"I lifted a secure radio from one of Al's men. He's not going to miss it."

"If you'd thought of that earlier, perhaps you wouldn't have had to throw Mitch over the side," Blackwood said.

"The opportunity didn't present itself until recently, and I would have tossed Mitch anyway. He was worthless and I didn't trust him."

This was followed by a long silence, which made Butch nervous.

"I don't trust him, either," Blackwood finally said.

Butch breathed a sigh of relief.

"He is a good swimmer, though," Blackwood continued, in an uncharacteristically chatty way. "And according to Mitch, he's very good with his hands. He was quite concerned about what was going to happen to him now that he's no longer a member of the eWolfe team. I told him that I have a perfect position for him in the basement with Henrico, so that problem is taken care of."

Ouch, Butch thought. *And Mitch is someone who* helped *Blackwood. Careful,* he told himself. *Remember who's on the scrambled line.*

"I'm just checking in to let you know I have a radio, so I won't be using the flare," Butch said. "When I have the package, I'll give you a shout."

"Excellent! Do you have any idea on the time?"

"Early, I think, and I have everything in place here. I'd have Pepper and his men on their way before light, which means the others need to be ready, too."

"They'll be ready," Blackwood assured him.

"Another thing," Butch said. "Tell Pepper that the Moon Pool doors will be wide open, so he shouldn't have any problem there."

"Do you have any more information on their plans for catching the giant squid?"

"Negative," Butch said. "And that has me a little concerned. I don't think they're using the dolphins to catch the giant squid. They changed the code to the Moon Pool for a while tonight. The only reason they would do that is because there is something in there they don't want people to see. They haven't even told the squid doctor what's going on. You'd think they would tell the world's authority on giant squid what their plans are."

"That is curious," Blackwood said. "But it shouldn't affect our plans. Bringing in a giant squid would be nice, but it's a distant third to our two primary targets. When this is all over,

I'm going to pay a visit to Ted Bronson on Cryptos, or have you go fetch him. He'll tell us what the plans were and we'll go out and capture our own giant squid."

Butch looked forward to *fetching* Ted Bronson.

"A couple of other things," Butch said. "They're shorthanded here, but you need to tell Pepper and the other guys not to let their guard down. The handful of people they have are pros and highly motivated. They could even the odds very quickly and turn this to their advantage."

"I already warned him," Blackwood said. "But I'll do it again."

"And finally, that reporter, or whoever she is, is going by the name Ana," Butch said. "She seems to have full access to everything, including the Moon Pool and probably Lab Nine. I also think she's in on the plans to catch the squid."

"Ana Mika," Blackwood said harshly. "She's an investigative journalist and an old friend of the Cryptos gang. I'm glad she's on board, because she's going down with everyone else. Make sure of it."

"No problem," Butch said.

INTO THE DEEP

Marty was sound asleep when he felt someone (or something) shaking his shoulder. It was Theo.

"Rise and shine, aquanaut," he whispered.

Marty sat up, rubbed the sleep out of his tired eyes, and looked around the cabin groggily.

Luther was sitting in an uncomfortable chair with his head thrown back, his mouth wide open, snoring in soprano. The Gizmo was sticking out of his shirt pocket. PD was in his lap with her tiny paws over her ears. Grace's door was closed to help block out Luther's high-pitched snores.

Marty swung his feet to the floor.

"You don't have to whisper," he said. "Luther and I have been roommates since we were kindergartners. You have to hurt him physically to wake him up."

"How do you sleep with that noise coming out of his mouth?"

"Weird, isn't it?" Marty stood and stretched. "You get used to it—after about five years."

"How did he do with the dragonspy?"

"He was better with it than I was when I started, and he

was still flying it when I fell asleep, which means he's probably better than I am now."

Marty pulled on a pair of cargo shorts and stepped into a pair of sneakers. "I'll wake him up."

"Let him sleep," Theo said. "We have at least an hour of prep before we launch. Bertha will bring him and Grace down before we take off."

Ana was outside in the hallway talking to Bertha.

Bertha looked at Marty. "For what it's worth," she said. "I was, and I still am, totally one hundred percent against you being turned into squid bait."

"And good morning to you, Bertha!" Marty said. "Thanks for planting that in my brain, but I don't think this is any worse than being pushed over a railing by Butch McCall."

"I wouldn't be so sure," Ana said, frowning at Theo. "Ted Bronson comes up with a lot of harebrained schemes, then talks people into joining him on his death wish."

Ana was dressed more casually than she had been the night before, but not by much. She was wearing designer jeans, a cashmere sweater, and about half a pound of gold jewelry.

"I couldn't agree more," Theo said to her. "Ted's intelligence is way overestimated, in my opinion. To him, people are nothing more than human guinea pigs. If the authorities knew half the things he's done in his life, he'd be sitting in a prison cell."

"Well put, Theo," Ana said. "You should pass that on to Ted."

"I will."

Ana looked at Marty. "Are you sure you want to do this?"

"Yeah," Marty said.

"Your funeral," Theo said, smiling at the still disapproving Bertha. "Here's the plan. We'll be ready to launch in about an hour. After they see us off, Ana and Grace will relieve Laurel in Lab Nine."

"Where's Phil?" Bertha asked.

"He's down at the Moon Pool, but he spent most of the night in Lab Nine helping Laurel rebuild the pens."

"What about Luther?" Marty asked.

"Wolfe said that he'll keep Luther with him down at the Moon Pool for the time being. And I'm afraid there's been some bad news."

"What?" Bertha asked.

"Roy is missing. He didn't report for his shift. Joe checked his cabin. His bunk hadn't been slept in, and he isn't answering his radio."

"Butch is still aboard," Bertha said.

"I think you're right," Theo agreed.

"Why wasn't I told?" Bertha asked.

"Because they just discovered Roy was missing," Theo answered. "Al and Joe and a few of the crew are scouring the ship for him right now. If Roy is dead, whoever killed him got his gun and his radio. Al changed the code." He handed her a slip of paper. "Here's the new one. If Butch got Roy, he probably already overheard an earful in the last few hours."

Bertha punched the new code into her radio.

"Wolfe wants everyone to stay in groups of at least two," Theo continued. "Whether it's Butch McCall or someone else, we are all vulnerable. Roy was a very tough guy. Whoever got him was tougher."

• • •

"I guess that does it, Yvonne," Wolfe said. "I appreciate your help."

They had just strapped the last camera on one of the three dolphins and were watching them circle the smaller holding pool.

"Do you want me to open the gate and let them into the big pool?" Yvonne asked.

"No, I'll do it later," Wolfe said. "Why don't you go to the mess and get some breakfast? Your work down here is finished. It's up to the dolphins now."

"I'd rather stay," Yvonne said. "I'm pretty fond of Winkin, Blinkin, and Nod, and I'd like to follow this through."

"I know," Wolfe said. "And I'm sorry, but you can't. There are some components of this capture that we would like to keep quiet. You've been great, Yvonne, but the truth is that we just don't know you very well."

"Meaning you don't trust me."

"Actually, I do trust you," Wolfe said. "I wouldn't have hired you to prep the dolphins otherwise. But there are degrees of trust, and you're just not there yet. You only come to Cryptos once or twice a year, and most of the time that you're there, I'm gone."

"Maybe you should hire me full-time," Yvonne said. "Then you'd see that I'm trustworthy."

"You'd come work for us full-time?"

"I love Cryptos Island and I would love to settle down there. I'm tired of traveling all over the world training other people's marine mammals. Make me an offer."

"I will," Wolfe said, ushering her to the door. "As soon as this is over and we're back on the island."

"I take that to mean I'm supposed to go now," Yvonne said.

"I'm afraid so, but I'm serious about talking to you about coming to work for us."

Yvonne gave Wolfe a sweet smile and exited through the sliding doors.

As soon as she was gone the control room door slid open and Phil stepped out.

"The dolphin vids are crystal clear," Phil said.

Wolfe nodded. "Did they find Roy?"

Phil shook his head. "I just talked to Al. He and Joe are still searching, but they're not hopeful."

Ana, Theo, and Marty walked through the sliding doors and joined them.

"It's hard to believe that Butch got the drop on him," Phil continued.

"You're talking about Roy," Ana said.

"He was a good man," Theo said. "I guess we should have listened to Al and put more security on board."

"Maybe they'll find him," Marty said. He felt terrible about Roy.

Theo shook his head. "I doubt it." He started stripping out of his disguise. "You were lucky, Marty. Very lucky. And I'm sure Butch figured out you survived. He wouldn't make the same mistake twice. If Butch threw Roy overboard, he waited to hear the splash."

Theo lay on the ground, with Ted Bronson standing above him wearing shorts and a T-shirt.

"Maybe we should delay the launch until after we get this worked out," Ted said.

"I'm not sure what that would gain us," Wolfe said. "We aren't going to find Butch unless he wants us to find him. What we need to do is catch a giant squid and get out of here."

Ted looked at Ana. "You've talked to some of the crew. Any idea how Butch is pulling this off?"

"Nothing concrete," Ana said. "But if I had to guess, I'd say he's posing as one of the scientists. They have no set hours, they have access to most of the ship, and no one questions what they're doing because no one knows what the scientists *are* doing. And a lot of the scientists are working alone. The regular crew members know each other and would recognize a stranger."

"It's hard to believe that Butch could pass himself off as a scientist," Ted said.

"Really?" Ana said. "Because I know a scientist who has passed himself off as a moron for years, and *he's* never been caught."

"Good point," Ted said. "It's your call, Wolfe. If you want to delay, just say the word."

Wolfe thought about it for a long time, then shook his head and said, "I think we should launch. Delaying will just give Blackwood more time to hurt us." He looked at Phil. "Bring the doctor down."

"Doctor?" Marty asked.

"The third member of our crew," Ted said.

Bertha went into Grace's cabin to wake her but found that she was already up, sitting at her desk with Congo perched on her shoulder, her stuffed monkey in her lap, reading a Moleskine.

"Don't tell me you haven't slept," Bertha said.

"I slept," Grace said. "I've only been up an hour or so. I'm reading one of my mother's journals."

"You might want to take it with you," Bertha said. "Because you won't be back here for a while. After we see your insane cousin off, you and Ana have dino duty. You might have to pull a double shift because we're a bit short-staffed."

Grace sighed. "And they're not getting any easier to take care of. In fact, they're getting more aggressive, except toward Luther, which is very annoying."

Bertha laughed. "That's one of the reasons we're short-staffed. Wolfe is taking him out of the rotation for the next twenty-four hours. He thinks that part of their aggression toward you and the others is a reaction to not having Luther feed them. He watched several feeding videos and believes that they've imprinted on Luther. With him gone, they might calm down and imprint on you and the others. Laurel and Phil fed them three times last night. By the third feeding they were as calm as if Mother Luther were there."

"Did you tell Mother Luther this?"

"Not yet. I'll wake him up."

"Good luck," Grace said. "Waking Luther is like waking Count Dracula at noon."

"Don't you worry," Bertha said. "I've rousted a lot of sleepy-headed troops."

But when Bertha saw Luther slouched in the chair with his head back as if his neck were broken and heard the inhuman sounds coming out of his mouth, her confidence stuttered. It seemed impossible that anyone could sleep in that position without experiencing permanent spinal damage.

PD jumped out of Luther's lap and dashed into Grace's cabin. Congo began screaming and PD began barking so loudly that Bertha had to cover her ears.

Luther did not move a muscle.

"Stop it, both of you!" Grace shouted from her cabin. "You two need to learn to get along."

Congo and PD ignored her.

Bertha gave Luther's bony shoulder a rough shake, which had absolutely no effect.

The shrieking and barking faded as PD and Congo headed off down the companionway.

Grace stepped into Marty and Luther's cabin. "No luck?"

"What's the matter with him?" Bertha asked.

"Aside from being Luther Percival Smyth the Fourth, nothing," Grace answered. "This sometimes works." She had a pair of sharp scissors in her hand.

"What are you going to do with those?"

"I would love to cut off his hair as a joke," Grace said. "Marty did that once, but it didn't wake him up, and Luther's hair was much longer back then. I'm just going to give him a little prick. That usually does the trick." She grabbed his hand and gave it a quick jab.

Luther's eyes snapped open. "Morning, Bertha! Hey, Grace."

"That is one of the creepiest things I've ever seen," Bertha said.

"My hair?" Luther said, seemingly unaware that he had just been stabbed in the hand. "Give me a break, Bertha. I just woke up. Let me at least give it a brush before you start criticizing it."

"I wasn't talking about your hair," Bertha said. "I was talking about how you sleep and what Grace had to do to wake you up."

He jumped up and cracked the kink out of his neck, then noticed the spot of blood on his hand.

"Did you stab me again, Grace?"

Grace nodded.

"It's okay." Luther looked at Bertha. "If you slept as well as I do, you could get by on two to three hours of sleep a night. That's a net profit of four to five extra hours to goof around every day. Where's Marty?"

"Down at the Moon Pool."

"What are we waiting for?" Luther asked, heading toward the door.

"Do you think his odd brain is the cause of his strange hair?" Bertha asked Grace as they followed.

"I heard that," Luther said. "Of course, I won't have much goofing-around time today because of those two little snappers."

"You won't be feeding the snappers today," Bertha said.

"Why not?"

Bertha explained Wolfe's theory.

"Fine with me," Luther said. "That will give me a chance to goof around with the dragonspy."

"That will be up to Wolfe. You'll be spending the day with

him in the Orb control booth watching him coordinate the dive, which will be about as exciting as watching a rock dropping down a deep well. If they come across a giant squid, it will get a lot more interesting."

"I have something for you to do," Grace said. "Congo and PD took off this morning. Maybe you could use the dragonspy to find them and bring them back to the Moon Pool."

"I'll find them," Luther said as they walked through the air lock, but the promise flew out of his mind as quickly as it had arrived when he saw the Orb floating in the Moon Pool like a giant golden egg. "Whoa!"

Standing next to the bobbing Orb, in gold aquasuits and black helmets, visors up, were Ted, Marty, and Dr. Seth A. Lepod.

"I should have brought my sketch pad," Luther said. "You look like superheroes! This is going to make an awesome panel in our next graphic novel."

Grace touched the side of the Orb and felt the fabric give. "You are not going down in that," she said.

"Yep," Marty said. "It's great. With the visors down and the cameras on, it's like sitting in a transparent bubble floating in air."

"Are you really Ted Bronson?" Luther asked.

"In the flesh," Ted said. "Well . . . in the aquasuit anyway. It's a pleasure to meet you, Luther. I hear you're pretty good with the dragonspy."

Luther flushed. "I'm okay. Thanks for letting me use it." Luther nodded at the Orb. "Marty said something about that thing being a nuclear sub, but of course I didn't believe him."

"It is a sub," Ted said. "And it is nuclear-powered, but it's configured differently."

"I can see that," Luther said. "It looks like a giant beach ball."

Ted smiled. "That's not exactly what I meant, but you're right, it doesn't look like a conventional sub."

"If we're going to do this, we'd better get this show on the road," Wolfe said. He pushed a button opening a hydraulic gate between the holding pool and the big pool. Winkin, Blinkin, and Nod rocketed through before the gate was all the way open. "Want me to leave the holding pool open or closed?" Wolfe asked.

"Leave the gate open," Ted said. "We might need the holding pool as a backup in case we can't get into the O-Tube quick enough."

"What's an O-Tube?" Luther asked.

"It's kind of a long parking garage for the Orb," Ted answered. "I got the idea from the lava tubes on Cryptos." He looked at Marty. "Remember what I was saying about all inventions being based on things that already exist in nature?"

Marty nodded. On his first trip to Cryptos he had spent a few hours exploring the lava tubes inside the island's extinct volcano.

Ted continued, "Obviously, I couldn't work on the Orb out in the open in the Moon Pool and keep its existence secret. There's a hatch under the water and a tube that leads to another pool on the other side of the control room. If we get a giant squid into the Moon Pool, we'll use the tube to get away from it. If the squid blocks the opening, we'll shoot into the holding pool. I can operate the gate remotely from the Orb."

Marty looked at Dr. Lepod for some kind of reaction. There was none. He had the same expression on his face that he'd had since he arrived at the Moon Pool: silent ecstasy, as if he had just learned he had won the biggest lottery in the history of the world. When Ted asked him if he wanted to join them in the deep, he had answered: "I would be delighted." And those were the only words he had uttered since Phil had brought him through the air lock, smelling like dead fish. Another good thing about the aquasuit was that as soon as Lepod put it on, the smell vanished. Apparently, the suit not only kept things out, it kept smells in.

Wolfe pushed another button. The bottom of the pool dropped away and fresh seawater bubbled in. Within seconds, Winkin, Blinkin, and Nod disappeared into the black beneath the ship.

Grace pushed the fabric of the Orb again.

"This will implode," she said.

Ted laughed. "I hope not," he said. "Orbs one through six *did* implode, but I'm pretty sure number seven won't cave."

Pretty sure? Marty thought. Ted hadn't said "pretty sure" during his first tour. And he hadn't said anything about this being the seventh Orb, which explained the *007* on the side, which he now realized was no ironic joke and had nothing to do with James Bond. It meant that the first six Orbs had *crumpled like a soda can being stepped on by an elephant.* He shuddered inside his golden aquasuit.

"Where are the doors?" Luther asked. "Can you get inside, or do you hang on for your life to the outside?"

"Do you want to do the honors?" Ted asked Marty.

Marty took the key out of his pocket, pushed the green button, and tore an opening in the side of the Orb.

"Now look what you've done!" Luther said. "You've wrecked Ted's Orb."

"How clumsy of me," Marty said.

Luther stuck his head inside. "Wow! It's like a space capsule." He pulled his head out so Grace could see.

Inside were three small seats — two in front and one in back — and an array of switches, buttons, and controls. As she pulled her head out, a call came over Wolfe's radio.

"The chimp's out," Cap said.

"How did that happen?"

"How would I know?"

"She probably figured out the combination to the lock," Marty said. "She did the same thing on the way to the Congo."

"She's on the warpath," Cap said. "She was just in the galley. Breakfast is going to be late."

Wolfe looked at Luther.

"Forget it," Luther said. "The clump she got the last time is just starting to grow back . . . and it's a different color."

"That might be good," Marty said.

"No," Luther said with finality.

"Okay," Wolfe said. "Phil, make sure the Moon Pool doors

are secure. We don't want Bo running amok before we launch the Orb." He got on the radio. "Get ahold of Yvonne. Tell her to corral Bo."

"I already tried," the man said. "She's not answering her two-way."

"Keep trying. Check the mess. If she isn't there, she might be in her cabin sleeping. Get someone to go down there and wake her up."

"Congo and PD are on the loose, too," Grace said.

Wolfe looked back at Luther. "Since you won't sacrifice your hair, you can try to find the fugitives with the dragonspy and direct their capture."

Luther saluted and said, "Aye, aye, Captain."

Wolfe rolled his eyes. "Okay, let's get this show on the road."

"You go first," Ted said to the still-stunned Lepod. "Get into the backseat and I'll get you strapped in and hooked up."

Lepod finally spoke. "I can't thank you enough for this historic opportunity." He climbed in.

Ted kissed Ana, then closed his visor.

"Be careful, you idiot," Ana said.

Ted climbed through the slit and strapped himself into the left seat.

Marty gave Grace a hug, shook everyone else's hands, then climbed into the seat next to Ted.

"Uh," Luther said, "can you hear me in those getups?"

"Loud and clear," Marty answered through a speaker in the control room.

"Good," Luther said. "Because there is, like, this big rip in the Orb and you are going to drown."

"Whew . . . that was close, Luther," Marty said. "Thanks for warning us. We might have died." Marty switched the key to red and sealed the rip.

"Nose-picker," Luther said.

"I can't even scratch my nose with this helmet on," Marty said. "See you around, nose-picker. We're going down to play some beach ball with *Architeuthis*."

The Orb started its descent into the pool. As she watched, Grace had the sinking feeling that this was the last time she was going to see Marty, but that wasn't all she was thinking about . . . her mother's Moleskine was on her mind. She looked at Wolfe. "Are you sure this is safe?"

"Relatively sure," Wolfe answered. "Come into the control room and you can see what they're seeing."

"Maybe Phil and I should take off and help look for Roy," Bertha said.

"What are you talking about?" Grace asked.

Wolfe told her about Roy's disappearance. This news, along with reading her mother's Moleskine, was too much for Grace. She started crying; Wolfe held her until she finished.

"We have to stop this," Grace said, wiping her eyes.

"Believe me, Grace, I would love to put an end to this," Wolfe said. "But Noah is determined to put an end to me, Marty, Ted—all of us except you. We have to protect ourselves." He looked at Phil and Bertha. "Phil, you can help Al look for Roy. Bertha, you've been up all night. I want you to bunk down in Lab Nine so you'll be close to Grace and Ana."

"What about Laurel?" Bertha asked.

"Tell her to stay in the lab. Until we find Butch, or whoever's on board, we need to stick together in well-defended groups." Wolfe looked at his watch. "I need to start monitoring the dive. There won't be much more to see until they get to the right depth, and that's going to take a while. I'll put a video feed into the lab so you can track their progress."

Bertha nodded and the four of them started toward the air lock. Luther launched the dragonspy and it followed them out.

Wolfe watched them walk down the companionway on Luther's Gizmo. "I'm sorry I got you in the middle of this mess, Luther."

"I don't mind," Luther said. "I'd rather be here than at some lousy summer camp."

"You don't even go home for the summers?"

"Sometimes for a couple of weeks, but then my parents fly off and find someplace to dump me until school starts."

"What do your parents do for a living?"

"I'm not sure," Luther said. "All I know is that they work 24/7 and have a lot of money. My dad knew all about eWolfe, and he was happy I was going to spend the summer with you."

"He wouldn't be happy if he knew what was really going on," Wolfe said.

Luther shrugged. "I wouldn't be so sure. He's kind of a tough guy. If he were here, he'd be right in the thick of things."

"Bring the Gizmo into the control room," Wolfe said.

Wolfe toggled through the cameras as the Orb descended into the deep.

"Marty was right," Luther said, glancing between the Gizmo and the monitor. "It looks like they're floating in a transparent bubble. What happened to the wall of the Orb?"

"You're seeing what they're seeing on their visor screens." Wolfe switched to another camera. It was a front view of Marty, Ted, and Lepod in their black helmets and aquasuits, surrounded by the gold Orb. "The Orb's skin is stippled with more than three thousand cameras and lights. When they get to a depth beneath the sunlight, they'll be able to see over a hundred yards, like it's daylight in every direction."

"Won't the lights scare the squid?" Luther asked.

"Not if they're like other squid species. Squid are attracted to light."

"Bertha, Grace, and Ana just arrived at Lab Nine," Luther said, looking down at his Gizmo.

"Good."

"Wolfe?" Cap's voice crackled through on the two-way.

"Go ahead."

"Yvonne isn't in her cabin or in the mess."

"Keep looking for her," Wolfe said, hoping that Butch hadn't gotten ahold of her, too. "What's the latest on Bo?"

"She just ran through the engine room. One of the guys tried to block her and she knocked him down and bit him."

"That's not like Bo. She can get wild, but she's never bitten anyone. What's gotten into her?"

"She's gone crazy," Cap said. "She's banged up a couple of people. She's going to seriously hurt someone."

"When you find Yvonne, have her get the tranquilizer gun,"

Wolfe said. "If she can't calm Bo down, tell her to immobilize her."

"Will do," Cap said.

Wolfe looked at Luther. "If you see Yvonne or Bo with the dragonspy, let me know immediately."

"Don't worry," Luther said. "I'll find them."

PASTS

After disinfecting themselves in the clean room, Grace, Ana, and Bertha found a very tired-looking Laurel watching two sleeping dinosaurs. The pen had been divided in half with a swinging gate. The gate was open and the hatchlings were lying next to each other with their necks entwined. The fan was running full blast.

Laurel explained that it was a lot easier feeding them separately. "You can keep better track of how much food you're feeding and it's harder for them to try to snap each other's heads off. When they finish you can open the gate so they can be together. I fed them about an hour ago, so they should be asleep for another couple of hours." Laurel noticed that Grace was holding a Moleskine. "You'll have some time to write in your journal."

"This isn't my Moleskine," Grace said.

"You opened the trunk?"

Grace nodded.

"That was a big step. Congratulations."

"I haven't gotten far," Grace said. "I looked at some of the photographs, then I decided to read the Moleskines in the order they were written. This is the first one. She wasn't much older than me when she wrote it. It's about my grandfather and living at the Ark." Grace hesitated. "My mother was happy. She loved her father and it sounded like she was living a perfect life. Noah Blackwood wasn't anything like the man you and Wolfe say he is."

"Your mother was young when she wrote all of that," Laurel said. "I'm not surprised she liked living at the Ark. It's a beautiful place. And being around animals all day must have been wonderful. How many Moleskines are there?"

"Thirty-two."

"I suspect things will change dramatically in the later Moleskines," Laurel said. "She probably hadn't figured out who her father really was yet."

"What are you two talking about?" Ana asked.

Grace told her about her mother's trunk.

"That trunk's a gold mine!" Ana said excitedly. "I know it's very personal, but I would love to read those journals and look at the photos. Sorry if that sounds insensitive, but I can't help myself. I'm a reporter."

"I'd like to read through them first before I make up my mind about that," Grace said.

"Of course."

Bertha picked up her shotgun, brought it over to the bunk, and sat down. "Wake me up if you need me to shoot someone." She lay down, closed her eyes, and was asleep within seconds.

"Did your mother mention having any friends?" Laurel asked.

Grace thought about it for a moment, then shook her head. "No one her age. She talked about a couple of the keepers she liked."

"School?" Laurel asked.

"She had a tutor whom she adored. An older woman she called Nana."

"Probably a nanny," Laurel said.

"Or a full-time guard," Ana added.

"Nana didn't sound like a guard," Grace said. "She sounded like a close confidante. When my grandfather was at the Ark, my mother spent all of her time with him. When he was away, she missed him terribly."

"Do you remember the conversation Wolfe and I had when I first arrived on Cryptos?" Laurel asked.

Grace nodded. She had been hiding up in the balcony of the library, eavesdropping on them. "He called my grandfather a wolf in sheep's clothing," she said, not mentioning that after reading the first fifty pages of her mother's Moleskine, she was beginning to wonder which man was the wolf.

"Just remember," Ana said. "Butch McCall is Noah Blackwood's thug. He tried to throw your cousin over the side and probably succeeded in throwing Roy over. I've been investigating him for years. Noah Blackwood is a monster."

Laurel gave Ana a cross look. "Grace needs to make up her own mind." She turned to Grace. "It took courage to open that trunk—to explore your past. I'm proud of you. Pretty soon you won't have any fears to overcome."

"That's not likely. Right now I'm worried sick about Marty going down into the canyon in that Orb. He'll probably provide me with new fears for the rest of my life."

"What's an Orb?" Laurel asked.

Ana switched on the monitor.

The aquanauts had reached the point of complete darkness and Ted had switched on the Orb's lights.

"A great white!" Dr. Lepod said.

"I see it," Ted said.

The shark swam straight at them with its mouth open in a toothy grin. Marty flinched as it gave the Orb an exploratory nudge, then backed away.

"It's going to hit us again," Lepod said.

Ted responded by turning on an electrical field.

The great white did hit them again, and a lot harder, but as soon as it touched the pod it did a complete backward somersault and shot away from them like a bullet.

Ted chuckled. "I love great whites, but they aren't the brightest bulbs beneath the sea. I set the field to its lowest setting. But that should be enough to discourage it from snapping at golden beach balls for the rest of its life."

Ted was right. The shark did not come back for thirds.

"What happens if you turn the field up to full power?" Marty asked.

"Death," Ted said. "But worse is the pulse matrix. Hopefully we won't have to use that. It will kill everything within fifty yards of us. But I would rather eject than use that option."

"Eject?" Marty and Lepod said at the same time.

"Our aquasuits are tailor-made versions of the Orb . . . without the defenses. They'll keep us alive for a good hour, which would give us ample time to reach the surface."

"What about decompression?" Lepod asked.

"We can go straight up without worrying about the bends," Ted answered. "Like the Orb, the suits adjust automatically to the pressure."

"Remarkable," Lepod said. "This will revolutionize undersea exploration. Perhaps we can coauthor a paper."

"All of this is experimental, Dr. Lepod," Ted said. "As we told you up at the Moon Pool, no one, and I mean no one, can be told about this."

"Of course," Lepod said. "I just meant when you're ready to release the information."

"Right. I'm going to switch to radio silence to conserve power." Ted punched a button and looked at Marty. "I just cut Lepod's speaker. He can't hear us. Maybe it wasn't such a good idea to bring him with us. We needed a squid expert aboard, but I'm not sure he'll be able to keep his mouth shut about all this."

"Have Al talk to him about it," Marty said. "Lepod will keep his mouth shut."

"Good idea. I'll have Al *debrief* him when we get back up. He'll scare him into silence."

"I have a theoretical question," Marty said. "Let's say we have to eject and on our way to the surface we get a visit from Mr. Humongous Hungry Great White Shark and he decides to eat us?"

"The aquasuit is absolutely impenetrable," Ted answered. "In other words, it's bulletproof *and* shark-tooth-proof."

"Good," Marty said.

"But," Ted continued, "it's not crunch-proof, meaning if a great white got ahold of you and started shaking you around, it wouldn't take long for the suit to turn into a golden bag of bones and guts."

"I think I'd rather be shot," Marty said.

"I hear you," Ted agreed. He switched on the dolphin cam. Winkin, Blinkin, and Nod were half a mile away, at a depth of sixty feet. They were smack in the middle of a school of tuna and gobbling them down like potato chips.

"They may not be serving a purpose," Marty said. "But they're having fun."

"They sure are," Ted agreed.

"Exactly why did you need them as decoys?" Marty asked.

"When you all got back to Cryptos from the Congo, we cleaned house, knowing that we had spies on the island. And not just Blackwood's people. I think we had corporate and foreign spies as well. We've invented a lot of things over the years, but nothing like the Orb. When something this revolutionary comes along, it's usually turned over to the government, which is better equipped to handle secrets. But as I told you before, we still haven't decided what we're going to do — or who we're going to share the discovery with. And that's why we brought Al in.

"The press and the scientific community wanted to know how we were going to catch a giant squid. We had to tell them something, so we gave them Winkin, Blinkin, and Nod to throw them off. We even went so far as to bring Yvonne aboard. She's probably the best marine mammal trainer in the world. This got everyone thinking about how we might use the dolphins to catch a giant squid, and it never occurred to them that we had something very different in mind."

"How long have you known Al Ikes?"

Ted laughed. "Al, Wolfe, and I went to kindergarten together. We lived on the same block. Except when Wolfe was off on safari with his father, the three of us were inseparable all the way through high school. Everyone was pretty happy when we split up and went to different universities. I went to MIT. Al went to West Point. And Wolfe went to vet school at UC Davis. But even though we were pursuing different interests in different parts of the country, we stayed in close touch, getting together whenever we could . . . and getting into a lot of trouble together just like when we were kids."

"So, you knew my mom when she was a kid?"

"Little Sylvia," Ted said. "Al had a crush on her his whole life and was devastated when she married Timothy. Wolfe's dad didn't take her on safari, so she filled in as the third trouble-maker when Wolfe was away. I was a little sweet on her myself, if you want to know the truth. She had as much grit as her big brother . . . maybe more."

Marty didn't want to think about his parents in the past tense.

"How did you end up with Cryptos Island?" he asked.

"Al was behind all that. He hasn't always worn a three-piece suit. He was recruited by the Central Intelligence Agency right out of West Point. Something came up that he needed Wolfe's and my help with. But I think it would be better for Wolfe to give you the details than me. All I can say is that the three of us got in trouble again, but it worked out well for everyone, including the U.S. Government.

"Now, let's get back to work. We have a squid to catch, and the sooner we get it, the sooner we'll be able to get away from Blackwood. I'm going to run a systems check." Ted started flipping switches and pushing buttons. "That's not good."

"What's the matter?" Marty asked.

"Hopefully, nothing," Ted answered. "We're having a communication glitch with the *Coelacanth*." He turned on Lepod's helmet speaker. "Have you punched any buttons back there, Dr. Lepod?"

"No," Lepod said. "I've just been enjoying the ride. It's remarkable . . . beautif—"

Ted switched off Lepod's helmet again.

"We have a major problem," Ted said.

CHAOS

Luther had no problem finding Bo, because Bo found him.

She was pounding on the outer Moon Pool door, and Luther didn't like the way she looked. He showed the Gizmo to Wolfe.

"What's gotten into her?" Wolfe asked. "She looks crazed. But don't worry, your hair is safe. That door is blast-proof."

"Yeah," Luther said. "But is it Bo-proof?"

Bo had given up pounding on the doors with her hands and was now taking running starts and hitting the doors with both feet. As they watched, they heard an odd sound, as if a turbine was powering off. The lights went out, replaced a second later by dim emergency lights.

"What the . . ."

Wolfe started hitting buttons on the control panel, to no effect. "You hear that?" he asked.

"I don't hear anything," Luther said.

"Exactly," Wolfe said. "The power's down throughout the ship." He keyed his radio. "Cap?"

"Yep, we're dead," Cap said. "I just talked to the engine room crew. They said they heard a series of small popping sounds, then everything went off. Our ship-to-shore radio is out, too. And our satellite radios have been jammed. Our secure radios work, obviously. And so do the crew's two-ways, but there's so much chatter you can't get a word in edgewise. I've tried to get them to calm down and shut up, but they aren't listening."

"How about the ship's PA system?" Wolfe asked.

"Dead."

"Butch," Wolfe said.

"No doubt," Cap replied. "Small explosives, perfectly placed. Professional job. It will take hours, if not days, to get the power back on. He blew the engines, too. We're up a creek without a paddle. I have some guys searching for other explosives just in case he has something bigger in mind."

"Good idea," Wolfe said. "If they find anything, get ahold of Al or Joe. They'll be able to defuse them. How long will the auxiliary power last?"

"Hopefully long enough for us to get the power back up. The only thing the batteries will run are the lights."

"How about the Moon Pool doors? Can we close them when we need to?"

"Maybe. But they use a lot of juice. If you try it'll probably drain the batteries dry and it'll be pitch-dark below deck. Can you get ahold of Ted? He might be able to come up with some way to work around this."

Wolfe looked at the blank monitors. "Ted's not available. He's on his own—I mean *we* are on our own." Cap had never met Ted Bronson and didn't know he was aboard disguised as Theo Sonborn.

Al broke into the conversation. "We're suspending the search for Roy," he said. "The lights are probably just a prelude to something much worse. I'm sending all available hands topside to set up our defenses."

"Good," Wolfe said. "I'm going to have to stick down here for a while and try to get in touch with our friends."

"No problem. We'll have it covered up here." Al signed off.

During this exchange, Bo had given up on the Moon Pool doors and was scampering down the companionway on all fours looking for her next victim. Luther followed her with the dragonspy while Wolfe tried to figure out a way to get at least the radio communication back online with the Orb.

It was harder to fly the dragonspy in the dim emergency light, and it wasn't helpful that the ship was now in chaos. Crew members were running in all different directions, and confused scientists were emerging from their labs asking why they had lost power. Some of the answers Luther over-heard were:

"We're under attack!"

"There was an explosion!"

"Hide! The chimp has rabies!"

Wolfe was right about Bo's behavior. When she'd been trying to yank out Luther's hair, she'd looked liked she was enjoying herself. It was a game. But there was no joy now and this was no game. She was in a rage, banging on the doors she passed and slapping aside anyone standing in her way. It looked as if she had lost her mind.

Bo ran into a dark corridor, and Luther had to slow the dragonspy down so he didn't smash it into a wall. When he reached the next turn, Bo was gone.

"What do we do?" Grace asked in the dimly lit lab.

Bertha was out of the bunk with her shotgun in one hand and her radio in the other, monitoring the situation.

"We stay right here," the former general answered. "Butch, or whoever blew out the power, is trying to create chaos. And by the sound of the radio chatter, he's doing a pretty good job of it. Bo didn't get out of her cage on her own. Someone let her out just as sure as someone cut the power. He's probably done some other things to maximize the pandemonium. When it peaks, he's going to show up here and try to grab you and the hatchlings."

"That might be a good reason for us not to be here when he shows up," Ana said.

Bertha shook her head. "He's close by. He knows where we are. He's waiting for us to open the door and come out."

One sat up, which roused Two. They both yawned and started mewing.

"And it's feeding time again," Laurel added.

PREDATORS

"I don't like it," Ted said. "Everything checks out here, which means the problem's aboard the *Coelacanth*. There are three backup systems on the ship. The only way they could lose all of them is a complete power failure. Maybe we should—"

Their ears were assaulted by a nearly deafening pinging noise followed by a series of equally loud clicking sounds.

"What is that?" Marty shouted, putting his hands on either side of his helmet.

"You don't have to shout," Ted said. "And it won't do you any good to cover your ears through your helmet. Just turn your speaker volume down." He pointed to the switch.

Marty turned it down, but his ears were still ringing. "So, what is it?" he repeated.

"Sperm whales," Lepod answered. "Five or six of them. All females, if I'm not mistaken."

"How do you know that?" Marty asked.

"I'm fluent in sperm whale," Lepod said.

"Do you mean sperm whale, as in Moby-Dick the sixty-foot behemoth? The kind of whale that swallowed Jonah in the Bible? The largest toothed whale in the ocean?" Marty asked.

"The same," Lepod said calmly. "And I can't tell you how delighted I am to hear that you have so much knowledge of this wonderful predator."

Marty wished he didn't know so much about them. "Think they're interested in gulping down an Orb?"

"That's an excellent question," Lepod said. "By the sound of their echolocation, they are definitely hunting, but I don't know how they would respond to our little ball."

"Don't worry about it," Ted said. "If they come after us, we'll be able to outmaneuver them. Oh, and I should warn you both. If we have to do that, you might get a little queasy. Try not to vomit in your helmets. It won't hurt any of the electronics inside, but it will be kind of unpleasant."

Marty was happy he hadn't eaten breakfast before they left.

"I wouldn't be so sure about your ability to outmaneuver them," Lepod said. "They are excellent group hunters."

"We're not going to give them a chance to try," Ted said. "We're going back up to see what's going on aboard the *Coelacanth*."

"I think that would be a mistake, Dr. Bronson," Lepod said.

"Call me Ted. And why would that be a mistake?"

"We should get closer to the whales," Lepod answered. "They're among the most intelligent predators on earth. They would not have expended the energy to get to this depth without a high expectation of finding food. If they are here, there are squid nearby. In fact, one of their echolocations was a sound I haven't heard before, and I'm very familiar with their lexicon. The unusual sound may have been emitted to actually bring a giant squid out of its lair. I'm speculating, of course. We know virtually nothing about giant squid and sperm whale interaction, but this may be a once-in-a-lifetime opportunity to learn something about their predator-prey interaction and share it with the scientific community."

Not without a way of communicating that information, Marty thought. *And not if the Orb becomes the prey and gets crunched in their powerful jaws.*

"We're going back up," Ted said, to Marty's relief. "If everything's okay, we can come back down."

"But the whales may not still be here," Lepod persisted. "They're doing our work for us. Without them we could search this canyon for months without seeing a single giant squid. The whales are our beacons. After they get their fill, they'll move on."

Ted didn't say anything for a long time, which Marty took as a bad sign. Lepod's argument made sense, but it was clear that Ted had a bad feeling about what was going on aboard the *Coelacanth*. Noah Blackwood and Butch McCall were not in the area on a pleasure cruise, as Butch had already proven.

"Thirty minutes," Ted said. "Forty-five tops, then we go up."

"Excellent decision!" Lepod said.

Terrible decision, Marty thought.

Ted turned the Orb in the direction of the hunting whales.

The predator aboard the *Coelacanth* could not be more pleased about how his prey were responding. They were running back and forth along the corridors like blind cats. His old pit bull, Dirk, would have loved this.

Wolfe had changed the code on the secure radios, but it didn't matter anymore. Butch had switched back to Blackwood's frequency and had talked to him several times in the past hour. Everything and everyone was in place, waiting for Butch's word. He put Roy's radio to his clean-shaven face and said, "Come and get 'em."

"Copy," Blackwood responded. "We're on our way. We'll give them a fifteen-minute head start, then the fun will begin."

Butch clipped the radio to his belt and stuck the earphone in his ear. He chambered a round in his automatic and stuck it behind his back into the waistband of his pants. He checked to make sure his green armband was securely in place and started to button his white lab coat, but thought better of it. He would need quick access to his gun and radio. He adjusted his wig and eyeglasses.

"Dr. O'Connor's goin' huntin'." He started down the companionway toward Lab Nine.

"Dr. Wolfe?"

Wolfe was lying on his back under the control panel with a flashlight clamped in his teeth, trying to figure out a way to reroute what little power they had to the Orb's communication system, when Yvonne's voice finally broke through on the two-way. With difficulty, he unclipped the little radio and brought it to his lips. "Where have you been, Yvonne?"

"I was in the infirmary with Dr. Jones playing chess. I didn't have my two-way on. He said it disturbed his concentration. As soon as the lights went out I turned it back on, but there was so much chatter I couldn't get ahold . . ."

The inane chatter interrupted Yvonne's transmission.

Wolfe cursed and waited for a lull in the frantic exchanges, wishing he had given Yvonne an encrypted radio. The lull finally arrived and he keyed the mic and held it down so no one could interrupt the transmission.

"Yvonne, switch to channel eighteen," he said. "And if I hear anyone using channel eighteen in the next ten minutes, I will personally keelhaul you. In fact, stay off the two-ways unless you have something urgent to communicate."

He switched to channel eighteen. "Are you there, Yvonne?"

"Yes," Yvonne said. "What do you want me to do?"

"Bo is loose."

"I heard."

"But there's something the matter with her. She's hurting people, which isn't like her. I think she's been drugged."

"Who would do something like that?"

"Someone who wants to hurt us," Wolfe said. He told her about Butch McCall.

"What does he look like?"

"We don't know exactly," Wolfe answered. "He's a big guy and he could be posing as a scientist. You need to stay clear of him."

"Don't worry, I will," Yvonne said.

"I need you to go up to my cabin on the bridge. There's a tranquilizer pistol under my bunk. Have you ever used one?"

"Of course."

"Load a couple of darts with ketamine. The drugs are in the fridge under the lab bench. You need to find Bo and tranq her ASAP. And no messing around with trying to coax or manipulate her into her cage. She's way beyond that. She's causing us more trouble than being dead in the water is. I want you to knock her out and drag her back into her cage."

"I'm on my way to your cabin right now," Yvonne said. "Where is she?"

"Hang on." Wolfe scooted out from under the control panel and saw Luther staring down at the Gizmo.

"I've been listening," Luther said, without looking up. "I lost her."

"What?" Wolfe shouted.

"Hey," Luther said. "The dragonspy isn't easy to fly in the dark."

Wolfe took a deep breath and calmed himself. "Sorry. I know you're doing the best you can."

"Duh *du jour*," Luther said. "I'll find her again. All I have to do is follow her path of destruction."

"I'm in your cabin," Yvonne said over the two-way.

"Is Cap at the helm?" Wolfe asked.

"Yes. He tried to stop me from going into your cabin. I shouted him out of the way."

"Good. Give him your two-way while you load the darts."

"Cap here."

"There's a spare secure radio in my desk. Fire it up and give it to Yvonne. She's a member of the team now. And everyone else monitoring this call should treat her as such. She has full access to everywhere and everything. Do you all copy that?"

Al, Joe, and Bertha all acknowledged.

"Good. Now put Yvonne back on the two-way."

"Hang on," Cap said. "She has her hands full loading darts."

While Wolfe waited he watched Luther concentrating on the screen. "Any luck?"

"Not yet," Luther said. "But I just spotted Congo and PD."

"The darts are loaded," Yvonne said. "Where is she?"

"Luther's tracking her."

"With the tags?"

"No," Wolfe said. "The tags are offline, and she didn't have one on anyway."

"I didn't know that," Yvonne said. "So how's he tracking her?"

"I'll tell you later," Wolfe said. "You'll be able to stay in touch with Luther on the radio Cap gives you."

"Tell her to head down to the lab deck," Luther said. "That's the direction Bo was heading when I lost her and that's also where Congo and PD are going."

Wolfe filled Yvonne in, adding, "You're officially my full-time animal behaviorist and trainer, Yvonne . . . that is, if you still want the job."

"Are you kidding?" Yvonne said happily. "It's a dream come true. I won't let you down."

"You never have. Thank you and good luck."

Wolfe looked at Luther. "Park the dragonspy for a second. I need to configure your Gizmo so you can talk on our radios."

Luther landed the dragonspy on a ceiling pipe. Wolfe punched in some numbers, then spoke into the speaker.

"Can you hear me, Yvonne?"

"Loud and clear."

"Good. I'm handing you back to Luther."

TWENTY MINUTES

Lepod was wrong. There were eight whales, and to Marty's relief they were only mildly interested in the Orb, which looked like a salmon egg next to their gigantic, gray, barnacle-encrusted bodies.

"Do you see the squid suction marks on that one?" Lepod was practically jumping out of his seat.

The marks were hard to miss. The whale was only inches away from the Orb and the marks were as big as garbage can lids.

"By the size of the scars I'd say the squid was at least thirty feet long," Lepod said.

The whales circled the Orb for about three minutes, decided it wasn't appetizing, and resumed their journey through the canyon in search of something more to their taste—like giant calamari.

"Are squid blind?" Marty asked.

"On the contrary," Lepod said. "Their eyes are the largest of any animal on earth. The size is thought to be an adaptation to the dark realm in which they live. The large surface of receptors gathers what little light there is. Essentially they can see in the dark."

"Then they must not be very smart," Marty said. "The whales are not exactly using stealth to hunt them. Why would a squid come out of hiding to take on something the size of a house with teeth?"

"No one knows," Lepod said. "My guess is that the whale doesn't always win. Squid have an advantage over a whale. They don't need to surface to breathe. If a squid got its arms and tentacles around a whale in the right way, it might be able to hold the whale under until it drowns. A sperm whale can stay underwater for an hour and a half. We don't know how long this pod has been down here, but let's say that they've been in the canyon for an hour. A squid would only have to keep one of them from surfacing for thirty minutes. And that isn't taking into consideration the aerobic energy the whale would have to expend battling the squid.

"The whales are certainly hunting *Architeuthis*, but *Architeuthis* might also be hunting the whales. We know nothing about how *Architeuthis* hunt. They might hunt in packs. Three or four giant squid could easily overwhelm a single whale. It wouldn't stand a chance. A whale carcass could feed a pack of giant squid for days. Not only would they be able to feed off the carcass, but the carcass would attract fresh food for the squid to eat. Clearly, the battle is worth the risk for both species."

"We might not find out how they hunt on this dive," Ted said. "In twenty-five minutes we're heading to the surface."

"This is a very deep canyon," Lepod said. "Perhaps the walls are blocking the *Coelacanth*'s transmissions."

"Not a chance," Ted said. "We're not using a radio signal you'd be familiar with, and I can't tell you how it works for proprietary reasons."

"Fair enough," Lepod said. "But perhaps you could tell me how you plan to keep the squid alive if you're lucky enough to get it aboard the *Coelacanth*? I've asked Dr. Wolfe several times and he's refused to give me any details. I was brought aboard to help keep *Architeuthis* alive. This dive alone has certainly been worth the trip, but I can't help you if I don't know what the plan is."

Ted laughed. "Actually, the reason you're here is because it's your plan, Dr. Lepod. We stole it from you. Three years ago you published a paper on the pressure chamber you built for giant squid."

"Baby giant squid," Lepod corrected. "Someday someone will catch a young squid. I built the chamber for that eventuality."

"We kind of improved on the design and scale," Ted said. "The Moon Pool is actually a giant pressure chamber. A closed system where we can re-create almost any atmospheric condition. We hope to get a squid inside the pool and match the conditions down here. On the way back to the States we'll see if we can slowly acclimate the squid to a pressure more suitable for exhibition purposes. If that doesn't work, we have an identical chamber at the Northwest Aquarium. It won't work for exhibition, but we can keep *Architeuthis* alive in it until we figure out what to do. And since it was your idea, you can write as many scientific papers on it as you like."

"Marvelous," Lepod said giddily. "Absolutely marvelous."

"What about the dolphins?" Marty asked.

"They'll be kept in the holding pool, which is outside the chamber."

"You've thought of everything," Lepod said.

"Not everything," Ted said. "I didn't think we'd lose communication with the *Coelacanth*. We have twenty minutes."

PIRATES

"What?" Wolfe shouted. He was still tinkering under the control panel while Luther continued to search for Bo.

"Pirates," Al repeated over the radio. "A couple dozen of them. Nine speedboats that we've counted. Well armed. They're shooting at Blackwood's yacht. Blackwood is returning fire, but not very effectively. His cooks and waiters must be terrible shots."

Wolfe scooted out from under the panel again and got to his feet.

"We have to help them," he said.

"Are you crazy?" Al said. "This is the best thing that ever happened to us. If we're lucky, they'll sink both of Blackwood's ships. It's called Manifest Destiny, Wolfe. Or tough luck."

"Knock it off, Al," Wolfe said. "We can't let them sink his ships."

This was followed by a long silence.

Luther continued flying the dragonspy below deck, but he could imagine clearly the exasperated expression on Al Ikes's face. Luther thought Wolfe was nuts, too.

"I'm sure I don't have to remind you," Al continued. "But

Noah Blackwood is the same guy who had Roy killed, attempted to kidnap your daughter, and tried to have your nephew thrown overboard."

"He's done a lot more than that over the years," Wolfe said. "And I'm still not willing to let him go down like that."

"Okay," Al said. "How about if we let the pirates have their way with him for a while? Let them mess up his ships like he's messed up ours. Level the playing field a bit."

"No," Wolfe said.

"For crying out loud!" Al shouted. "A few weeks ago you stranded him in the middle of the Congo to die!"

Wolfe shook his head. "I knew Noah wouldn't die. Butch was with him. And Butch McCall could make his way out of the jungle shackled and blindfolded."

"Hang on a second," Al said. "Four of the boats have broken off the attack and are headed this way."

"I'm coming up," Wolfe said, looking at Luther. "Let's go."

"What about Bo?" Luther asked.

"Park the bot. Maybe we'll get lucky and she'll run by. Right now we have bigger problems than a berserk chimpanzee."

Luther landed the dragonspy on a ledge on the lab deck, just above one of the emergency lights. The little bot's batteries were getting low and could use the time to recharge.

Wolfe got Yvonne on the radio as they made their way to the upper deck.

"Yvonne? Did you catch Al's transmission?"

"Yes."

"Luther's with me. You're on your own."

"Don't worry. I'll get her," Yvonne said. "I think I know where she is."

Noah Blackwood was on the deck of *Endangered One* with cameras rolling, enjoying himself immensely.

When he was a kid he loved buccaneer movies — couldn't get enough of them — and now he was right in the middle of one. The star, as a matter of fact. Rifle blazing. His face grim and determined as he repelled the horde of filthy cutthroats. The right sleeve of his khaki shirt was torn at the shoulder where a bullet had grazed him. Bright red blood dripped onto the deck from the terrible wound. He ignored the pain, which was easy because there was no pain. The rip in his sleeve had not been caused by a bullet, but by his personal makeup artist. The pirates firing at his beautiful ship were his own men firing blanks. The blood *was* his own blood. He never went anywhere without it. If he got in an accident that required a transfusion, he was not about to let his body be tainted with someone else's blood. He had enough of his own blood stored in a special refrigerator aboard the yacht to fill himself up twice over.

He gave a signal.

The pirates broke off their attack and headed toward Wolfe's dilapidated freighter.

"Get the boats!" Noah shouted. "They're going after the *Coelacanth*. We have to stop them!"

He bounded over the rail as if he were jumping into a black Zodiac and landed on a king-sized mattress. He looked up at his cinematographer. "How'd that look?"

"Beautiful," the cinematographer replied. "All we need now are a few tight shots of you in the Zodiac firing your rifle, shouting orders, and we'll have a wrap."

Noah stood. "Let's get it over with, then. I have an appointment in a few minutes, and I don't want to be late." The footage would be carefully edited and played on television for the next decade. Noah smiled at the thought. Reality TV at its best.

Luther and Wolfe arrived on deck out of breath.

"They're all heading this way now," Al said. "Broke off the attack on Blackwood completely."

The three-piece suit was gone. Al was dressed in full camouflage battle fatigues with a flak vest, helmet, and enough weapons strapped to his body to take on the nine boats of pirates single-handedly.

There were at least a dozen crew members on deck, also in flak vests, manning the strangest weapons that Luther had ever seen. There were three bolted to the deck on the port side, three on the starboard, and one each on the stern and bow. Each weapon had what looked like a small satellite dish on the front and a swivel seat protected by steel plating on the back. Men were strapped into the seats, looking through scopes, pivoting the units, and getting used to the controls. Joe and Phil were running from one unit to another shouting instructions on how to operate them.

"What the heck are those?" Luther asked.

"Sonic cannons," Al said. "With pinpoint laser sights. We can blow up a pirate's brain from the inside out if we want to."

He looked at Wolfe. "But I don't suppose Dr. Pacifist here is going to let us do that."

"Very astute, Al," Wolfe said, mildly irritated. "We'll start by blowing out their eardrums and just scramble their brains a little. If that doesn't work, we'll turn up the heat."

"Fair enough," Al said.

"Are these one of Ted's inventions?" Luther asked

"No," Al answered. "They're military, but Ted has fiddled with them a bit to make them more accurate. He just can't keep his hands off things."

"Can I try one?" Luther asked.

"No!" Wolfe and Al said in unison.

"Do you have any spare flak vests?" Wolfe asked Al.

"There's a pile of them over there." He pointed.

"Put one on," Wolfe told Luther. "Then go up to the bridge and stay there. And stay away from the windows."

Disappointed, but not surprised, Luther put on the vest and tromped up to the bridge, which was abandoned. He peeked out the window, saw Wolfe staring up at him, and ducked down quickly. Then he remembered that there was more than one way to see outside. He took out the Gizmo.

EIGHT MINUTES

The Orb followed the pod of whales as they slowly swam through the canyon, singing. Along the way, Marty and Ted saw several sunken ships and debris from the contents spread out along the bottom.

"If you want to make gas money for eWolfe, why don't you use the Orb to explore some of these old wrecks?" Marty said. "I bet there's a ton of loot down here."

"We've talked about that," Ted said. "It's on our to do list. Someday we'll come back here for a better look, but first we have to fix the communication malfunction. I also have to figure out some kind of air lock, or expulsion system, to get in and out of the Orb while it's underwater. The keys are the only way in and out. We're safe in our aquasuits, but put a tear in the fabric and the Orb would fill up like a water balloon. The instruments are completely waterproof. All I have to do is come up with a way of blowing the water out after we reseal it. Right now we have some other priorities. Like—"

"Excuse me," Lepod interrupted.

"Go ahead."

"We have some company behind us."

Ted and Marty turned their heads and had a perfect high-definition view of at least six gigantic reddish bullets coming up behind them like race cars.

"They hunt in packs!" Lepod said. "I thought they . . ."

Ted pulled the controls back and the Orb shot up like a ballistic missile. Their stomachs dropped to their toes. Lepod started gagging.

"I warned you about vomiting," Ted said.

Like anyone can control that, Marty thought, trying to swallow the bile sneaking up his own throat.

"I also told you the Orb was quick," Ted added proudly, pausing it about two hundred feet above the canyon floor and flipping on the powerful lights.

They had a perfect ringside view of the greatest tag-team event ever witnessed by a human being. The whales had whipped around and were charging the charging giant squid. When they collided, the bottom sediment erupted into a gigantic plume of gray murk and defensive squid ink. Even with the bright lights, all they could see were flashes of flukes, teeth, arms, and tentacles.

"Are you recording this?" Lepod croaked.

"Yep," Ted confirmed. "Pretty amazing. I've never seen this much violence in one place."

It was over as quickly as it had begun. When the water cleared, the score was Whales, 3; Squid, 1. Three of the whales had squid clamped in their mouths. A fourth whale was on the bottom, engulfed by the long arms and tentacles of four more squid. There was no sign of the four other whales.

"They probably took off in the confrontation," Lepod said, having difficulty speaking with the contents of his stomach stuck in his helmet. "They're probably heading to the surface for air. The question is, were the squid after the Orb, or was the Orb simply in their path to getting to the whales?"

"I don't know," Ted said.

Marty was still shocked by how quick the squid and the whales had been. On television documentaries, whales always looked so laid-back and calm. There was nothing laid-back and calm about what he had just witnessed.

"There's one way to find out," Lepod said. "There are two smaller squid lying in wait about ten feet to the right of the suffocating whale."

"I see them," Ted said.

Marty saw them, too, but they didn't look that small to him.

"They are probably subdominant to the larger squid, waiting their turn to eat," Lepod continued. "You might want to take the Orb down and see if you can get one of them to come after us."

"Before I see if I can hook them, how are you doing, Lepod?"

"I'm all right. I mean, it's a little disgusting to have your head stuck in a bowl of regurgitation, and my eyes are stinging a bit from the gastric acid, but I've had worse things on my face."

What could possibly be worse? Marty wondered.

Ted laughed. "You're a good sport, Lepod. I guess I'll have to work on a way of expelling vomit from the helmets like water from the Orb. I'll put it on the list. One good thing: You probably got rid of everything in your stomach during that last maneuver."

"I hope so," Lepod said. "Because there really isn't much room inside here for more. If I might make a suggestion . . ."

"Go ahead," Ted said.

"Your best technique will be to tease them to the surface, like you are jigging for them with bait. I would stay just in front of them. If they fall behind, slow the Orb down so they can catch up. If you think it's safe, you might even allow them to touch the Orb with the tips of their tentacles from time to time. You have to keep their hopes up. I think the quick maneuver you made scared them off. Common squid are very smart. Giant squid may be even more intelligent. They'll eliminate their energy expenditure the moment they think they can't catch their prey. I would never let them get in front of you, though. Their tentacles and arms, as you've just seen, are like lightning bolts."

"Good safety tip," Ted said. He looked at the digital clock on the control panel. "We'd better cut bait. Tighten your seat belts. We have eight minutes."

SCUTTLE

Butch knew that Grace was in Lab Nine. He also knew that Laurel, Ana, and Bertha were in there with her. What he didn't know was how he was going to get her or the dinosaurs out.

Three of Blackwood's men were already aboard. Pepper was down at the Moon Pool coordinating the placement of C-4 plastic explosives. (But it would be Blackwood pushing the plunger on the remote detonator. He wanted to take out Travis Wolfe personally.) Butch had radioed one of the men to Lepod's lab to bring him a little chunk of C-4. As a last resort he was going to blast his way into Lab Nine and hope that Grace or the dinosaurs weren't anywhere near the door when he blew it off. If any of them were injured, he might as well swallow the C-4 and detonate himself. Because that's what Blackwood would do to Butch, or to anyone else who harmed them.

Butch was pretty confident that he could shape the charge around the door's locking mechanism, which would minimize the damage on the inside. But on the other side he still had a big problem named Bertha Bishop. And she just might be more formidable than the door.

As he considered all the pros and cons, he heard a loud shrieking noise outside Lepod's lab. He stuck his head out the door and came face-to-face with a parrot—the same parrot he'd thrown against a tree at Lake Télé. Apparently, the parrot hadn't forgotten. It landed on his shoulder and latched onto his earlobe with its sharp black beak. It was Butch's turn to shriek now. He tried to shake off the bird, but it hung on like a parrot earring. Then he felt something tugging at his pant leg. He looked down and saw Wolfe's tiny poodle latched onto his cuff. He reached for the parrot to rip it off his ear, but it dodged him, jumped on his head, grabbed onto his wig, and flew down the hallway with it clutched in its sharp little talons.

Butch tore his lab coat off in a rage. His earlobe throbbed, and blood dripped onto his tattooed forearm. He heard something rushing up behind him, and this time it wasn't a poodle or a parrot. Butch turned around and Bo, running at full speed, jumped and planted both feet into his stomach, knocking him against the wall and taking every ounce of oxygen from his lungs. As he gasped for breath, she tore his glasses off his face, pummeled him with her hands, bit him twice on each leg, dislocated two fingers on his left hand, then continued down the hall. He reached for his gun with his right hand and took a shot at her, but missed by a mile. Butch was left-handed.

Yvonne came running around the corner and stopped in shock upon seeing the injured Butch McCall.

Luther watched the pirate battle on the Gizmo from the comfort of Wolfe's cot. Within a matter of minutes the sonic cannons had taken out six of the pirates' speedboats, or at least the pirates piloting them. The boats were running in crazy circles without anyone steering them. The cannon operators centered their lasers on the driver of each boat, pushed a button, and a second later the pilot released the wheel, grasping his ears with both hands and reeling over backward. If another pirate took control of the boat, he, too, got the laser and sonic blast with the same disastrous effect.

The three remaining boats—all Zodiacs—seemed impervious to the cannons. There were two men in each boat, and they didn't look like the other pirates. They were dressed in black combat gear. As one steered, the other systematically shot out the dishes of the sonic cannons.

Who are these guys? Luther thought. *And why don't the blasts hurt their ears?*

"Blackwood's guys," Al said to Wolfe. "Paramilitary. Professionals. They're wearing sonic earplugs. Somehow they knew about the cannons. What do you want to do?"

"Shoot them," Wolfe said flatly. "Head shots."

"Joe!" Al shouted. "Get your sniper rifle. Take 'em out. Pilots first."

"Wolfe!" Yvonne's breathless voice crackled on the radio.

"Did you find Bo?"

"No, but I found your stowaway and he's after me!"

"Where are you?"

"On the lab deck."

"Go to Lab Nine," Wolfe said. "Bertha?"

"Got it," Bertha said. "I'm in the outer room waiting for her. She's here. Talk to you later."

Bertha was looking through the peephole at a panicked Yvonne pounding on the door. She jacked a shell into her shotgun and opened the door. Yvonne nearly ran her over pushing through the doorway.

Bertha slammed the door shut behind her. "How far away is he?"

"He's at the end of the hall," Yvonne answered, gasping for breath. "He's carrying a pistol."

"What does he look like?"

"Big and bald. He's bleeding from his ear. It looks like he's been in a terrible fight."

Bertha turned back toward the door and looked out the peephole. "It sounds like Butch McCall," she said into her throat mic. "Yvonne says that he's in rough shape and has a pistol. Want me to deal with him as he runs by?"

"Negative," Wolfe said. "As soon as we take care of the situation up here I'll come down and we'll see what we can do about running him to ground."

Bertha felt a stinging sensation in the back of her leg. As she turned around, Yvonne hit her in the head with Butch's telescoping baton and yanked open the door to Lab Nine.

The battered Butch stepped into the doorway and looked down at the crumpled Bertha. She had a tranquilizer dart sticking out of her leg and was bleeding from the head.

"Nice work, partner," Butch whispered. "But I'm ticked about the chimp you drugged." He had popped the two dislocated fingers back into place, but his left hand still ached.

"You told me to create chaos," Yvonne said. "I didn't know she would attack—"

"Forget it," Butch cut her off. "Go into the other room and dart Ana. Leave Laurel and Grace to me."

Yvonne slipped another dart into the tranquilizer gun and walked into the other room with the gun behind her back.

Grace and Laurel were standing on the other side of the dinosaur pen. Ana was in front of the stainless steel food prep table.

Yvonne could not believe her eyes. Butch and Blackwood hadn't said anything about baby dinosaurs!

"Are those what I think they are?" Yvonne said.

"Yes," Grace said. "Mokélé-mbembé."

"I had no idea," Yvonne said. "How could that—"

"You didn't take a shower before you came in here," Ana said, raising an eyebrow. "And you're not wearing scrubs."

"Bertha just told me to come in," Yvonne said. "She didn't say anything about—"

She whipped out the tranquilizer gun from behind her back and fired a dart into Ana's thigh. Ana ignored the dart and made a lunge for her. Yvonne sidestepped her and snapped out the baton, but it was Butch who put an end to it. He stepped into the room and hit Ana in the forehead with the butt of Bertha's shotgun. In his other hand he held Bertha's radio.

"Good to see you again, Grace," Butch said. He looked at the two dinosaurs. "Wow, they're bigger than I thought they'd be."

He threw two cloth laundry bags to Grace, who let them fall to the floor without even trying to catch them. "Bag 'em."

"No," Grace said.

He pointed Bertha's shotgun at Laurel. "If you don't bag them, then I bag your friend Dr. Lee."

Grace picked up the bags.

Bertha's radio went off.

"Bertha?"

It was Wolfe.

Butch handed his pistol to Yvonne. "This is a little more permanent than the dart gun. All the tranquilizer is going to do is to give them strange dreams and a terrible headache when they wake up. If Dr. Lee moves a quarter of an inch, shoot her."

Yvonne took the pistol and nodded.

"Bertha, are you there?" Wolfe asked.

"I can't believe that you work for Noah Blackwood," Grace said to Yvonne.

Yvonne laughed. "I've worked for Dr. Blackwood since I was a girl. He's gotten me every animal-training job I've ever had. And now it looks like I get to train a couple of dinosaurs. If he'd told me about them, I would have done this job for free."

"Bertha?"

Butch held the radio to Grace's mouth. "You'd better make this good. Because if Wolfe comes down here, I will personally kill Laurel, Ana, and Bertha. I'm going to key the mic. Ready?"

Grace took a deep breath and nodded.

"It's Grace," she said.

"Where's Bertha?" Wolfe asked.

"She and Yvonne are in the shower. Sorry I didn't answer sooner, but I was in the nursery and didn't hear Bertha's radio at first."

"How's Yvonne?"

"She's scared, but fine," Grace answered.

There was a moment's hesitation on Wolfe's end. "Is everything okay?"

"Yes," Grace said. "We're fine. Bertha said that Butch ran right past the lab and didn't even look at the door."

"Good," Wolfe said. "Have Bertha give me a shout when she gets out of the shower."

"I will. How's everything going on deck? I mean, with the pirates and all."

"It's under control," Wolfe said. "All we have to do is find Butch and we'll all be safe."

Butch took his finger off the SEND button. "That's what you think," he said, smiling, then looked at Grace. "End the transmission." He pushed the button.

"I guess I'd better get back to feeding the dinosaurs."

"Good," Wolfe said. "I'll see you soon."

"Impressive," Butch said. "You're a chip off the old block. By that I mean your grandfather, not Wolfe. Convincing lying must be genetic. Now, bag the dinosaurs. We have a flight to catch."

"Why don't you just take the dinosaurs and let her go?" Laurel pleaded.

"Why don't you just shut up before I shoot you in the head?" Butch answered.

TWO MINUTES

The two squid took the bait, but it wasn't nearly as easy to stay away from them as Ted had anticipated. He tried to hover just out of their reach, but it was difficult to judge how long their reach was. Twice one of them got ahold of the Orb, and both times Ted was about ready to punch the electrical field button but Lepod stopped him.

"Don't!" Lepod yelled. "If you shock them, they'll disappear into the deep."

Instead, Ted made a quick maneuver and was able to roll the Orb out of their grasp.

Lepod puked again, and so did Marty, but only a little. Then things got complicated.

"Whales," Lepod gurgled. "Just one. She's after the squid."

But the squid only had eyes — very big eyes — for the Orb, and appeared completely unaware that they were being pursued.

"What do we do?" Ted asked.

"We'll know if we have them hooked in a minute," Lepod said.

"What do you mean?"

"The light," Lepod answered.

Marty and Ted looked up. Just above them the sunlight was beginning to penetrate the water.

"If you get to the light and they're still in hot pursuit, not slowing down, they'll follow you all the way into the Moon Pool."

Marty looked behind. The whale was gaining on the two squid. "We'd better pick up the pace or they're going to be calamari."

"Continue to play with them," Lepod said. "They've already seen the light. They're leery of it, but they're more concerned about not catching you. When you get to the light, you can speed up. Not as fast as you did in the deep, but enough to keep them ahead of the whale."

They reached the light and the squid did not slow down.

"We have them," Lepod said. "Speed up."

Ted did. So did the squid . . . and the whale.

The hull of the *Coelacanth* came into view and, seconds later, the open entrance to the Moon Pool. The squid were about thirty feet behind the Orb. The whale was about fifteen feet behind the squid.

STANDOFF

Joe had managed to take out two of the men in Zodiacs, but not before they had taken out every sonic cannon. When they blew out the last cannon, they turned and sped back to Blackwood's ships.

There were still a couple of pirate boats with no one at the helm, looping around and around in circles.

Wolfe watched the Zodiacs through binoculars until they pulled behind Blackwood's ships.

"What do you think that means?" he asked Al.

"I don't know," Al said. "But I don't think this is over. In fact, it might not have even started yet. Blackwood knew we had the sonic cannons, but he sent the pirates out without ear protectors. Sacrificial lambs. He's not stupid. He's up to something."

Wolfe keyed his radio. "Bertha?"

No answer.

"Grace?"

No answer.

"Anyone in Lab Nine, pick up."

Silence.

"Blackwood's chopper is lifting off," Al said. "He's headed this way."

Wolfe tried reaching Bertha—anyone—in Lab Nine again. He got a response, but it wasn't the one he wanted.

"Hey, Wolfe," Butch said into Wolfe's earpiece. "I'm coming out on deck, but you need to tell your guys to stand down. I have Grace, two dinosaurs, and your sweetheart, Laurel Lee. You know I'm not going to hurt Grace or the dinosaurs, so that leaves Laurel. When I get on deck, if I see anyone with a weapon in their hand, I'll shoot your girlfriend right in front of you. Can I make that any clearer?"

"No," Wolfe said.

"Oh, and I'm not alone. I got a couple of guys with me and another girl you know. They're not nice people."

"The Moon Pool," Wolfe said.

"Bingo. Thanks for opening the door for them."

Wolfe took his finger off the SEND key, then turned to Al and Joe.

"What do you want to do?" Al asked.

"Put your weapons down," Wolfe said.

"We can take them," Al insisted.

Wolfe shook his head. "No. Stand down. Everybody."

Reluctantly, Al, Joe, and everyone else on deck complied.

Butch came out first, holding a bound Laurel Lee by her forearm, with a pistol pointed to her head. Yvonne emerged next, holding on to Grace. Two other men dressed in black wet suits followed. Each held a laundry bag slung over his shoulder with something struggling inside.

Blackwood's helicopter landed on the helipad.

"You took out our helicopter to make room for his," Phil said.

"I sure did," Butch said.

"Where's Bertha?"

"Asleep, along with that annoying journalist, but they're both fine, which is more than they deserve," Butch answered.

Blackwood stepped out of the helicopter before the rotors stopped.

"How's it going, Travis?" he shouted over the din of the blades.

Wolfe didn't answer.

Butch looked at his men. "Take the bags up to the chopper! And where's Pepper?"

"Last time I talked to him he was still down at the Moon Pool," one of the men answered.

"Tell him to get up on deck," Butch said. "We're out of here."

The man spoke into his radio. "We got all the cargo. Come on up."

"Be there in a minute," Pepper answered back.

The two men climbed to the helipad, put the bags inside the helicopter, then covered the group with their assault rifles.

Wolfe looked at Yvonne with complete disgust.

"Save it, Wolfe," Yvonne said. "I didn't need your job. I already have one."

ONE SECOND

Ted brought the Orb into the Moon Pool so fast it went airborne.

Pepper, who was putting his gear into his satchel, was so startled when he saw it that he nearly wet himself. The gold ball was followed into the pool by something huge and red. A second later, something hit the ship so hard Pepper was thrown to the ground.

"What was that?" Ted shouted.

"The whale snagged the second squid and slammed into the hull!" Marty answered.

The ship rocked.

In the confusion, Grace yanked herself out of Yvonne's grasp and ran over to Wolfe.

Al dove for his gun and came up shooting. He hit Butch in the shoulder. Butch managed to hold on to Laurel Lee in spite of the wound.

"Drop your gun," Al said. "I won't miss twice."

Butch looked at him and smiled. "I won't miss once. I'll

have a bullet in Laurel's head before your bullet reaches me."

"That's right," Al said. "And you'll both be dead."

As soon as the Orb splashed back down into the Moon Pool, a red tentacle wrapped itself around it.

"Now would be a good time to use the shocker," Lepod said, staring in horror at the gigantic barbed suckers squeezing the Orb.

"It might scare the squid out of the pool," Ted said.

"I don't think so," Lepod said. "It's disoriented. Hit the button!"

Ted did.

The tentacle disappeared like it had touched a hot stove.

"Hang on," Ted said.

He dove the Orb under the surface, shot into the holding pool, and slammed the door behind them.

Pepper picked up his radio. "We have a situation down here," he said into Butch's earpiece.

"Yeah," Butch said into his throat mic. "Well, we have one up here, too. What's the problem?"

"There's a giant squid in the Moon Pool. At least I think that's what it is. And this round golden thing that looks like some kind of spaceship."

"What are you talking about?"

"I'm just tellin' you like I see it."

"Get up here," Butch said. "Or we're going to leave you behind. And that wouldn't be too good for your health."

"I'm on my way," Pepper said, and he was, until he saw the gold fabric on the ball rip open and what looked like three spacemen step out. He watched them remove their black helmets.

As they took them off, weird liquid spilled out of two of the spacemen's helmets, followed by the distinct smell of vomit.

Pepper got back on the radio. "Three guys just got out of the gold ball. Well, two guys and a kid. Two of them are covered in what looks like vom—"

"What kid?" Butch interrupted.

"Marty O'Hara."

Wolfe and the others could hear what Butch was saying, but they couldn't hear the person on the other end of the transmission.

Butch smiled. "Bring him up here on the double." He looked over to Blackwood. "Looks like they have a giant squid." He looked at Wolfe. "And we have Marty."

Blackwood processed this new information and came to an instant decision. With the hatchlings in hand, he would send the giant squid back to the bottom of the canyon — along with the *Coelacanth*'s crew. If he had it transferred to the *Endangered Too*, he'd have to incarcerate everyone on the *Coelacanth* before he sank it. The longer he remained on board, the more that could go wrong.

"Congratulations, Wolfe!" he said. "It's the catch of the century. I hope you get it back to NZA in good shape. I got what I wanted . . . what was rightfully mine. And you have what you wanted. Let's forget all of this other business and call it even." He looked at Butch. "We will proceed as planned."

Pepper walked over to the threesome.

"Who are you?" Ted said.

Pepper answered by shooting him in the chest, then turned

the pistol on Lepod and shot him. Both men went down.

"You get to live," he said to Marty. "For the time being, that is."

From the floor, Ted kicked Pepper in the knee. As he fell, his radio and pistol skidded across the deck.

Both men were on their feet within a second. Pepper pulled his knife and rammed the blade into the gold man's belly. The man stepped away. Pepper was shocked to see no gaping, bloody wound and no reaction to the vicious knife thrust.

"What the—"

"Mistake," Ted said, and kicked him in the head. Pepper stumbled backward and fell into the pool. A tentacle wrapped itself around him and pulled him under. The water bubbled and turned black with squid ink and pink with Pepper's blood. Ted didn't even glance at the gruesome show. He ran over to Pepper's satchel and started rifling through it as Marty helped Lepod to his feet.

"That man just shot me at point-blank range and I'm perfectly fine," Lepod said, amazed.

"How about that," Marty said.

"Get over here," Ted said. He showed them a package of what looked like clay. "C-4," he said. "Plastic explosives. They're going to sink the ship." He pulled out a diagram and scanned it. "There are nine charges. Six in here, one in the bow, two in the stern." He tore the diagram into three pieces. "Lepod, you get the charge in the bow. Marty, you get the two in the stern."

"I don't know how to disarm a bomb," Lepod said.

"Well, you're going to have to learn quick. The C-4 detonators are radio-controlled. I don't know who has the radio, but all they have to do is punch a button and the *Coelacanth* is going down. Come with me."

Using his section of the diagram, Ted led them over to one of the charges. "Two wires. One blue. One yellow. Pull the blue wire first, the yellow wire second. Just remember this: Blue is cool. Yellow will kill a fellow. Now go."

"What about *Architeuthis*?" Lepod asked. "The Moon Pool door is still open. It'll get away. If we don't change the pressure it will die."

"We can't do anything without power," Ted said. "And if the ship goes down, it doesn't matter. I'll pull the wires in here, then I'll try to scab in power from the Orb to the ship. As soon as you defuse the C-4, come back here. We'll figure out our next step."

Marty and Lepod ran out through the air lock.

Ted grabbed the dead man's radio as he hurried over to the second packet of C-4 and pulled the blue wire.

He typed in a code and put the radio to his lips as he pulled the yellow wire.

"Wolfe? If you can hear me, don't say anything. Just key your mic so I know you're there."

Ted heard the click as he raced over to the third charge.

"One click for yes. Two for no. You got bad guys up there?"

Click!

"Are they monitoring this frequency?"

Click! Click!

"They've wired the ship to explode. C-4. Nine charges. I'm taking out the six in the Moon Pool. Marty and Lepod are disarming the three in the stern and in the bow. The explosives are hooked up to a remote." Ted pulled out the yellow wire and started toward the fourth charge. "I took out a guy when we surfaced. He's being dined on by a giant squid at the moment. They won't try to blow the ship while they're still on board. You need to stall them. I need five or six minutes to disarm the explosives. I'll let you know when we have everything defused." He pulled another blue wire. "Key your mic again if you understand." He pulled the yellow wire.

Click! Click!

Lepod found the C-4 quickly, pulled the wires, and got back just as Ted disarmed the last charge in the Moon Pool, hoping Blackwood's men hadn't decided to install a couple of extra charges that weren't on the diagram.

"Where's Marty?" Ted asked.

"I don't know," Lepod said. He walked over to the pool. The squid was still there, feeding on the man Ted had kicked in.

"Go!" Ted said. "Help him find those explosives."

Lepod hesitated.

"It's either that or I go," Ted said. "Do you know anything about how to hook up nuclear power to a conventionally powered ship?"

Lepod shook his head.

"Then go help Marty. If you and he aren't back here in three minutes, I'm going to come help you and your squid is going to get away."

Lepod ran back through the air lock.

He found Marty frantically searching the stern of the ship.

"I found the first one," Marty said. "But the second one isn't where it was supposed to be."

Lepod grabbed the diagram and looked. Marty was right. It wasn't where it was supposed to be.

TIME'S UP

"Let Laurel go," Wolfe said.

Butch smiled. "Only if you let Grace get onto the chopper with Yvonne."

Wolfe shook his head.

"Here's another incentive for you," Butch continued, still smiling. "We have a man below and he has Marty. Be a shame if something bad happened to your nephew."

"They have Marty?" Grace screamed.

Wolfe clamped his mouth shut. He wanted to tell her that they didn't have Marty after all, but he couldn't without tipping his hand.

"I'll go," Grace said.

"No," Wolfe said.

"They'll kill Marty and Laurel," Grace said. "I couldn't live with that. *You* couldn't live with that, Wolfe. We need to stop this right now. This feud has to end."

Wolfe took her hand. "It's not a feud. And you don't know everything that's going on. Grace, you can't go with Noah Blackwood."

Luther was watching everything unfold on the Gizmo. He had even heard the exchange between Ted and Wolfe. He wanted to help, but what could he do? To get to the Moon Pool he would have to walk right past everyone on deck.

He pushed a button on the Gizmo. "Ted?"

"Yeah. Who's this?"

"Luther."

"Where are you?"

Luther told him, along with everything else that was going on.

From the helipad, Blackwood motioned to the pilot to start the chopper, then looked back at Wolfe and shouted, "Let her go, Travis! You lost this one. Admit it. Cut your losses. You have your giant squid. eWolfe is secure. I have as much right to have Grace as you do. If you don't let her go, Dr. Lee will die. Marty will die. And for what? You know I'm not going to give up until Grace is with me. You can't win."

"You can't have her, Noah," Wolfe shouted back. "I'm her father. She belongs with me. I promised Rose you would never get her and I'm not going to break that promise."

Grace looked up at her father and knew he meant what he said. She looked at Laurel, who had not flinched through this whole ordeal; she looked as calm as she had the first day Grace had seen her in the library on Cryptos. She looked at Butch. She had no doubt that Butch would kill Laurel and Marty, when his man dragged him up on deck. All it would take was a simple nod from her grandfather.

She jerked her hand out of Wolfe's and ran back over to Yvonne. "I want to go with my grandfather," she said.

Yvonne grabbed her by the arm.

"You can't mean that," Wolfe said.

"I mean it!" She looked at Yvonne. "Let's go before I change my mind."

Butch started to make his way to the helipad with Laurel.

Wolfe stared in helpless disbelief.

Luther ran down to the deck and shouted at Grace, "Are you crazy?"

"Remind Marty that he squeezed Monkey's arm!" she shouted back.

"What?"

"Just tell him!"

"Yeah, fine!"

But Luther had not raced down from the bridge to determine if Grace was crazy. He had come down to delay Blackwood's departure because he knew Marty, Ted, and Lepod hadn't found the last packet of C-4. But now he wasn't so sure about Grace's sanity. What was she talking about? He wanted to tell her that they didn't have Marty, but just like Wolfe, he knew he couldn't.

The men lifted Grace up to the helipad. Noah Blackwood took his granddaughter's hand. He tore off her blue tracking tag and dropped it on the deck. "You won't be needing this collar anymore. At the Ark we don't treat people like dogs."

There was another reason Luther had come out of hiding. "Grace!" he shouted. "Don't let that old man bug you. Be a dragon."

"What?"

"I said, *Be a dragon!*"

Grace felt something move in her shirt pocket but, to avoid attracting her grandfather's attention, didn't look down. "I will, Luther. Thanks."

"What about Pepper?" one of Noah's men shouted.

Luther swore under his breath. *No point in hiding anything now*, he thought. *They're about ready to take off.*

"He can't make it," Luther shouted back. "He's having lunch with a giant squid."

"Guess that makes us even," Butch said, smiling. "I got Roy. You got Pepper."

Butch was the last to board the helicopter. As he got in, he thought about shooting Laurel just to see the look on Wolfe's face, but he let her go. Wolfe already looked devastated at the loss of his daughter, and they'd all be dead soon enough anyway.

The helicopter took off.

PD, Congo, and Bo came scrambling onto the deck.

Bo was carrying a brown wig in one hand and what looked like a clump of gray clay in the other.

Luther took refuge behind Al, but Bo didn't seem interested in his hair. Nor did she seem nearly as crazed as she had a few hours ago.

Wolfe walked over to her. She hid the wig behind her back.

"You can have the hair," Wolfe said. "Just give me the other thing."

Bo handed it to him. It was a brick of C-4 with two wires dangling from it. One yellow, one blue.

Wolfe threw the brick over the side in angry disgust, then keyed the radio. "We have the final charge. Bo had it."

"Lucky she pulled out the wires in the right order," Ted said.

"There is nothing lucky about this day," Wolfe said. "Blackwood has Grace."

"I'm sorry, Wolfe," Ted said quietly. "I'll be up soon."

AMAZING GRACE

Ted found Marty and Lepod frantically searching the stern for the last charge.

"Bo found it," he said. "She brought it up to the main deck and Wolfe tossed it over the side."

"So we're safe?" Marty asked.

"We're not going to sink, if that's what you mean," Ted answered.

"What about the giant squid?" Lepod asked.

"Secured and doing fine. I spliced power from the Orb to the Moon Pool. The door's closed and the room is pressurized."

"I better get down there and monitor the squid," Lepod said happily, and quickly headed in that direction.

"What's the matter?" Marty asked. He could tell by Ted's somber mood that he hadn't told them everything.

"Blackwood got the hatchlings," Ted answered.

"How did that happen?"

"That's not all," Ted said. "Blackwood also has Grace."

Marty stared at him, not sure he had heard correctly. "What?"

"She's gone. Butch must have grabbed her from the lab."

Marty took off running. On his way up to the main deck he ran into a concerned-looking Phil Bishop.

"Is it true?" Marty asked.

Phil nodded. "Blackwood won. He got the hatchlings and Grace. He just took off with them in his helicopter along with Butch and Yvonne."

"Yvonne?"

"She was working for Blackwood all along. She's the one who drugged Bo and let her loose. I'm on my way to Lab Nine to check on Bertha and Ana. Yvonne drugged them, too, with a tranquilizer gun."

"I hope they're okay," Marty said, continuing up to the main deck.

What he found there was a grim group of people staring at a helicopter hovering about a half mile away. Bo was hanging over the rail, hooting at Winkin, Blinkin, and Nod. PD and Congo had joined her and were barking and screeching at the dolphins.

Wolfe and Laurel were holding hands.

Luther was standing a few feet away from them, looking down at his Gizmo.

"I lost her," Wolfe said. "I'm sorry, Marty."

"We'll have to get her back," Marty said.

Luther glanced up from the Gizmo. "Just before she took off, she told me to tell you that you squeezed Monkey's arm."

"Huh?"

"Didn't make sense to me, either," Luther said, and looked back down at the Gizmo.

"We'll get Grace and the hatchlings back," Al assured them. "And I'm going pay *Butch* back for killing Roy if it's the last thing I do."

"How did he get her?" Marty asked.

"She got away from me and went with him willingly," Wolfe answered.

"No way," Marty said.

"She didn't have a choice," Laurel said. "Butch had a gun to my head and would have killed me. She thought they had you, too. Grace gave herself up for us."

Endangered One and *Endangered Too* had pulled their anchors and were moving away. The remaining pirates had boarded the fishing trawler, and it, too, chugged away. Theo Sonborn came up on deck with his hands in his pockets and stood about ten feet away from the group.

"Why is Blackwood just hovering there?" Marty asked.

"Because he thinks the charges are still in place and he wants to see us blown out of the water," Al answered.

"I can't believe Grace is gone," Marty said.

"Maybe not for long," Luther said.

"What are you talking about?" Wolfe asked.

"What's the range between the dragonspy and the Gizmo?"

"I don't know," Wolfe answered, glancing at Theo. "Maybe five miles, but it's like a tracking tag. With the satellite we can find it anywhere, and we can see what it's seeing. We're building more of them. As soon as they're finished we're sending a swarm down to the Amazon to look for Marty's parents. Why?"

"The dragonspy is in her shirt pocket," Luther said. "And she knows it. She just looked down at it and winked at me."

Wolfe grabbed the Gizmo. He and Marty and Laurel stared at the screen. All they could see was pink fabric. Wolfe turned on the audio, but he couldn't pick up their voices. The helicopter rotors were too loud.

HOVERING

Grace saw the sun reflecting off Marty's golden aquasuit. She couldn't see him clearly, but she knew it was him. And she knew how frustrated he was right now with her so close, yet unreachable. She hoped he'd been looking at the Gizmo when she'd winked. She hoped he knew why she really left.

She was in the back of the helicopter with the two soldiers, Butch, and Yvonne, who was treating Butch's shoulder wound. Her grandfather was in the copilot's seat. He looked back at her and pointed to his headset, indicating for her to slip a pair on herself. She did.

"Are you doing all right?" he asked cheerfully.

"Yes," she answered.

"I'm glad to finally have you with me, Grace. This is how it should have been from the very beginning. We're going to have a wonderful life together. But I do have a question for you."

"What is it?"

"Why did you decide to come with me?"

Grace knew this question was coming and she was prepared for it. "Curiosity," she answered. "I landed in the middle of this family feud, but I'm not a part of it. Someone had to put an end to it. I don't want anything bad to happen to Wolfe, or to you."

"Wolfe is going to come after you," Noah said. "He's going to come after the dinosaurs."

"I decide who I stay with," Grace said. "It's not up to either of you."

"I have another question," Noah said. "What did you mean by squeezing the monkey's arm?"

"It's a private joke between Marty and me. Bo doesn't like it when we squeeze her arm."

"For your information," Noah said, "Bo is a bonobo chimpanzee, therefore she is an ape, not a monkey."

"Wow," Grace said, although she knew full well that a chimpanzee was an ape.

"Oh, the things I'll be able to teach you," Noah said.

He turned back to the front, his hand resting on the remote detonator, debating with himself. He wanted to see the *Coelacanth* explode, but he might have to forgo that pleasure. If he blew up the ship in front of Grace, he would probably lose her forever, even though he had her in hand. The detonator had an effective range of fifteen miles. At that distance he wouldn't be able to see or hear the explosion, but neither would Grace. "Let's head out," he told the pilot, taking note of their exact position on the chopper's GPS.

"Where are we going?" Grace asked.

"One of my private jets is waiting for us in Wellington, New Zealand. We'll fly back to the States. We need to get our two friends to a proper facility as quickly as we can."

"Good idea," Grace said. "I'm sure they're not very comfortable in those bags."

Grace allowed herself a small smile. *Noah had people working for him on Cryptos Island,* she thought. *Now Wolfe has someone working for him at the Ark.*

This was the only way she could save Laurel and Marty, protect the hatchlings, and find out who her grandfather really was.

At exactly fourteen miles, Noah Blackwood pushed the button on the detonator. He closed his eyes and imagined the explosion and the expressions of surprise on the crew's faces. He allowed himself a small smile, too.

HOVERING

TENTACLES

Five minutes after the detonator was pushed, Theo Sonborn said, "I guess I better get down to the engine room and see if I can get this rusty bucket of bolts started. I could use some help."

"I'll go," Luther volunteered.

"I'll help you, too," Laurel offered. "But first I'm going to check on Bertha and Ana."

Wolfe said he would be down in a few minutes. He joined Marty at the rail, where he was staring at the empty sky where the helicopter had been.

"We'll get her back," Wolfe said. "And we'll find your parents."

Marty kept his eyes fixed on the sky and did not respond.

"I should have left you and Grace at Omega Prep," Wolfe continued. "I should have never come back into your life. If I'd stayed away, you'd both be safe. None of this would have happened."

Marty looked at his uncle. "You're right," he said at last. "But the thing is, if you hadn't showed up, we'd still be living a lie. I know now that Grace and I aren't twins, but we're still connected like we are. I know what she's thinking. She went with Blackwood to save me and Laurel, but that's not the only reason. She went because she wants to know the truth. And the only person who knows the whole story is Noah Blackwood. Grace had to go with him. We'll get her back, but not until she gets what she wants."

Marty let go of the rail and started to walk away.

"Where are you going?" Wolfe asked.

Marty stopped and looked back at his uncle. "Grace knew this was going to happen."

"How could she know that?"

"She just knows things," Marty said. "I don't know how and neither does she. What I *do* know is that I squeezed Monkey's arm."

"And what was that all about?" Wolfe asked.

"A promise. I told Grace I would untangle the things in that old trunk. Ted snagged a giant squid. Blackwood snagged Grace and the hatchlings. It's time I put out *my* tentacles to see what *I* can snag: 'Below the thunders of the upper deep . . .'"

"Tennyson," Wolfe said. "From the poem 'The Kraken.'"

"Right," Marty replied. "Do you want to help?"

"I guess I'd better," Wolfe said.

They went below to see what they could discover in the upper deep.

ACKNOWLEDGMENTS

I've said this before, but I have to say it again . . . "Novels are written in solitude, but they are never written alone." I don't have the words to thank all the people who helped me with this long-awaited sequel to *Cryptid Hunters*. My fantastic editor at Scholastic, Anamika Bhatnagar, who "labored" over this under difficult circumstances. Siobhán "Dash" McGowan, who picked up the story and ran with it. Suzanne Murphy, who was always willing to talk, even when she had the flu. My wonderful agent, friend, and fearless advocate, Barbara Kouts. Ed Masessa, friend, fan, and (okay, I'll say it, Ed) #1 *New York Times* Bestselling Author. Larry Decker, who always makes me sound and look better than I am. My wonderful readers, Joan and Doug Arth, Naomi Williamson, Scout and Kim Hornkohl, Hannah and Melanie Gill, J. R. and Bethany Culpepper, and, of course, my wonderful wife, Marie, who makes it possible for me to write all of my novels. Thanks also to everyone else at Scholastic for your support, enthusiasm, teamwork, and intelligence. And finally a special acknowledgment to Meena, who was along for the ride throughout the entire voyage.

Roland Smith is the author of numerous award-winning books for young readers, including *Zach's Lie, Jack's Run, Sasquatch, Cryptid Hunters, Peak, Elephant Run, I.Q.*, and, most recently, *Storm Runners.* For more than twenty years he worked as an animal keeper, traveling all over the world, before turning to writing full-time. Roland lives with his wife, Marie, on a small farm south of Portland, Oregon. Visit him online at www.rolandsmith.com.

ABOUT THE AUTHOR

Chase Masters and his father are "storm runners," racing across the country in pursuit of hurricanes, tornadoes, and floods. Anywhere bad weather strikes, they are not far behind. Chase is learning more on the road than he ever would just sitting in a classroom. But when the hurricane of the century hits, he will be tested in ways he never could have imagined.